A STAR IS DEAD

A STAR IS DEAD

Elaine Viets

This first world edition published 2019
in Great Britain and 2020 in the USA by
SEVERN HOUSE PUBLISHERS LTD of
Eardley House, 4 Uxbridge Street, London W8 7SY.
Trade paperback edition first published
in Great Britain and the USA 2020 by
SEVERN HOUSE PUBLISHERS LTD.

British Library Cataloguing in Publication Data
A CIP catalogue record for this title is available from the British Library.

ISBN-13: 978-0-7278-9016-0 (cased)
ISBN-13: 978-1-78029-674-6 (trade paper)
ISBN-13: 978-1-4483-0373-1 (e-book)

All Severn House titles are printed on acid-free paper.

Severn House Publishers support the Forest Stewardship Council™ [FSC™],
the leading international forest certification organisation.
All our titles that are printed on FSC certified paper carry the FSC logo.

Typeset by Palimpsest Book Production Ltd.,
Falkirk, Stirlingshire, Scotland.
Printed and bound in Great Britain by
TJ International, Padstow, Cornwall.

To Nan Seimer – Merry Christmas!

ACKNOWLEDGMENTS

I'm fascinated by death investigators, a fairly new profession. Death investigators work for the medical examiner's office. They are trained, but they are not physicians. I'm not a death investigator, but I did take the Medicolegal Death Investigators Training course in St Louis.

Many people helped with A Star Is Dead. Most important is my husband, Don Crinklaw, my first reader and rock.

Thanks also to my agent, Joshua Bilmes, president of JABberwocky Literary Agency, and the entire JABberwocky team.

Thanks to the Severn House staff, especially Carl Smith, commissioning editor (who writes the most delightful notes on my manuscript), assistant Natasha Bell, and copyeditor Loma Halden. Cover artist Jem Butcher perfectly captured my book.

I'm grateful to Bill Hopkins, Detective R.C. White, Fort Lauderdale Police Department (retired) and licensed private eye, Krysten Addison, death investigator, Harold R. Messler, retired manager-criminalistics, St Louis Police Laboratory, Gregg Brickman, Ruthi Sturdivant, Greg Herren, Will Graham, Alan Portman, Joanna Campbell Slan, Jinny Gender and Carolina Garcia-Aguilera, and many librarians, including those at the Broward County library and St Louis and St Louis County libraries.

Sarah E.C. Byrne made a generous donation to charity to have her name in this novel. She's a lawyer from Canberra, Australia, and a crime fiction aficionada.

Special thanks to Sharon L. Plotkin, certified crime scene investigator and professor at the Miami Dade College School of Justice, who read the crime scenes for accuracy.

Any mistakes are mine.

Enjoy Angela Richman's latest adventure. Let me know what you think. Email me at eviets@aol.com

ONE

No one knew Jessica Gray's real age – not until it was published in her obituary.

I knew Jessica wasn't young – she couldn't be. 'Ageless' was the word used most often to describe her. That's a code word for a bare-knuckle fight with Father Time . . . and almost winning. Jessica was a sixties beauty who'd starred in two classic films from that era, *Flower Power* and *Eternally Groovy*, and had a torrid affair with Johnny Grimes, a rock star who OD'd in 1968.

I did Jessica's death investigation, and it was ugly.

I'm Angela Richman, death investigator for Chouteau County, Missouri. Jessica had her final seizure in Chouteau Forest, the largest town in the county. Now the Forest will be branded as the place where Jessica Gray was murdered.

I'm one of the people who serve the Forest's old guard. I work for the county medical examiner. At a homicide, I'm in charge of the body and the police are in charge of the scene.

Back to the murdered star. Jessica first burst on the scene in 1966 with *Flower Power*. Pauline Kael, then a powerful reviewer for the *New Yorker*, called the movie 'a pure emotional high, and you don't come down when the picture is over. Jessica Gray is luminous, magical. You want to see more of her.'

And so we did, in *Eternally Groovy*, in 1967. That's when we saw *all* of Jessica, dancing naked at a decadent party in a scene in that movie. Rumor had it that the drugs in the film were real.

Jessica and Johnny Grimes had a passionate, drug-fueled romance. His star was ascending with hers. While Johnny was singing his way up the charts, Jessica could be seen with her flowing locks and fringed vest, dancing at Whisky a GoGo in Hollywood and the Peppermint Lounge in New York. She always wore the latest Carnaby Street fashions, and tried all the fashionable drugs.

Rumor was she'd killed her lover. Like many rock gods, Johnny Grimes died of a heroin overdose at age twenty-seven, joining the '27 Club,' including Janis Joplin, Jim Morrison, Amy Winehouse and other dazzling talents who died too young. Jessica was said to have given him the fatal dose – she'd scored some unusually pure H. She stayed out of sight for a few months, then re-emerged with a stunning perform-ance in *Powerline!*, a movie that set the standard for the seventies.

By the time Jessica came to Chouteau Forest, she was famous for being famous – and for relentlessly peddling her beauty treatment, a dried kale concoction called Captivate. She also sold a Captivating Finishing Spray for women to spritz on their face after they put on their make-up. Jessica claimed it gave them 'the dewy look of youth.'

I thought Jessica looked more embalmed than eternally young, but she was fashionably emaciated. Her fans saw her as a sweet, beautiful actress still mourning her lost lover. The woman I saw was bitter and caustic.

She surrounded herself with an entourage of has-beens and wounded people. Somehow, she managed to convince America that she was a sweetheart.

That's why I thought Jessica was a great actress. I didn't like anything about the woman – her politics or her cruel jokes. She attacked other women, and said if Joan Rivers 'had another facelift she'd be bikini waxing her upper lip.'

Jessica was a queen bee who decided pretty women got their success because they slept with an important man. Some called her a feminist because she was a show business pioneer, but I felt that feminists didn't tear down other women. Because of her AIDS charities, Jessica had a big following with gays.

That winter, Jessica was touring the country in a one-woman show called 'Just Jessica.' St Louis was the last stop on the twelve-city tour, and Chouteau Forest was thirty miles west of the city. Jessica was booked to play three nights at the Lux Theater in February. My hairstylist, Mario Garcia, was chosen to be Jessica's local stylist. Mario was over the moon at this invitation. He had an extra ticket to Jessica's last St Louis show, and invited me. We were also invited to the after-party at Old Reggie Du Pres's mansion.

Mario was honored and excited by the double invitation. I wasn't sure I wanted to go. But I feared I had no choice.

TWO

One bone-cold February evening, I was at home, trying to think of excuses that would get me out of going to Jessica Gray's show at the Lux, when I got a surprise visit from Clare Rappaport.

Clare dropped in on me two or three times a year and always said the same thing, 'Forgive me for not calling, my dear. I'd been lunching with Old Reggie and thought I'd stop by to see you.'

I lived in a former guest house on the Du Pres estate. Shortly before my mom went to work as the Du Pres family housekeeper, she'd worked briefly for Mrs Rappaport. Clare and my mother became friends – at least as friendly as a servant and a wealthy employer can be – and Clare stayed in touch with me after Mom died.

I always pretended I'd expected her visit and said the same thing, 'I'm making some coffee, Clare. Would you like some?'

We fell easily into the old pattern this visit. 'That would be nice,' she said, and followed me into the kitchen. She tossed her mink coat on the couch.

'Still take it black?' I asked.

'Haven't changed,' she said, but she seemed pleased that I'd remembered.

I poured two cups of coffee and started to take them into the living room.

'No, let's sit in your kitchen,' she said. 'It's homier.'

She propped her cane against the wall and sat down at my round maple table. I knew then that she wanted to ask me for advice. Clare had the touching belief that my mother gave good advice and that I'd inherited Mom's practical view of the world.

I set down a plate of cookies, and she took one. I set the table with Mom's rose-patterned dessert plates and silver, and two linen napkins. I'd have to iron them, but if anyone would appreciate that touch, it was Clare.

It took a half hour of small talk, three chocolate chip cookies and a cup of coffee for Clare to announce, 'I'm going to disinherit my children.'

Now her shocking words hung in the air.

Clare was eighty-three. She was prickly and independent, and still buzzed around the Forest in her beat-up green Land Rover, and walked with a silver-headed cane. She never seemed to change. Her snowy hair was in an elegant French twist. She wore a black St John knit pantsuit, the favorite designer for well-bred Forest dowagers. Small pearl earrings and a gold wedding band were her only jewelry. Her face was as wrinkled as fine tissue paper, and she wore light pink lipstick.

I was stunned by her announcement. The Forest ran on two powerful forces: blood and money. It was almost impossible to separate the two.

Disinheriting both children was the most drastic action any Forest dweller could take. Clare's decision would reverberate through Chouteau County for years.

Clare was incredibly rich, even by Forest standards, and believed people like me – who didn't need her – would give her honest advice.

During the long silence, Clare gently patted her mouth with a linen napkin and then said, 'I know my husband Roger only married me for my money, though we were quite fond of one another.'

'No!' I said. 'That can't be true.'

'The young are so romantic,' she said, and looked at me sadly.

'I'm not young. I'm forty-one.'

'Not young! Wait till you get to be my age.' She laughed.

It wasn't funny. Like many of the rich, elegant Clare was haunted by the thought – however hard for the rest of us to understand – that people only loved her for her money.

'Now I have the same concern about my children.'

'Trey? I went to school with him.'

'Yes, he's your age. Jemima is two years younger. This

last year they've both been very neglectful. Jemima hardly ever comes to visit, and she used to see me at least once a month.

'I know she has a career and two children, but she was too busy to come for Christmas, and I wanted to see her and my precious grandchildren. And Trey' – that's Roger the third – 'forgot my birthday. Those were the straws that broke this camel's back. They know both those occasions are important to me.'

I'd lost track of Jemima and Trey after I'd left school. 'Where do they live now?'

'In St Louis. Both of them. That's only thirty miles away. It's not like they're on the East Coast.'

'I can understand how they can get caught up in their careers,' I said.

'Trey works for a big law firm. He has a secretary. She could have kept track of my birthday!' Clare picked up another cookie and quickly dispatched it, then looked at me. Her faded blue eyes were bright with determination, and maybe unshed tears.

'I'm going to give them a test,' Clare said. 'I'm telling them they must come home this Saturday – it's imperative.'

She crunched on the last cookie and it sounded as if small bones were breaking.

'Then I'll tell them that my attorney says I'll be broke within a year and ask them what I should do. I'll see which child loves me when I'm penniless.'

'And if they fail the test?' I asked.

'I'll leave my money to the Forest Humane Society! I'd rather it went to the dogs than to my ungrateful children.'

She stuck out her jaw, but one hand trembled when she set down her flowered cup.

'Isn't that a bit drastic?' I said.

'Perhaps. But it's a good test.'

'I'm sure both children love you,' I said.

I knew my words sounded hollow and useless. Clare brushed them aside. 'It's always better to know the truth.'

Clare was determined to test her children and for some reason, she wanted to tell me all about it. Maybe I had underestimated Clare. There was a tough woman under that genteel exterior.

I wanted to change the subject. 'How's Old Reggie?' I asked.

'In a tizzy,' she said. 'He's giving a party for Jessica Gray – the actress – after her third performance on Saturday. He didn't know whether it should be catered! I told him of course he'd have to cater it, and have a bartender, too. Otherwise, I know what he'll serve – those awful deviled eggs, pigs in blankets, and rat cheese on crackers.'

'That's the standard menu for Forest parties,' I said. I'd swallowed my share of cheap, dry yellow cheese on semi-stale crackers. You had to drink at a Forest party, just to get the food down.

'Well, I told him it was time to hire a caterer. Otherwise, we'll all look like hicks.'

'Did he agree?' I asked.

'Finally. It took some talking. Reggie will squeeze a nickel till it begs for mercy, but he did say yes. The party's only four days away. He's lucky he could get someone. I gave him three names and made sure he called the caterer while I was in the room. And a good florist, while he was at it. Otherwise, he'll put out a couple of supermarket bouquets in Waterford vases.

'Really, the reputation of the Forest is at stake here.'

I saw Clare's determined chin quiver, and could just imagine her giving tight-fisted Old Reggie a lecture. The old man thought his presence at a party more than made up for any lack of amenities. His children did as they were told. Only an equal like Clare could confront him.

She demurely sipped her coffee, and took a small bite of a cookie. I asked her the one question that everyone in the Forest had to answer. 'Are you going to Jessica's show at the Lux Theater?'

'No. I have season tickets but I gave this one away. I'd prefer to remember Jessica as she was in the sixties – young, vibrant and full of life.'

'You talk about her as if she's dead,' I said.

'She is. At least, the Jessica I admired is dead. I don't like this new incarnation. She's a scrawny old woman now, peddling that face junk. Kale, for heaven's sake! And her so-called comedy show is mean-spirited.'

She took a decisive crunch of her cookie, and a long drink of her coffee.

'I guess I'll have to go to the after-party,' Clare said, 'after I made such a fuss.'

'Mario, my hairdresser, wants me to go to the show with him, and the party at Reggie's afterward,' I said. 'I'm dreading it.'

'You should go, dear,' Clare said. 'It's a Forest occasion, our turn in the limelight. Don't miss it.'

THREE

The local media fawned all over Jessica Gray. She gave facials with her Captivating Youth Mask to all the major news anchors – on the morning show, the noon show, and the five and six o'clock news. The cameras took tight shots of the city's TV celebrities covered with green goo, then celebrated their 'amazing transformations.'

They looked the same to me, but I didn't want to sound like sour grapes. Or kale.

A radio shock jock drank the Captivating Youth Solution on air and made gagging noises. 'Tastes like lawn clippings!' he said.

'Well, you're acting younger already,' Jessica said. The sharpness in her voice subdued the jock.

'I'm sure it's good for me,' the jock said. 'Does it go well with leftover pizza?'

'And stale jokes,' Jessica said.

The interview was quickly back on track and Jessica wound up giving an infomercial on the city's most popular morning show for millennials.

The local paper, the *St Louis City Gazette*, had a full-page feature, even quoting a St Louis dermatologist who declared that Jessica's potions were 'all-natural.' That was definitely true. He couldn't quite bring himself to say that the products would make anyone look younger. But her show at the Lux Theater, 'Just Jessica', got rave reviews, and the final sold-out show this Saturday night promised the city a 'special event.'

I hadn't seen Mario, my hairstylist, since Jessica flew into town, so I was eager for the details of his triumph. I met him for an early dinner at Gringo Daze, the Forest's most popular Mexican restaurant. Actually, its only Mexican restaurant, but the food was superb.

We had a corner booth, and piled our coats on a chair. The restaurant was nearly empty at four-thirty, so Mario could dish. The server, a handsome twenty-something whose name tag said he was Glenn, couldn't keep his eyes off Mario. I couldn't blame the lad. Black-haired, dark-eyed Mario was a stunning man, who turned the heads of both sexes. Tonight he looked like a Spanish gunfighter in black Gucci and a heavy silver belt. Glenn the server took our order – chicken fajitas and white wine for both of us – and left.

'I have something for you.' Mario gave me an elegant glossy green bag filled with jars and bottles. 'Jessica's products.' He said the two words reverently, and presented them to me like a cat proudly giving me a dead bird. I had to hide my surprise. Mario was too sophisticated to be sucked in by Jessica's over-priced green glop. His regard for her had overruled his normal good taste.

One jar, a pretty swirl of frosted glass, was the Captivating Youth Mask. A tall glass bottle held Captivating Finishing Spray. 'You put that on after your make-up,' Mario said. The third bottle was the Captivating Youth Drink. 'Mix that with spring water,' he said.

'Thank you.' I tucked the bag next to my purse. 'Now, spill.'

'Everyone is so nice,' Mario said. He always started like this, whether they were nice or not. Then he'd get down to the real information. A Mariel Boatlift refugee, Mario had a slight Cuban accent, which grew thicker when he was under stress. Right now, he was relaxed.

'How many people does Jessica travel with?' I asked.

'Only three. Tawnee Simms, her understudy and dresser. Her assistant, Stu Milano. Her make-up artist, Will London – he's very sweet.'

Hm. Mario usually said that when he was attracted to a man. I kept quiet. He'd tell me sooner or later if he was having a fling with Will.

'Tawnee sounds vaguely familiar,' I said.

'She is,' Mario said. 'She had a chance at stardom back in the sixties, but it didn't work out. It probably never would have. She doesn't have Jessica's magnetism.'

The waiter brought our wine. I waited for him to leave, then said, 'OK, Mario, what's Jessica really like? And don't tell me she's "nice." She's anything but.'

'No, she is nice. Very nice. And it's an honor to work with her. I'm lucky – I got the job through a friend of a friend.'

'Come off it, Mario. You're internationally known. Lots of major celebs have you do their hair when they're in town. You've flown to New York, Paris, and Brazil for jobs.'

'True,' Mario said. 'But I live here in the flyover, the Midwest. That's not good for my cachet.'

Sad but true. Both coasts thought we in Middle America lost twenty IQ points simply by living here.

'So what's really happening?'

Mario was dying to tell me. I could sense it. He looked around the restaurant, and confirmed no one was within earshot, not even the dazzled server Glenn.

'I had to sign a nondisclosure agreement,' he said. 'But I know you never talk.'

I nodded, confirming my silence.

'Jessica depends on her make-up artist, Will. He's the best. Maybe even better than me.'

Will must be fantastic. Mario would never admit to anyone but me that someone else's skills were superior to his. I kept my silence, which encouraged him to continue.

'And Jessica has had plastic surgery.'

'You're joking! That's her whole campaign, that she's naturally beautiful.'

'Sh! Keep your voice down.' He looked alarmed, though there was no one around.

'Jessica is beautiful,' Mario said. 'And she believes she's never had plastic surgery. She told me so. But I saw the scars – and felt them – when I washed her hair.'

He shut up abruptly and Glenn delivered our drinks, a basket of tortillas, and bowls of salsa, guacamole and sour cream for our fajitas. 'I brought you extra tortillas,' he said to Mario, who smiled at him. I waited for the server to leave, then asked, 'What did you do when you found out she'd had a facelift, Mario?'

'Pretended she was telling the truth.'

'You said she believes she's never had plastic surgery. How can she believe that?'

'I think she's said she hasn't had surgery so many times, she does believe it,' Mario said.

'Right.'

'That's how I treat all my clients – as if they're always telling the truth. Jessica has had very artful nips and tucks. I'd like to know the name of her doctor, but of course, I can't ask.'

'What about that hair? That thick blond mane can't be all hers.'

'It's not,' he said. 'It's a hairpiece and extensions. Her own hair is very thin.'

'But you can't say that, either.'

'Why would I? I made it look as natural as possible. She has a very good hairpiece. The best.'

Glenn the server was back with two sizzling platters of fajitas. Mario and I carefully built our fajitas. I spread my tortilla with dabs of sour cream and guacamole, then just enough chicken, onions and peppers so my dinner wouldn't spill into my lap. I took a bite. Delicious, as always. Mario and I ate in silence. While we were preparing the second round, I asked him, 'What happened while you worked on her hair?'

'She kept quiet, and sipped water through a straw. When I finished, Jessica said she was pleased with my work. Tawnee came in to help her finish getting dressed. I stayed backstage, talking with Will. He told me he wants to have his own line of cosmetics and to open a salon in Bel Air. He asked me how I did it, how I ran my salon.'

Mario seemed proud to give Will advice.

'Bel Air? That's going to be expensive – and there will be lots of competition.'

'Yes, but Jessica is talking about backing him. He'll either have to hire a manager or close the salon when he travels with her.'

'Sounds like he has his future planned out.'

'He does. Life on the road is hard, and he misses California. Then Stu came back and asked me to do a favor for Jessica.'

'What kind of favor?'

'She needed some Percocet and Xanax, and I had both with me.'

'Mario! You didn't!'

'Who's going to know?' He tried to look innocent. He was an American citizen, but a Cuban-American would be suspect if Jessica's drug use was investigated.

'What if something happens to Jessica?' I asked.

'It won't. You worry too much. She needed to relax, because people are so mean to her.'

I thought Jessica was pretty nasty herself, but said nothing. 'Then what happened?'

'Jessica was ready. Will touched up her make-up and I sprayed her hair once more, and she went on-stage, where she was a huge success. Three standing ovations after the show! While she did her routine, I got a chance to have a drink with Will.'

His voice seemed to soften slightly at the mention of Will, but that could have been my imagination.

'What's Will like?'

'Very sweet,' Mario said.

'Seriously?'

'He's an artist, and we talked about make-up tips. He believes in bringing out a woman's natural beauty. Jessica has gorgeous brown eyes and he emphasizes them.'

'What color are Will's eyes?'

'Also brown. He has a terrific body and very thick red hair. But he's so smart, Angela. It's fun talking to another professional. And when Tawnee and Stu were around, we were perfectly professional.'

'I'm sure you were.'

'Stu used to be a magician. He still does magic tricks all the time, and makes things disappear. He disappeared two of my brushes.'

'That sounds annoying.'

'No, they reappeared just before I needed them. He seemed to sense exactly when I would. His timing is perfect.'

'What happened to Stu's magic career?'

'Who knows?' Mario shrugged. 'Maybe he wasn't very good. Stu says he's lucky now that he can work with Jessica. It's his way of staying in show business.'

'I'd find it painful to be on the edge of someone else's success,' I said.

'Stu seems happy enough,' Mario said. 'Jessica pays well. He says he's saving money for another show in Vegas – a comeback – and Jessica will help him.'

Glenn returned and took our plates. 'May I get you another drink?' the server asked. 'Some dessert? Our flan is good.'

'I know.' I smiled at the server. 'But not tonight, thanks. You've fed us too well. Just the check.'

Mario nodded, and grabbed the check when Glenn put it on our table. 'This is on me,' he said. 'I want to have a cigarette before we leave for the theater. Jessica made Stu, Will, and Tawnee stop smoking and switch to e-cigarettes. She said their cigarette smoke bothered her.'

'What if they smoked cigarettes outside, like you do?' I asked.

'She says she can still smell it on their hair and clothes, and it would get into her clothes. She's right, of course. They're all forbidden to smoke.'

'But she doesn't mind you smoking?' I asked.

'No.' He shrugged. 'I try not to smoke around her assistants. That would be cruel. They really miss cigarettes – they all smoked at least two packs a day – but they want to keep their jobs. She says vaping is healthier. Maybe it is, but she's never had to deal with smoker's cravings.'

We were in the restaurant parking lot now. 'Since I'm not allowed to smoke around Jessica, this is my last chance.' Mario brought out his cigarettes and fired up, nearly frantic for a nicotine fix. It was two degrees, way too cold for me.

'I'll wait in the car. We've got time before the show,' I said.

'I hope there is a show,' he said. 'Jessica has a terrible cold. Last night she was coughing and feverish. She could hardly stand up, but she went out and gave a brilliant performance.'

'Do you think she'll cancel tonight?' I said.

'If she's feeling as bad as she did last night, she should. But she won't. Jessica is determined. Nothing stops her once she's made up her mind.'

FOUR

The Lux Theater's official name is the Fabulous Lux, and that isn't hype. The theater, a twenties' fantasia of red and gold twisted pillars, roaring lions and fantastic light fixtures, lives up to its name.

That's why Jessica's 'surprise' for the city the last night of her run was such a shock. No, not a shock. An extended middle finger.

All the Forest's movers and shakers were there, and most had Lux Club luxury boxes. They had their own reserved parking lot, a private entrance, a private place where they could eat and drink before, during and after the show. They also had private bathrooms. Lux Club members did not have to pee with the peasants, even though those bathrooms were pretty swanky, too.

All this privilege didn't come cheap. An eight-seat luxury box was $64,750 – and they were sold out. With a wait list.

I waited in the theater while Mario went backstage. I never tired of wandering around the Lux. Each time I went I discovered another marvelous detail – a gold filigree lamp here, a grinning gold griffin there.

Mario and I had the best (non-Lux Club) seats in the house. Mario joined me just as the curtain went up.

The theater smelled of cold fur, wool, face powder and flowery perfume. Fluffy white heads dotted the audience like a field of chrysanthemums. The evening was also an infomercial for Captivating, and every theatergoer got a small leaf-green bag of samples and a tiny spray bottle. These were examined with excited oohs and playful squirts of the Captivating Finishing Spray. I left my bag under the seat. I wasn't going to have kale forced on me in any form.

There was a fanfare, the lights dimmed, the great gold and red curtains swung open, and then there was wild applause as Jessica appeared in a smashing black sequined gown.

She looked gorgeous. Her blond hair was thick and full, her face unlined. Her arms were toned and one long leg showed in the slit on her sparkling black gown.

The audience laughed at her jokes and applauded her one-woman skits. 'The President declared a war on poverty, so I threw a hand grenade at a bum.'

How could anyone think that was funny?

I disliked the show – no, I loathed it. Jessica mocked the poor and immigrants. Mario laughed. Never mind that he was an immigrant himself. I put a tight smile on my face and left it there, like an abandoned For Sale sign.

Finally, we came to Jessica's surprise. 'Vogue magazine likes to run stories about street fashion,' she said. 'Well, they ain't seen nothing yet. Let me show you the fashions I found on the streets of St Louie – right around the good ol' Lux Theater.'

Uh, oh. I held my breath. The area around the Lux was problematic, to be kind. The homeless people scared the crap out of the suburbanites who'd paid a hundred bucks for their tickets. The Lux Club members were protected, but only if they didn't go off the reservation.

Jessica, slim and glamorous, said, 'Let me introduce my top three street fashion finds.'

The orchestra played tinkling music and Jessica said, 'Here we have our first model, Suzy. She's wearing two dresses, and a cape in a fashionable shade of gray, accessorized by a single Rosie O'Grady bottle.'

A woman who could have been anywhere from thirty to sixty staggered out, shrouded in two stained dresses. The heavy beige wool dress had a loose hem that flapped around her dirty legs. A lighter white summer dress topped the wool one. It had yellow stains down the back that looked like urine. Suzy wore a Salvation Army blanket thrown over her scrawny shoulders. Suzy's smile revealed a toothless mouth. She waved her bottle cheerfully, and cheap wine arced over the stage. The audience howled with laughter. Suzy plopped down by the footlights like an abandoned doll and took a long pull on the bottle.

The audience applauded.

'Thank you, Suzy, dear,' Jessica said. 'Next, we have Denise. She also favors the layered look.'

Denise's haunted eyes looked out from under a baseball cap. She wore a black hoodie and a green Army jacket. Denise pushed her loaded shopping cart in a wide circle around Jessica, as if the glittering star would steal her trash-bagged bundles.

The audience laughed.

'Don't worry, Denise darling,' Jessica said. 'No one will take your worldly goods.'

'Why are these people laughing?' I said to Mario. 'This isn't funny.'

'Relax,' he said. 'She has something for all of the models.'

'Humiliation,' I said, as the third woman came out.

'And last, but not least, we have Becky,' Jessica said.

Becky, bleary-eyed and greasy-haired, managed a lopsided smile. She looked like she was wearing most of a Goodwill store. Her shaggy coat made her into a gray, lumbering bear.

'What's under that coat, dear?' Jessica asked. 'Show us.'

Becky fumbled with the single remaining button and tossed the coat on the stage. A wave of stink overwhelmed the people in the first rows, including me. Jessica fanned herself. The audience laughed.

Underneath, Becky wore a floppy man's plaid flannel shirt.

'Take off the shirt,' Jessica said.

Becky flung it off, to loud cheers. She smiled shyly at the audience and they cried, 'More, more!'

Becky threw off the gray hoodie, next a stained blue work shirt, and a once-white T-shirt, while the audience chanted 'More! More! More!'

Her eyes were dull and her smile was lost. Now Becky was wearing a blue blouse. The sleeves had been cut off.

'What's this around your neck, dear?' Jessica's voice was sweetly mocking as she fingered a rhinestone G on a greasy blue ribbon around Becky's neck.

She stood over Becky like an evil queen, sparkling, commanding and so beautiful. 'Why, it looks so sparkly. Is it a diamond pendant?'

'No, I found it in the parking lot,' Becky said.

'And what's the G stand for?' Jessica asked. 'Grubby?'

Jessica was mocking her, but Becky answered seriously. 'Good luck.'

'And we can see how lucky you are,' Jessica said. The audience roared with laughter. Becky smiled, as if she didn't quite get the joke.

Jessica checked out Becky's lumpy lower body.

'Good heavens, girl, you must be exhausted carrying around all those clothes,' Jessica said. 'How many pairs of pants are you wearing?'

'Four,' Becky mumbled.

'Take them off! Take them off!' chanted the audience.

Becky sat down on the stage and took off her down-at-heel work boots, then stood up and stepped out of a pair of men's baggy khakis. Underneath was a pair of striped pajama bottoms. The audience laughed. 'Take them off!' they cried.

Becky did, and revealed dirty red sweatpants.

'Take them off!'

She did. Becky was down to baggy brown jeggings and her sleeveless blouse.

'Take it off! Take it all off!' the audience screamed. Becky looked confused.

I couldn't stand any more. I got up to leave. 'Where are you going?' Mario asked. He grabbed my hand.

'Away,' I said. 'I can't watch this.'

'Stay,' he said. 'For me? Please?'

He was still holding my hand. He looked so handsome. I glanced again at dirty-haired Becky, who looked like a lost child. 'It's almost over,' he said.

I stayed. Later, I hated myself for that decision.

'Becky, dear, will you take off your clothes for ten dollars?' Jessica asked.

'No.' Becky's voice was small.

'Fifty dollars?'

Becky shook her head no.

'What about a hundred dollars?' Jessica's smile sparkled and her sweet voice made you see the riches a hundred bucks could bring.

A man stood up in the audience, his belly hanging over

his baggy suit pants. 'Hell, for a hundred bucks, I'll take off my clothes!'

'Thank you, sir,' Jessica said. 'But judging by your physique, I'd pay you to keep your clothes on.' The audience laughed, and he sat down red-faced.

'What about you, Becky?' Jessica's voice was seductive. 'A hundred dollars is a lot of money.'

'Do I have to take off my underwear, too?' Becky's voice was so small only those of us in the front rows could hear her.

'What?' Jessica said. Becky repeated her question.

'What do you say, folks? Underwear on or off?'

'Keep it on and take it off! Keep it on and take it off!' Thank goodness for St Louis reserve. If this was any other city they'd want the poor woman totally naked.

The audience kept chanting 'Keep it on and take it off!' Old, white-haired women and bald men chanted that sentence together. I was sickened. Enough. I started to stand again, but Mario grasped my hand tighter. 'Don't go,' he begged.

Becky unbuttoned the sleeveless blue blouse, revealing a drooping circle-stitch cotton bra holding her pendulous breasts. Then she slipped out of her sagging jeggings and revealed sad grayish granny panties. The G around her neck sparkled under the stage lights.

'Well, it's certainly your lucky night, Becky,' Jessica said. 'Stand up, dear.'

Becky stood, shivering slightly.

'There you have it,' Jessica said. 'Everyone has their price!'

The audience applauded as Tawnee appeared with a silver platter piled with envelopes. She wore a glittering red dress and a toothy smile.

'Here are the prizes for our models,' Jessica said. 'Becky, you get this crisp new one-hundred-dollar bill and seven gift cards for McDonald's meals.'

Becky had already slipped on her jeggings and was buttoning her sleeveless shirt. She took the envelope, gathered up the rest of her clothes and hurried off the stage.

Denise and Suzy each got ten dollars and five McDonald's gift cards.

'And as a special treat,' Jessica said, 'I've hired a limo to take our three models to the party at Reginald Du Pres's home in Chouteau Forest tonight.'

The audience applauded wildly, some standing. I looked to see if Old Reggie was in his box. 'The old boy will have a heart attack when those three bag ladies show up at his mansion,' I said to Mario.

'He already knows,' Mario said. I found that hard to believe.

Stu and Tawnee helped the other two homeless women offstage to another round of applause.

'And now, ladies and gentlemen,' Jessica said to the audience, 'before we go, let me introduce you to the people I can't live without. First, my friend, understudy, and assistant, Tawnee Simms. If that name sounds familiar, she had a part in *Eternally Groovy* as the endless party girl. If you didn't notice her, it was because – unlike me – Jessica kept her clothes on during the party scene. Take a bow, Tawnee.'

Tawnee came out, a fake smile plastered on her face.

'Next, we have my assistant, Stu Milano. Stu was a Las Vegas magician, who somehow made his career disappear. Tonight, he magically muscled Denise's cart on-stage. Come out, Stu.'

Stu, wearing a black tux, skipped out smiling, and bowed. His long, brassy blond hair, pulled into a ponytail, emphasized his noble nose. From some angles, his handsome features had a feral look.

'Then there's my magic make-up man, Will London, who brings out my natural beauty. Will wants his own line of make-up, and if he kisses my ass enough, he may get it. Come on out, Will.'

Will's smile was stretched across his face as the audience laughed at her comment. Like Stu, he wore a tux, but Stu's was better cut.

'And last, but not least, my local hair bender, Mario Garcia. Come on stage, Mario. Folks, didn't he do a fabulous job with my hair?' She ran her fingers through her long mane.

By now the whole audience was standing. Mario looked surprised. I nudged him and he ran up the side stairs and soon was on-stage, glowing with happiness. Jessica and her crew took three bows, then headed backstage. Mario came out and got me. 'You can come to Jessica's dressing room with me,' he said.

The star's dressing room was an opulent affair with vases of red roses, red velvet chaises longues, and gold mirrors. Jessica was coughing like she was about to lose a lung. Tawnee handed the sickly star tissues and a throat spray. 'I'm making you warm tea with honey, Jessica,' she said.

'To hell with the tea, get me a drink!' Jessica said, gasping for breath. The coughing fit was nearly over. She spit something nasty into a tissue and Tawnee took it.

Next, Tawnee poured a hefty slug of bourbon into the tea, turning it into a hot toddy. Jessica downed it. 'That worked,' she said. 'We leave tomorrow morning, thank gawd. I have to get out of this freezing shit-hole and home to California.' Tawnee looked pale and tired. I suspected she wanted to leave, too. Mario fussed with the star's hair, and Will touched up her make-up, while Jessica sipped a second toddy through a straw.

'Stu, did you put those disgusting, smelly creatures into the limo?' Jessica asked.

'Yes. Denise refused to leave her shopping cart and stayed behind, but Suzy and Becky are both going.' He bared his white teeth in a smile, but it didn't reach his flat, cardsharp's eyes.

'I can't wait for Old Reggie Du Pres to see those two – and smell them,' Jessica said. 'I told him I was bringing the models from the show. He said he'd be honored. He also said he'd only invited the "best people" to this party. Wait till he sees my models. Haw, haw, haw.'

Her cruel bar-room laugh ended in a second coughing fit. It took ten minutes for her to recover from the coughing. I was no doctor, but her cough sounded deep and dangerous.

Jessica patted the satin-lined pockets of her sable evening cloak, then said, 'Dammit, Stu, did you make my gloves disappear?'

'Only to make them reappear, milady,' he said. A mocking smile played across his thin face, and he produced the fur-trimmed gloves with a flourish.

Jessica angrily snatched them out of his grasp and slid her hands inside them. 'I've had enough of your third-rate tricks, Stu,' she snapped.

Then she whirled around, the glossy dark cape spreading out like wings and said, 'OK, let's get the hell out of here, and tomorrow we can get the hell out of here for good.'

FIVE

W e'd almost made it out of the Lux dressing room when Stu's phone rang. He looked at the caller ID and said, 'It's Reggie Du Pres.'

'Gee, I wonder why he's calling?' Tawnee's voice was mock-innocent. Jessica laughed, then erupted into another coughing fit. Tawnee handed her the throat spray.

Stu put his cell phone on speaker so we could all hear the conversation and answered, 'Yeah, Reg, what's up?'

I almost choked. Nobody ever addressed the Forest patriarch as 'Reg.'

We heard Old Reggie spluttering. Then he got control of himself. His speech was dangerously slow. 'There are two bums here in a limo. They said Jessica sent them.'

Jessica grabbed the cell phone from Stu. 'I did, Reggie. I told you some models from the show might be coming to the party.'

'Models?' Outrage burned through the phone. 'One's drunk and neither one has bathed in some time!'

'That's ambience, Reg. They're part of my show tonight.'

'I can't let those people in my home!'

'Then I won't come,' Jessica said. 'I'll go straight to my hotel. I'm exhausted, anyway.'

The silence stretched for nearly a minute. I could almost hear Old Reggie calculating the cost of the caterer, the florist, the open bar, not to mention the damage to his prestige. His house was some eight thousand square feet – he had plenty of room to stash the unwanted guests.

'All right,' he said. 'As a courtesy to you.'

'See you soon, darling,' Jessica cooed, and clicked off the phone.

'Let's go,' she said, and we were finally outside the theater.

Even though it was eleven at night, Jessica was given a police escort to the Du Pres mansion: A car in front and one in back. Mario and I joined the entourage, following Jessica's black stretch limo.

I congratulated Mario but said little else. He was thrilled with his on-stage accolade, and I didn't want to spoil his fun. I was still appalled by the way Jessica had used and abused those poor homeless women.

When we reached the city limits of Chouteau Forest, a spot-lit banner said, 'Welcome, Jessica!' From there, it was a short drive to Reggie's mansion.

The nineteenth-century stone castle looked like it had been frosted with white icing. Every light was on, and we could hear a string quartet playing. Reggie himself came out through the black lacquered double doors to greet Jessica. The old man looked distinguished in black tie. He kissed Jessica's hand. I was close enough to see the old man's flinty eyes. He had his prize. Jessica gave him a syrupy smile and Reggie led her inside.

The rest of us followed, dazzled by the lights and sparkling chandeliers. Candles flickered, and hot house flowers were everywhere: sculptural arrangements of waxy white calla and sweet-smelling Stargazer lilies, cheerful bouquets of Gerbera daisies, colorful poppies and showy peonies.

The entire Forest aristocracy had turned out at Reggie's, a glittering array of local grandees. The women brought their jewels out of vaults and put on their evening gowns shining with bugle beads and sequins. The men added festive touches to their evening wear – a daring cummerbund or colorful bow tie.

All waited in a long line to meet Jessica. She sat in a throne-like chair next to a table of leaf-green goodie bags. Jessica was in full sales mode, graciously greeting the guests and pushing her products. The Forest creatures looked thrilled to receive the free samples.

Mario stopped to talk to some clients and I headed for the food. The array was amazing for a culinary conservative Forest dweller. Small, handwritten signs labeled each appetizer: baby boiled potatoes with caviar and sour cream, lobster ceviche, lamb lollipops, grilled watermelon caprese skewers, grilled baby octopus, and an enormous platter of cheese – a real

English Cheddar, blue-veined Roquefort, Swiss Pecorino, and Italian Asiago.

The Forest dwellers went for the more conventional choices: the lamb, the caviar potatoes, and the cheese. I wasn't surprised to find Clare Rappaport in elegant silver lace, helping herself to the baby octopus. I waved at her.

'Isn't this amazing?' she said. 'The old boy has done us proud, and I've told him so.' She skimmed off to a table of her friends.

Becky, the 'model' who'd won a hundred dollars, had a plate piled high with appetizers. 'These thingies are good,' she said, through a mouthful of lamb lollipop. She'd washed her face and combed her greasy hair.

'I'll try some,' I said, filling my own plate. We picked up napkin-wrapped silverware. Becky sat at a small table covered with a pink cloth.

'May I join you?' I asked.

'Do you want to?' she said. 'I haven't had a bath in a while. The old man didn't want me and Suzy in his house. He told us we could shower in the pool house and take a nap there, and he'd send over food. Suzy took him up on his offer. I told him to fuck himself.'

I nearly choked on a caviar potato.

'I wish I'd told that bitch that, too.' Anger flared in her eyes – and hurt.

Becky stabbed her lobster ceviche. 'I hate her,' she hissed. 'I hate her. I hate her. She wanted me to get naked so they could laugh at me, but I kept my underwear on.'

She seemed proud of this small victory. 'Why does she do that – make people feel bad – when she has everything?'

'I don't know,' I said. 'She's leaving St Louis tomorrow.'

'Good riddance,' Becky said. She stabbed her grilled octopus. 'I hope she feels the same pain she inflicts on others.' The words felt like a curse.

We ate our food in silence, and then Becky said, 'I didn't used to be like this. I had a husband and a house and a good job. I was a nurse's aide at an old folks' home. I like working with older people. Then I lost the job and my world turned to shit. That's why I did it, you know – that's why I let her make a fool out of me. I was hoping someone would see me and give me a job. It's hard living on the street. Hard and dangerous.'

'Were you robbed?'

'Worse. Robbed and raped. I started drinking after I got raped.'

I put my fork down. 'You were raped? When?'

'Three years ago last December. In an alley off Olive, not too far from the Lux. The bastard beat me up and took my stash – ten dollars.'

'Did you report it?'

She snorted. 'Won't do any good. I never saw the guy's face. He was wearing a ski mask.'

'I'm sorry,' I said.

'Happens a lot, you know.' She seemed so matter of fact about that terrible event. Maybe telling her story that way helped diminish the horror.

'I'd do anything for a job,' Becky said. 'Well, almost anything. I'm no hooker. But I'd sober up if I could get work again and get my life back.'

She patted her glittering rhinestone G. 'That's why I always wear this. Always. And no matter what that evil bitch says, it did bring me good luck. With that hundred dollars she gave me, I'll get a week in a hotel. That's all I want, a warm room and a job.'

I gave her the name of Women's Work, a local organization that helped homeless women find jobs. Becky promised to contact them. 'They're not far from the Lux,' I said. 'When you get your ride back to St Louis, maybe the limo can drop you off there.'

Becky snorted. 'I don't think we're going back by limo. But thanks. This information gives me some hope.'

A server took my empty plate. 'May I get you something to drink, Becky?' I asked.

'No, thanks,' she said. 'I'm off the sauce, starting now. I will get more food, though.'

She was back at the table. I went looking for the bathroom. I knew the house from when my mother was housekeeper here. I wandered down the grand hall, which deserved its name. White marble. It was lined with feathery palm trees and marble statues of Roman gods and goddesses. In daylight, the stained-glass ceiling was stunning.

I heard someone crying in a darkened salon next to the bathroom, and peeked in. It was Tawnee and Stu. Even in the soft light, Tawnee looked haggard, her blond hair flat and her face lined and pale. Her make-up was smudged and her mascara left muddy trails down her face. Up close, her sparkly red dress looked shabby and worn.

Stu seemed to have lost his usual chipper demeanor. His tux was rumpled and his long, brassy hair was slipping out of his ponytail holder. From this angle, I could see it was a silver death's head. Quite the player, Stu. Only Will seemed confident, crisp and cheerful. None of them saw me.

I slipped inside the bathroom. I could still hear Tawnee weeping about her on-stage humiliation. 'It goes on night after night,' she said. 'I can't take it, Stu. But what am I going to do at my age?'

'Oh, for gawd's sake,' Stu said. 'Most people would be thrilled to be in your shoes. As my mother used to say, I hate a whiner.'

'I hate Jessica,' Tawnee said, and punched something soft. A pillow? A sofa cushion?

'I wish she was dead. She ruined my life. I got good reviews in that movie, and she made sure I never got another part.'

'Same with me,' Stu said. 'I know Jessica got me barred from the Vegas and Tahoe casinos so I'd have to work for her.'

If he knew that, I wondered, why was he working for her – and confessing it? Didn't the man have any self-respect?

'And I know how the bitch convinced the producer of *Eternally Groovy* to hire her instead of me,' Tawnee said. 'I was too proud to go down on him. I should have given him a hummer.'

'But what choice do we have now?' Stu said. 'Even if I knew whose ass to kiss to get something better, I'll be damned if I'll do it. We're both wearing golden handcuffs.'

'At least I can get away,' Will said. He sounded smug. 'Jessica is talking about backing me in my own business.'

'Hah! Don't bet on it,' Stu said. 'She makes those promises to get what she wants, and then forgets them.'

With that, I heard the click of heels on marble. I slid out of the bathroom, and peeked around the corner.

'I heard that,' said an angry voice.

Jessica. A glittering goddess of destruction, death rays beaming from her hard eyes.

'All of you are no-hopers.' She sounded like a judge pronouncing a sentence. 'You aren't has-beens. You never worked hard enough to achieve that. If you were any good, you would have succeeded on your own. You're never-weres!'

I winced at her cruelty.

'Stu, the only thing you ever make disappear is your paycheck! The way that vanishes, it has to be magic.'

'Not true!' Stu said. 'The timing was bad. Magic is a big deal. If I had a comeback in Vegas, I could make it.'

'Hah!' Jessica said. 'Not a chance. You're no David Copperfield. You'll be doing children's birthday parties for the rest of your miserable life.'

Stu moved back as if Jessica had struck him.

Jessica turned her wrath on Tawnee next. 'Tawnee, quit whining about that movie from 1967. You didn't get the part because you can't act your way out of a paper bag.

'And Will, forget the idea of starting your own make-up line. You're a loser, like these other two. You'll never get a nickel out of me.

'I'm firing all of you when we get back to LA. Tawnee, where's my goddamned spray?'

I saw Jessica grab the red spray bottle from Tawnee, then blow her nose and stick the used tissue in Tawnee's outstretched hand. Yuck. Then she flounced off.

I was horrified. I waited for their reactions. Stu showed no emotion at all. He could have been a wax figure. Will looked worried. 'Are we really fired?' he asked. 'I've never seen her so furious.'

Tawnee shrugged it off. 'Don't worry, she doesn't mean it. She fires us all the time, especially at the end of a tour when the strain is getting to her,' she told Will. 'After she's home a week, we'll regroup and get ready to go back on the road and she'll have forgotten all about it.'

Stu finally came out of his trance. He narrowed his eyes and said, 'But don't bet you'll ever see any of her money for your make-up line, Will. It ain't gonna happen.'

There was a scream from the main salon, and we all rushed out.

Jessica was lying on the floor by her throne, surrounded by her green goodie bags. A woman in blue sequins was cradling Jessica's head. 'She's fainted,' she said. 'Call an ambulance.'

Soon sirens screamed up the drive and Jessica was loaded onto a stretcher, bound for Sisters of Sorrow Hospital.

Becky materialized next to me. 'Is she dead yet?' she asked.

SIX

'**A**ngela, you've got to help me!' It was Mario, calling me at six the next morning. I heard the panic in his voice. Also, his Cuban accent had thickened, a sure sign he was upset. He'd called me on my personal cell phone. I had two phones, like some egotistical titan: one for personal calls and one for work. If my work phone was ever subpoenaed, I didn't want my personal calls and texts to wind up in court.

'You've got to drive me to the hospital,' Mario said. 'My car won't start. Jessica wants me to fix her hair before she leaves.'

'Leaves? Mario, she can barely stand up.'

Last night, Jessica wasn't dead, but darn close to it. She had double pneumonia. Mario and I found out when we followed her entourage to the hospital. Jessica didn't have to wait in the ER like everyone else. She was examined, diagnosed, pumped full of antibiotics, given oxygen, then rushed up to SOS's finest private suite. Stu, Tawnee and Will slept on cots and couches in her suite. Mario and I left about two in the morning, once she was settled.

'She wants her hair done. I should be there now,' he said.

'I'm on my way. But I'm on call as a death investigator today, from six to six. I might have to suddenly leave. How will you get home?'

'If I get stranded, I'll call Carlos at the salon. I can't find him this morning. And you know the last cab I called took forever to show up and the driver was drunk. Just get here, please. I'm at my salon.'

I wasn't looking forward to Jessica and her meanness, but Mario was my friend. I threw on my black death investigator pantsuit and rushed over. Mario ran out of the salon and threw his bag of gear in the back of my Dodge Charger. He was wearing his customary black pants and shirt and a fantastic black fake fur coat.

On the way to SOS, he tried to fix my hair.

'I'm driving,' I said. 'Stop that.'

'But you're with me, and your hair looks terrible.'

I slammed the car into a parking space, and gave him a moment to brush my dark hair until he was happy with it. Then we ran through the cold to the hospital lobby, past the waiting TV reporters. Judging by the forest of cameras, Jessica's hospitalization had become a national story.

Stu, in a sharp navy business suit, met us in the lobby, and got us through hospital security. He showed no emotion.

'How is she?' I asked, as we elbowed our way through the crowd of reporters.

Stu waited until we were in the back stairs before he answered. 'She's still sick, but she insists on going home. The doctor is trying to talk her out of it.'

'After last night? Is she fit to travel?'

Stu shrugged. 'Jessica doesn't follow the rules.' He was puffing a bit by the time we got to the fourth floor – we all were. We'd run up the stairs, Mario still lugging his heavy black styling case, as if we were responding to an actual emergency. We waited in the hall outside Jessica's suite.

The door was closed, but we heard raised voices.

'I cannot release you,' a woman said. This voice was deeper than Jessica's, and impatient. A doctor?

'You'll have to leave here Against Medical Advice,' the doctor said. 'If you opt for an AMA discharge, you'll need to sign a document. This will state that you understand that you are leaving against our advice.'

'Bring it on!' That sounded like Jessica, a wheezy, angry Jessica.

'Your insurance may not pay for your care,' the doctor warned.

'I don't give a damn!'

'The long flight will aggravate your symptoms,' the doctor said. 'With an AMA discharge, you have a four-time higher risk of readmission to the emergency department.'

'I want out of here.'

'You have a higher likelihood of dying within the next six months,' the doctor warned.

'If I don't get out of this shit-hole I'm going to die. I'm going home to sunny California.' Jessica's outburst resulted in a fit of coughing that sounded like her lungs were being ripped apart.

'That wracking cough is exactly what I mean, Jessica. What if this happens on your flight home?'

Jessica took two wheezy breaths and said, 'I'm doing this. I'm fine and I'm leaving. I want to go home.'

'As you wish,' the doctor said, clearly offended.

We scattered away from the door as the angry doctor stomped out – a tank-like brunette in a starched white coat. I slipped around the corner and ran into Becky. At least, I thought it was Becky – she was clean and wearing a blue pantsuit with a pink top, a pink-and-blue checked scarf, and matching blue Crocs with a coffee stain on the right shoe.

'Becky?' I said. 'Is that you?'

'I clean up good, don't I?' she said. Even her good-luck G sparkled around her neck.

'You look terrific. Nice clothes.'

'I found them,' she said.

I didn't ask where.

'She's still alive, isn't she?' Becky asked.

'She's going home today,' I said.

'She looks like shit,' Becky said. 'I got into her room when everyone was asleep, and snagged an e-cigarette case that's real silver, some cool vape juice, and some cash. I got out before anyone noticed.'

'You stole things out of her room?'

'So? They deserve it. They were all in on it. What happened last night was like being raped, except hundreds of people watched, and laughed at me.'

'I'm so sorry,' I said. 'It must have been horrible.'

'It was. I'll remember it for as long as I live. But I got my revenge.' Her sad smile showed crooked, yellow teeth. 'She'll pay for what she did to me.' *She*. Becky couldn't bring herself to say Jessica's name.

I was grateful when Mario called my name.

'Angela! If you want to stay here at the hospital, you have

to be my assistant,' he said. 'Will is almost finished with her make-up.'

'What do I do?'

'Hand me brushes, clips and spray when I ask for them,' Mario said. 'I'll point them out.'

Jessica was sitting in a tall-backed hospital chair by the window, where the light was best. She wore a blood-red turtleneck, tight black pants and stylish black high-heeled boots. Her veined hands were purple with bruises from the IV sticks. Her mane of hair was crushed into a turban, while Will worked on her face.

Will looked a little rocky this morning. His rusty red hair needed combing and he had bags under his brown eyes. But he did a fine job of making the star look glamorous.

Stu got in the way, making Will's brushes and make-up disappear with his magic tricks, until the two nearly came to blows.

'Stop with the stupid tricks, Stu, and go sit on the couch,' Jessica ordered through gritted teeth, as if he were a disobedient child. Stu sat next to Tawnee, and sulked like a child.

Tawnee, her hair a rat's nest, demanded, 'Stu, did you make my e-cigarette disappear?'

'No,' Stu said.

'You liar.' I could feel the heat in her voice. 'It was a good one. Real silver.'

'No, honest, I didn't. Someone swiped my vape juice, too. And sixty dollars out of my wallet.'

Tawnee glared at him, but said nothing. Neither did I, though I could have solved that mystery.

'That's what you get for leaving your things lying around in a hospital room where anyone could come in and take them,' Jessica said. Never mind that they were at SOS because of her.

Will did a final dusting of powder on Jessica's face and said, 'All done.'

'Good job,' I said.

Jessica glared at me and said, 'Who the hell is that woman?'

'She's my assistant,' Mario said.

'Long as she's not with the press,' Jessica said. 'Will, there's a shadow under my left eye.'

Will touched the imaginary shadow with a brush, and finally the star was satisfied. Mario stepped up to her chair. I lugged over his styling case. It must have weighed fifty pounds. He plugged in a powerful acid-green dryer, and started brushing out her hair. He sectioned it, and pointed out the brushes and clips he needed, his words short, his manner serious.

'Round brush.'

'Clip.'

'Second round brush.'

'Clip.'

I felt like a nurse assisting a surgeon in the OR.

Finally, the star was ready. Her cold symptoms were no longer visible. Jessica shrugged into a fabulous white fake fur, fit for a forties movie queen, and covered her bruised hands with white leather gloves. I had to admit she looked dazzling, and I didn't even like her.

Will powdered her nose again and she said, 'Let's go while I can still breathe. I need to get out of this hellhole. Stu, do you have everything ready for the demonstration?'

He held up a tall glass of what looked like liquefied grass clippings. 'All ready,' he said.

'I'm ready, too,' Jessica said, and we headed for the elevator.

The dark gray marble lobby of SOS was crammed with reporters, doctors, hospital staff, and visitors. Security had to clear a path for us through the scrum.

'Jessica! Jessica, what do you think of St Louis?' asked a red-haired TV reporter in a chic blue dress.

'Such a friendly city,' she said, her voice slick with false sincerity. 'Thank you for the sold-out shows and good reviews.'

'What's next?' a second blond reporter in shocking pink asked.

'I'm going home to recover and then I'll hit the road for the East Coast leg of "Just Jessica."'

'Why are you checking out against medical advice?' asked a reporter in baggy khakis and an old tan coat. By the way he was dressed, I suspected he was a newspaper reporter.

'I loved it here,' she lied, 'but now I need some healing

California sunshine. Let me show you what else will heal me.'

The media crowded around, hungry for a photo op. I caught a glimpse of Becky at the edge of the scrum, watching with avid eyes, and thought of her question, 'Is she dead yet?'

Stu produced the tall glass of green stuff with a magician's flourish.

'This is Captivate,' Jessica said, holding up the glass. 'It's packed with nourishment. This is why I look so good. My personal fountain of youth not only keeps me young – it will cure me of this cold.'

Cameras clicked as she drank the whole glass of green gunk. I tried to hide my disgust. Nothing could make me drink a glass of cold ground-up kale. The woman's greed was astounding.

Stu handed her a clean handkerchief to pat her lips, whisked away the glass and stuffed it into his leather travel bag.

'That's it, people,' Stu said. 'The press conference is over. Jessica has to catch a plane. Thank you!'

Jessica waved goodbye and got into her black stretch limo. Mario started to head to the parking lot with me. Stu ran up to us. 'Mario, there's going to be more press at the airport. Jessica will need you in her limo for a touch up.'

'Can I bring my assistant?' Mario asked.

'There's no room,' he said, though the limo looked to me like it could seat ten comfortably.

'I'll follow behind you,' I said, 'and give you a ride home, Mario.'

'I'll leave my cell phone on and video everything. You can watch it in real time, so you don't miss anything. I'm even going to record it,' he whispered. 'Thank you.'

'Can you do that?' I asked. Mario was even less tech-savvy than me.

'Of course.' He gave me a kiss on the cheek and I ran for my car.

But before I reached it, I was stopped by his frantic cry, 'Angela, my recording app is not working! And my battery is down to 37 percent. My phone is useless. Can I use yours?'

'Do you really need this, Mario?'

'Yes,' he said, his voice low, fast and frantic. 'I told you, I am stuck here in the Midwest where my work is not taken seriously. But a recording of me styling a major star would help my business. Please, Angela. *Es muy importante.*' His brown eyes pleaded with me, and he'd regressed to Spanish, a sure sign. Mario was desperate.

I said, 'OK.'

'Hurry!' he said. 'I have to go! I'll download a video app on your phone, OK?'

'Sure,' I said and handed him my personal cell phone.

'Thank you,' he said. 'I'll make sure you can watch it, too.' He called my office phone. I answered and he said, 'Leave it on, so you can see, too.' My hated second phone was finally coming in handy after all.

'Mario!' Stu shouted. 'Are you coming or not?'

'Yes!' Mario said.

'Then get your ass in here so we can get the hell out of here.'

I ran to my car, glad Jessica was finally leaving the Forest.

SEVEN

Plumber Bob Ross was late for work that morning. He ran a red light on Gravois Road and plowed into the side of a white box truck. Bob wasn't hurt, and neither was anyone in the truck. But Bob's minor fender bender would have a major impact: it would destroy the Forest's reputation.

Mario had kept his promise to record everything. He had the cell phone sticking out of his shirt pocket. Jessica was too busy ordering her staff around to notice.

Thanks to him, I could see the inside of Jessica's black Mercedes stretch limo as it sat in the hospital parking lot, and I was right. There would have been plenty of room for me. The stretch limo had a long black leather bench seat, a bar fully stocked with drinks, and a TV. The sound system played the late sixties music of Johnny Grimes, Jessica's long-dead lover, his guitar squealing like a vacuum cleaner. I liked his music. Johnny was harder edged than the Beatles, but not quite as abrasive as the Stones. I wondered if the music was a tribute to Jessica from the driver.

Mario was squeezed in a side seat next to Stu, his styling case at his feet. Jessica spread herself out on the long leather main seat, her fluffy white fur coat taking up most of the room. Tawnee and Will were on either side.

The long-gone Johnny Grimes song was 'Sometime Girl'; the ballad he supposedly wrote for Jessica at the height of their passion. His words wafted softly, thoughtfully, around the limo. 'Sometimes you're mine / sometimes you belong to the world / please be mine / all the time / my sometime girl.' Even through the iPhone's tinny speakers, the sound was soulful. It was hard to believe the singer had been dead for forty years.

'Turn that shit off,' Jessica yelled, and Johnny Grimes was gone.

The limo departed the hospital at a stately pace. 'Thank God we're out of here,' Jessica said, her voice a snarl. 'Goddamn

rubes. Never again. Never again will I go to this hellhole. I
don't care if they pay me double.'

Stu, Tawnee, and Will stayed silent during this tirade.
I couldn't see Mario, but the phone was so still, I knew he
was frozen in his seat.

'How much longer till we're at the airport?' Jessica shouted
to the driver. A fishwife would have admired her screech.

'We should be at Lambert Field in twenty minutes, ma'am,'
the limo driver soothed. 'Plenty of time for your ten o'clock
flight to Los Angeles.'

With that, the limo halted. It was caught in the aftermath
of Bob the plumber's fateful accident, stuck in the morning
rush hour traffic. I was two cars behind the sleek black machine.

'Then why the hell aren't we moving?' Jessica screamed.

'A minor accident up ahead,' the driver said. He sounded
like a pilot assuring his passengers they'd be encountering a
little turbulence. 'From here, it looks like just a fender bender.'

'Well, drive around it,' Jessica screeched.

'Can't, Miss Gray. The police have the road blocked and
there's no alternate route. But the intersection should be cleared
in a minute.'

Jessica turned back to her staff. 'Fix me up,' she commanded.
Will opened his black make-up case. He outlined Jessica's lips
in a neutral color, and began applying fresh red lipstick with
a small brush.

That's when the video showed Jessica started coughing
again – horrible hacks that sounded like her lungs were coming
apart. She gasped for breath and held her chest. Finally, she
managed to say, 'Tawnee! Where's my throat spray?' Her
voice was a croak.

Tawnee dug in her purse and handed Jessica more tissues
and cough drops.

Jessica coughed into the tissues and shrieked. 'Shit! I'm
bleeding. Get my goddamn spray.'

Even I could see the blood on the tissues, thanks to the cell
phone feed from inside the limo. The tissues were bright
crimson.

Tawnee looked terrified. 'Let's get you back to the hospital,'
she said.

'I'd rather die.' Jessica's voice was a gurgle. 'Tawnee, call Dr Albion and make an appointment for as soon as we get home. If I need a hospital, I'll go straight to Cedars.' Cedars-Sinai Medical Center in Los Angeles, hospital to the stars. Jessica erupted into another burst of chest-wracking coughs.

I remembered the doctor's warning: Jessica had a good chance of dying within six months if she checked out against medical advice. She sounded like that prediction could come true any moment. Stu looked worried. Tawnee was digging through her purse with a craziness that was almost cartoonish. Tissues, mints, a hairbrush, and two packs of tissues flew onto the seat, but no spray.

'Where's the goddamned throat spray?' Jessica demanded between hacks.

Tawnee frantically searched, tossing out her wallet, three pens and an iPhone. The debris was piling up on the leather seat.

'Dammit, Stu,' Tawnee said. 'Did you make that spray bottle disappear?'

'No.'

I couldn't see Stu clearly, but I could hear his offended innocence.

'Where is it?' Jessica demanded. 'I need it now.'

'I'm looking,' Tawnee said. 'I carry two bottles, one for back-up.' Tawnee resumed ransacking her purse, tossing out a lacy pink thong.

Will looked embarrassed. 'Hey!' he said. 'Enough! Let me look!'

He put his lipstick brush in his make-up case and gently took Tawnee's black purse, the size of a microwave oven. Will dug around and came up with another iPhone and a box of tampons.

Stu, disgusted, said, 'Will, you couldn't find your ass with both hands. Give it to me.' He grabbed the purse and pulled out a blue spray bottle.

'Stu, you asshole, you were playing your stupid tricks,' Tawnee said.

Jessica reached for the bottle with shaking hands. 'It's about goddamn time,' she said between racking coughs.

She sprayed her throat, and the grating coughs stopped. She took several deep breaths to recover. In the loud silence, she looked pale and exhausted, even with Will's skillful make-up. Jessica swallowed two cough drops and yelled at the driver, 'Hey, I thought we were going to the airport.'

'We are, Miss Gray. The tow trucks have just arrived. As soon as the intersection is cleared we'll be on our way.'

'Damn hicks,' Jessica muttered. 'I'll never get out of this fricking dump.'

Those turned out to be Jessica's last words. Suddenly, she sat up as if she'd been electrified. A stream of green vomit shot out of her mouth and her arms and legs flailed wildly. I heard the sound of breaking glass, and saw Jessica's high-heeled boot plunge through the TV screen. Tawnee screamed as it shattered.

Stu shouted, 'Driver! Jessica's sick. We need to go to the hospital! Now!'

With that, I quit watching my cell phone screen. From my car, I saw the limo make a wild U-turn and rush back to the hospital. The driver was going at least seventy miles an hour. I followed, able to keep up. I was glad most of the traffic was going in the other direction.

I couldn't see what was going on inside the limo – I was going too fast to watch the scene on my phone. I imagined a frantic Mario, Tawnee, Will and Stu desperately trying to help Jessica. I could see her arms and head thrashing around.

The road back to SOS was blessedly free of traffic, and the limo pulled up at the ER entrance in less than ten minutes.

Someone must have called ahead. A medical team was waiting with a stretcher. The limo screeched to a stop, a nurse flung open the back door, and Jessica was lifted onto the stretcher, a dramatic vision of long blond hair and white fur. She was briskly rolled inside, followed by Tawnee, Will and Stu.

I parked my car, and found a dazed Mario, green vomit on his fur coat, clinging to his black styling case like a life preserver.

'Here is your cell phone,' he said. It slipped out of his shaking hand and landed on the concrete with a clatter. We both scrambled to pick it up, but I could see the screen was now black and had a big diagonal crack.

'I broke it!' Mario said. 'I am so sorry.'

'It's just a phone,' I said, eager to cut off the flow of apologies. 'It can be fixed. What I really care about is you. How are you?'

He didn't answer. 'She is dead,' he said.

'You don't know that,' I said. 'She looked pretty awful last night, but she turned out to be OK this morning.'

'No, this time, she is really dead,' Mario said. 'She had terrible seizures. You don't get those from pneumonia. Somebody killed her.'

EIGHT

Mario was right: This time, Jessica really was dead. But murdered? That was another question, and it had no answer yet.

The press had followed the star's stretch limo back to the hospital like a pack of hounds after raw meat. Shortly after Jessica was rolled into the ER, the hungry throng of reporters followed, demanding to know what was wrong.

No-nonsense hospital security in navy blazers herded the reporters into the lobby, the same place where the TV reporters had taped Jessica downing her youth drink earlier this morning. They waited impatiently, interviewing one another and making cell phone calls to demanding city editors and news desks.

The SOS lobby was the perfect place for the grim announcement we were all expecting: It was dark as a cave, with cold charcoal marble walls and a funereal black floor. The stainless-steel cross was cold comfort – two slim pieces of steel.

Nearly an hour later, a hospital spokesperson – a scrawny sparrow of a woman in a plain brown suit – came into the lobby and made sure Sisters of Sorrow didn't take any blame for Jessica's death.

The SOS announcement was masterfully crafted: 'It is with great regret that we announce the death of the beloved entertainer, Jessica Gray.' Ms Sparrow's reading was flat and her eyes never left the paper in her hand. She was white with terror and her hands shook so hard the paper rattled as she read.

'Ms Gray was dead on arrival at Sisters of Sorrow Hospital, and efforts to revive her were futile. This morning at seven-thirty, she signed herself out of this hospital against her physician's orders, and insisted on flying back to California, despite warnings that this course of action could have serious – even fatal – consequences.

'Unfortunately, Ms Gray disobeyed her doctor's orders. By the time she was brought back to this hospital, it was too late to save her. The cause of death is under investigation, pending an autopsy. We extend our heartfelt sympathy and prayers to her family, friends, and many fans.'

The reporters threw questions like darts: 'What did Jessica die of? Was she murdered? Who poisoned her?'

'No questions,' Ms Sparrow said, and scurried back into the depths of the building. She refused to speculate on Jessica's cause of death.

A TV reporter shouted at Ms Sparrow's retreating back, 'I heard Jessica didn't die of pneumonia. She had seizures and vomiting. She was poisoned! They're running the tests now.'

The herd of reporters scattered to spread news and rumors. In no time, word was out that Jessica had been poisoned. On the TV news, 'special reports' showed a glamorous Jessica in the hospital lobby downing that green gunk – her 'fountain of youth' – and speculating that her last drink was poisoned.

One TV reporter called her death a 'locked limo mystery,' implying that everyone in the car with her – Tawnee, Stu, Will, and Mario – were suspects in her untimely death.

Since I was on call that day, Evarts Evans, the Forest's ME, ordered me to do Jessica's death investigation. His voice was imperious. 'This is just terrible,' he said. 'A horrible loss, and such bad publicity for our community. You'll be joined shortly by Detective Ray Greiman. He's on his way.'

Rats! I'd have to work with the most careless detective on the force.

'I need you to do an exceptional job on Ms Gray's death investigation,' Evarts said. 'And please be as careful as you can. The eyes of the world are on our community.'

'I can't do this death investigation, sir,' I said. 'I know the deceased. I went to the party at Reggie Du Pres's house last night. I'm at the hospital now. I was following her limo to the airport to give her hairstylist a ride home.'

Evarts wasn't buying it. 'Did you ever go to Ms Gray's home in California? Did you go to her hotel room? Are you on her Christmas card list?'

'No, sir.'

'Meeting Ms Gray at a party does not constitute knowing her, Angela. Our other death investigator on duty was called out on a case involving a two-car accident. You will do Jessica's death investigation.'

'But—' I said.

'That's a direct order.'

'Yes, sir.' That command meant I'd be fired if I said no. I fetched my DI suitcase, which I kept in my car trunk. Hospital deaths made my job easier. The victim had been pronounced dead and the staff would give me all the necessary paperwork.

First, I needed a quick look at the probable death scene. Examining the limo was the job of the police, but it would help me understand Jessica's death if I could see the scene. The driver had pulled the limo around to the hospital loading dock, between two delivery trucks.

He was standing outside the limo, blowing on his hands to keep them warm. I waved hello and showed him my DI credentials.

'I'm freezing out here, Miss, but I can't stand the stink in there and I've got orders to stay with the limo. I'm hiding from the press back here.'

The driver was maybe sixty, and white – very white. His thin face was drained of color, as if he were a vampire.

I introduced myself. He said, 'My name's Michaels. Bob Michaels. I'm kinda shaky. I never had anyone die on me before.'

'What happened?' I asked.

'I tried to welcome her, because she was a big celebrity. I made sure the inside looked extra good. I put in three kinds of bottled water. I put on music by her late boyfriend, or husband, or whatever he was, and she screamed at me to turn it off. I don't like speaking ill of the dead, but she wasn't very nice.'

I nodded, but I couldn't say anything. Bob took that as a sign of agreement. Talking about the trip was making him feel better. A little color was coming back to his cheeks.

'She didn't have the privacy window up, so I could hear everything, whether I wanted to or not. She yelled at her staff, and she called us hicks and rubes. She called our city nasty names. I thought St Louis treated her well. All she could say was she wanted to go home to California. I couldn't wait to get her out of our town.'

I'd already seen most of what he'd told me, thanks to Mario's video call.

'She had some kind of fit, throwing up all over everything, head flying back. She put her foot through the TV screen.

'That Stu guy hollered at me to head for the hospital and I did,' the driver said. 'I hate to say it, but I think Jessica Gray died in my limo. I called the hospital and nine-one one, and the ER staff was there to meet us. I hope I did right.'

'You did,' I said. 'May I see the inside of the limo?'

'If you want. It stinks to high heaven. This was a brand-new limo, too. The boss is gonna kill me.'

I opened my suitcase, put on a pair of latex gloves, and grabbed my point-and-shoot camera. It took better photos than both my cell phones, though my personal one still wasn't working after Mario dropped it.

Bob opened a back door and I saw the damage: The TV monitor was kicked out and the windows, carpet, and black leather upholstery were splashed with green vomit. A crystal glass was shattered on the thick black carpet. CSI would collect the shards and check them for food or drink. The vomit puddles on the floor had been stepped in by many different shoes.

Used tissues, some with bright red blood, were scattered about, along with the contents of Tawnee's purse. I saw two iPhones, hairbrushes, lipstick and more on the seat and floor. Will's make-up case was open on the floor, with a lipstick brush stuck straight up in it. The make-up would be collected and tested for poisons if the spray showed nothing. I didn't see Mario's case, or Stu's small black bag.

I photographed it all, and saw a small bit of red on the floor.

'What's that, way under the seat?' I asked.

Bob started to grab it, but I stopped him. 'No, the police will have to fingerprint that and analyze the contents.' I leaned closer for a look, then wished I hadn't. The odor was blooming in the warm car. The CSI tech would need a hazmat suit to work in here. Under the seat was a red plastic bottle – throat spray, according to the label.

'Don't touch anything back here,' I said.

'That's what they told me, Miss. I'm waiting for them now.'

I saw Detective Greiman pull up in his unmarked car, a spiffy black Dodge.

'The homicide detective is here,' I said. 'The rest of the team will be along shortly.'

I slipped into the hospital by a side door. Back inside, I watched Ray Greiman shoulder his way through the milling reporters in the SOS entrance. He was dressed for TV in a black cashmere coat, blue shirt and rep tie, his dark hair slicked back.

The press was pelting him with questions. When Greiman got to the front of the scrum, he said, 'Sorry, no comment,' and flashed a telegenic smile.

I was waiting in a back corner. His smile disappeared when he saw me. 'Where's the stiff?'

Typical Greiman. No respect for the dead. I was tired of lecturing him.

'The decedent is in the ER,' I said.

'I heard she had pneumonia,' he said.

'She did. She was hospitalized for it overnight. She checked herself out this morning against the advice of her doctor. I heard through the hospital grapevine that her death was murder.'

'Shit,' Greiman said. 'Just what I don't need. I'll have everybody crawling up my ass.'

'We'll have to be extra careful.'

'I'm always careful,' he said, and swaggered back to the ER.

NINE

Some people believe they can feel the departed soul hovering around a room where someone has just died. Not me. But I saw the debris from the battle to save Jessica. The floor was littered with used alcohol pads, tape, and other medical debris.

Jessica was lying on a narrow bed, wearing a faded blue hospital gown. She looked like a scrawny older woman with enormous breast implants. Jessica had been stripped of her expert make-up and hair styling, and her designer clothes had been cut off – reduced to smelly rags – and tossed in a corner.

Jessica would be furious that the 'hicks' and 'rubes' were in charge of her body, and knew all her secrets.

Her own hair was thin – barely enough bottle-blond strands to anchor her fabulous blond fall. The fake hair was flung on top of the pile of clothes, like an abandoned pet. She'd worn a beige body suit that must have strangled her mid-section, but it flattened her tummy. It was cut off and tossed on the pile. Good heavens. It had ass pads to round out her shape.

The clothes and hair would be bagged and tagged by the police.

One false eyelash clung to Jessica's cheek like a spider. The IV lines were still attached to her hands, and the ECG stickers were on her chest. The medical examiner would remove them.

Without Will's make-up, Jessica's face was wrinkled and yellowish, and her eyes were sunken. But she had a stunning bone structure. That was the real secret of her enduring beauty.

Karen, a trim, capable brunette nurse of about forty, arrived with Jessica's chart and records. She still seemed shaken by Jessica's death. Even the butterflies on her pink scrubs looked wilted. 'I was part of the ER team that met Ms Gray's limo,' she told me. 'She was covered with green vomit. We started CPR and the code protocol.'

The tiny room would have been boiling with nurses, techs, and respiratory therapists.

'The ER doctor ran in,' Karen said. 'He asked us to hold up. He checked her with a stethoscope and looked at the ECG tracing. He heard nothing and there was a flat line.'

The nurse gulped. Was she holding back tears? I couldn't tell, but losing a patient was always traumatic.

'He told us to continue the resuscitation for a few minutes. He told me, "Give the epi now." There was still no heartbeat and a straight line on the monitor.'

Even a jolt of epinephrine couldn't bring Jessica back to life.

'The doctor checked her pupils. They were fixed and dilated.'

I knew what that meant: Jessica had been dead a while.

'The ER doctor stopped the code and pronounced her dead. There was nothing we could do. She was probably dead when she arrived.'

'Do you think she died of pneumonia?' I asked.

'I doubt it,' Karen said. 'She'll have to be autopsied, but we think she might have been poisoned. And that's not for publication.'

'You know I don't talk,' I said.

'That's why I told you.'

'Why do you think she was poisoned?'

'Her symptoms: The seizures in the limo and the projectile vomiting. Those are all signs of poisoning, not pneumonia. We'll have the tox reports back shortly.' The hospital could test the vomit and get the results back faster than the ME's office.

'I have to go back to work,' Karen said. 'Here's my number. Call me if you need anything else.'

Jessica was in Room One, which was reserved for severe – often fatal – trauma. I was all too familiar with that room. That's where I found my beloved husband, Donegan. He'd had a sudden heart attack while teaching at City College. He was dead by the time I got to the ER. He'd only been forty-five. For a long time, I thought my life had ended with his. Only my work kept me going.

Since my husband died, I'd entered this room several times,

but it still tore my heart to walk into Room One. Even for someone like Jessica.

I reminded myself that I was a professional. Having the hospital records made my job easier. I turned on my iPad, and filled in the information. The time of death of was 8:47 a.m. On the hospital forms, Jessica was five feet six and weighed ninety-five pounds. Her age was listed as seventy-six. She was married. Did she still consider herself married to that rock star, Johnny Grimes? She'd listed her agent as her next of kin.

That was sad, but not surprising.

Hospital records gave her time of arrival at the ER as 7:42 a.m.

I opened my DI kit, a plain black rolling suitcase that contained the tools of my trade – thermometers, Tupperware for collecting specimens, paper bags and rubber bands for protecting fragile evidence on hands and feet, and more. I also had my camera.

First, I photographed Jessica – wide shots, medium, and close ups. The police would take their own photos and videos, but these would go to the ME.

Next, I pulled on multiple pairs of latex gloves for the examination. I'd strip them off as I examined the body, so I didn't contaminate the evidence.

I started my examination with the head.

The hospital had cleaned up Jessica just enough to work on her. I noted a patch of 'dried green fluid' near the right occipital bone, and checked her head for lacerations. I noted the telltale two-inch facelift scars in front of each ear. Her elongated earlobes had been hidden by her mane of honey-colored hair. The lobes were pierced, but she wore no earrings. Jessica also had a seven-inch scar along her frontal bone. No fillers and fat injections for Jessica. She'd had old-school facelifts, including a brow lift, and lied about it.

Jessica's attempted resuscitation was a violent, last-ditch fight to save her life. She did not die peacefully. She had what we called 'resuscitative artifacts,' and I had to note every one. I started with a three-inch abrasion on the right side of her neck, just under her ear, and another abrasion, a thin scrape two inches long, on her left cheek.

Her hospital gown was unbuttoned on the left shoulder, and I saw a yellow two-inch contusion from an IV puncture, and bruises on her sternum from CPR. She had a four-inch cardiac burn on her upper chest. I lifted her gown to check for other signs of the hopeless fight to save her. She had another four-inch cardiac burn on her left side, just under the sternum, and a four-inch bruise on her left hip. I caught a glimpse of the patch of sparse, gray pubic hair, and pulled the gown back down. I couldn't take her gown off. That was the ME's job.

I saw the trauma from the blood-pressure cuff on her stick-like right arm – it formed a yellowish armlet. Her right hand had a yellow-metal ring with a large, clear stone. The rock was probably a diamond and big as an almond, but I couldn't say that. I wasn't trained to appraise jewelry. Her blood-red nail polish was chipped on the third and fourth fingers.

On her left hand was a bruise, three inches by four inches, covering almost the entire top of her hand. That was probably from the IV while she was a patient at the hospital. She wore no wedding ring or other jewelry, but the nail on her second finger was broken.

Her toenails were painted red and she had a bunion on her right foot.

I needed to examine her back, and called Karen to help me turn the body. Even though Jessica weighed less than a hundred pounds, she was dead weight in the truest sense of the term.

A harried Karen returned, her dark hair sticking out. 'Car accident on the way,' she said. 'I've just got a minute.'

'I need help turning the decedent,' I said. We got Jessica on her front, and the gown exposed her flat, flabby bottom and lower back, which was starting to be covered in pinkish-purple patches. Now that Jessica's heart had stopped pumping, the blood was pooling in her body.

'Lividity is starting,' Karen said.

I noted a clear, two-inch butterfly-shaped sticky tape clinging to the back of her neck.

'Did you do some sort of procedure on her neck?' I asked.

'No, that's a short-term neck lift,' Karen said. 'Her make-up person did that. See how her hair is shaved on the back of the neck? That's so the adhesive will stick. Then he pulled her neck tighter and taped it in place. I'm using that in a couple of years when my neck goes – I'm not going under the knife.'

There were no other bruises on Jessica, and we turned her over.

Karen's phone buzzed. 'The ambulance is here. Gotta go,' she said. She was gone before I could thank her.

I was packing up my DI kit when Greiman entered. He wrinkled his nose in disgust.

'Good gawd,' he said. 'Is that old bag Jessica?'

TEN

'**M**ost murder victims don't look good,' I said to Greiman. I sounded sanctimonious, but I hated that he'd insulted a dead woman.

'Yeah, but Jessica was supposed to be this hot babe.'

'She looked damn good on stage,' I said. Why was I defending her? I didn't even like the woman. I forced myself to calm down and not get in a pissing match with the detective.

'Did you find anything when you looked at her?' the detective asked.

'Just the usual signs of resuscitation – cardiac burns and the resuscitation artifacts. The hospital put up quite a battle to save her, but the nurse suspected she was DOA. The nurse also thought Jessica had been poisoned.'

'That's already on TV,' he said. 'I'm waiting on the tox results and autopsy. I don't need to spend any more time in here, do I? It stinks.'

It did, but not as bad as some death scenes. I wondered if he was afraid he'd get vomit on his cashmere coat.

'Did you talk to the limo driver?' he asked.

'Yes.'

'I had to impound his limo. He's not happy. His company is picking him up.'

'I need to talk to the people who were in the limo,' I said. 'They're witnesses.'

'Already talked to them,' Greiman said. 'They didn't have much to say.'

Not to you, I thought. But they may talk to me. I didn't want Greiman around during my interviews, glowering at four witnesses who'd been through a shattering experience.

'Why don't you get some coffee in the cafeteria?' I said.

'That swill? Are you trying to poison me?'

'How about the coffee at the nurses' station? It's better.'

'Yeah, maybe I'll try some – and talk to that little blond.' He acted as if his presence would make the woman's day. He straightened his tie and marched off toward the nurses' station, adding, 'The wits are in the family room by the elevator.'

Wits. That was cop talk – mostly TV cops – for witnesses.

Stu, Will, Tawnee, and Mario looked like shipwreck survivors huddled on the hard orange plastic chairs in the family room, adrift on a sea of pale scuffed tile. They held foam cups of coffee, and Fox News blared overhead. I reached up and pulled the plug on the TV.

'Thank you,' Tawnee said. 'I couldn't take much more of that.'

'I'm really sorry this happened,' I said.

'We are, too,' Will said. 'It was terrible. The police officer said we'll have to miss our ten a.m. flight.'

'I'm sorry about that, too,' I said. 'But if I can talk to you about what happened in the limo, maybe we can speed things up a little.'

All four started talking at once.

'It would help if I interviewed you one at a time on the couch in the corner,' I said. 'Tawnee? Will you go first?' The couch was in the far corner, and the family waiting room was big enough I didn't think they would hear one another's interviews.

Tawnee and I settled on the hard black plastic couch. She seemed to be taking Jessica's death hard: her eyes were red from crying, and her skin was sallow. Her thin, frizzly hair gave her a witchy look.

'What happened when you left the hospital this morning?' I asked.

'Jessica was unhappy when we had to stop for a car accident. She was anxious to go to the airport. She wanted Will and Mario to fix her up. Will was freshening her lipstick when she had a coughing fit. She needed her throat spray – it's the only thing that stops that terrible cough. I started looking frantically for the spray bottle in my purse, and couldn't find it. I was dumping stuff all over the seat. That big purse turned into a bottomless pit. Jessica was getting impatient, and

I accused Stu of making the spray disappear. He denied it. Will saw that I was half-crazed. He put down his lip brush and dug around, but he couldn't find it, either. Then Stu took my purse and produced the bottle. He found it too fast. I still think he was pulling his stupid magic tricks.' She didn't hide the bitterness in her voice.

'Do you have it?'

'No, it seems to have disappeared in the confusion. But I can describe it. It's an over-the-counter spray in a refillable blue plastic pump bottle. That's the back-up bottle. I also carry a red bottle. Both are three ounces,' she said. 'So we can take them on the plane. She uses that spray all the time.'

'I'll need the bottle to show the ME,' I said. 'Do you have any of Jessica's other medications?'

'They're in the limo, too, but I can list everything she takes. She had a bottle of Levaquin capsules. They're antibiotics. She's taken them before.'

'Any cough medicines?'

'She didn't like the stuff the hospital doctor prescribed and threw it out in her room. She said she didn't trust any hick . . .' Tawnee stopped quickly, then said, 'uh, any local doctors. She wanted to see her own doctor in Los Angeles. She also had cough drops. In a yellow bag. Ricola brand, lemon-mint flavor.'

'Any other medications for blood pressure, cholesterol?' I asked.

'Yes, she took Lipitor for cholesterol. Ten milligrams. That's in her suitcase.'

The police would handle that. I noted the medication name and dose.

'That's all?' I asked. Tawnee nodded.

'She was remarkably healthy,' I said.

'That's what allowed her to keep that grueling tour schedule.'

'Was Jessica really seventy-six?' I asked.

'Yes. She was two years older than me, but Will kept her looking much younger.' She pushed her blond hair out of her eyes, and I saw the age spots on her hand.

'Jessica didn't even have any age spots,' I said.

Tawnee's face reddened. She knew I'd noticed her hand.

'She went to a dermatologist once a year and had the spots burned off. I have too many.'

'What happened after you found the spray?' I asked.

'Jessica used it, and I thought her cough would stop. Instead she went rigid, then started throwing out her arms and legs. She kicked out the TV screen with her boots and broke it. I screamed, I think. Then Stu shouted for the driver to go to the hospital. Mario, Will and Stu helped me hold her arms and legs so she wouldn't flail around and hurt herself. She was throwing up all over the place. As soon as we got here, the medical team took her inside and told us to wait in here. I cleaned up a little. The next thing we knew, the doctor said she was dead.' I saw where she'd tried to scrub green stains off her beige pants and dark coat.

She followed my eyes. 'I'm going to have to shop for new clothes,' Tawnee said. 'I can't wear these anymore.'

I brought her back to the case. 'Do you think Jessica was poisoned?'

'Poisoned?' Tawnee looked surprised. 'No. Of course not. I think she had a stroke. Poor Jessica. This traveling was just too hard on her at her age.' Tawnee started sniffling again.

'Thank you, Tawnee.' She looked broken. I guided her back to the rest of the group. Mario patted her shoulders and gave her a tissue.

Will was next. He told pretty much the same story, except he added, 'It was really hard to cover up the signs of pneumonia, and her eyes kept watering. I use waterproof make-up, but it still smeared.

'When the limo was held up by the accident, I was working on her lipstick. She started coughing – horrible wracking coughs. Tawnee couldn't find the spray bottle, and Jessica was getting upset. Have you seen Tawnee's purse? It's the size of a small city. No wonder she couldn't find anything. I took it away from her, but I didn't get a chance to find the spray bottle. Stu grabbed it. He says it was tucked in a fold. That spray works like magic, better than anything the hospital gave Jessica. Except this time, everything went weird, and Jessica started kicking and throwing herself around. Tawnee, Stu, Mario and I had to fight to keep her from knocking her head on something. She was puking all over the place. Totally ruined my coat. I tossed it. I'll have to buy a new one.'

He stopped as if he wanted sympathy. I mumbled something and he continued.

'The driver took us straight to the hospital, the medical team met us, and here we are.' He was talking way too fast. I looked at his pupils, to see if they were dilated. I suspected drugs, but didn't see any signs. His manner was oddly casual, but people react to death in different ways.

'Do you think Jessica was poisoned?' I asked.

'Nope,' he said. 'She had a stroke. That's how my Aunt Edna acted when she died from a stroke. Are you done?' Will was scratching his arm as if he had poison ivy. I was almost sure he was on something. He sat down next to Mario and they began talking. Mario seemed dazzled by Will's clean-cut good looks and that swoosh of bright red-gold hair.

Stu was next. He looked tired and his blond hair was oily. It had escaped its usual ponytail and fell limply to his shoulders. His blue-checked shirt was rumpled and had a large brown stain that I hoped was coffee. His suit jacket was on a chair in the corner. I saw green vomit on the sleeve. He was distant, without a trace of emotion. I wondered if he was in shock.

'I saw what everyone else did,' he said. 'Jessica was in a hurry to go to the airport. She wanted out of this place really bad. Then we were stalled because of that accident and she decided to use the time to freshen up. Will was working on her make-up when she had a bad coughing fit. Tawnee couldn't find the spray, and got hysterical. She lost it and accused me of making it disappear.'

I didn't like the look on Stu's face: slitty-eyed and mean.

'Did you?' He could have slipped it into her purse during the confusion.

Stu sounded offended. 'Of course not. That spray is the only thing that stops Jessica from coughing. Tawnee gets like that when she's upset – she starts accusing everyone.'

'But you do make things disappear,' I said.

'Just for fun,' he said. He gave me a cold smile. 'Work can

get tense. I try to break the tension with little magic tricks. But not this time. This was serious.'

A shadow slid across the room, and I saw Greiman leaning in the doorway, listening. The 'little blond' nurse must have sent the detective on his way.

'Can we go home now?' Stu asked. 'Back to California? I'm cold. I had to toss my coat because of the mess.' He looked disgusted.

The 'mess' made by Jessica's death throes. He had no sympathy for her at all.

'That's up to Detective Greiman,' I said.

'Well?' Stu looked at Greiman. 'We've answered your questions. We want to go home to LA.'

'And I want to solve a murder,' Greiman said. 'You four are suspects.'

'Suspects!' Tawnee looked like she was going to cry. Will seemed stunned.

'I'm a suspect, too?' Stu was suddenly alert. His eyes were hooded, calculating. 'I want a lawyer,' he said.

'Be my guest,' Greiman said.

Now Stu's voice was cold with anger. 'You have no right to keep us. You can't prove Jessica was murdered. I want to go home and take my wife with me.'

'Your wife?' I said.

'What wife?' Greiman looked confused.

'Jessica,' Stu said, with a flourish, as if he'd pulled a rabbit out of a hat. Then he carefully enunciated every word. 'Jessica. Gray. Is. My. Wife.'

ELEVEN

'What the fuck? You're married to Jessica?' Greiman said it, but it could have been any of us. Mario looked stunned. I couldn't believe it, either.

Tawnee's mouth dropped open. 'But you never said anything, Stu.' Jessica's stand-in sounded hurt and her voice wavered, like she was going to cry again. 'We didn't get to celebrate your wedding.'

'We wanted to keep it secret, because of the age difference,' Stu said.

'Which is what? Forty years?' Will said. His face was lobster-red with anger.

'Thirty-eight,' Stu said. I'd never really thought about it, but now I realized that despite his shifty manner, Stu was good-looking, with a square jaw and thick hair. Muscles bulged under his checked shirt. 'But age didn't apply to Jessica.'

Except it did. I'd seen her worn, bony body and sagging skin. Also, that sparse gray pubic hair. Did Stu's duties include bedding Jessica?

'Why didn't you tell me you were married to the vic?' Greiman's voice was low and menacing. I wished he didn't sound like a TV caricature.

'You didn't ask,' Stu said.

'I DIDN'T ASK!' Greiman was so mad he was spitting. 'YOU SHOULD HAVE TOLD ME, DIPWAD!' He took a deep breath, and that seemed to calm him.

Greiman's voice went back to that low, dangerous tone. 'I could arrest you for interfering with an investigation! You know the husband is always the main suspect when a wife is murdered. Always! Especially when a young buck marries a much older woman. Why didn't you say you two were married? I assume you inherit everything?'

'You have no proof Jessica was murdered,' Stu said. He

was icy calm. 'I want to speak to my lawyer. Then I want to go home and take my wife with me.'

Stu had avoided Greiman's question. Did he inherit Jessica's fortune? Did Stu trade his so-called golden handcuffs for a wedding band? That's when the idea popped into my head: Stu killed Jessica. I considered it again – yes, it fit. Stu was the killer. He was free of his old, nasty wife. He'd have her money. He could restart his magic career in Vegas. I hoped Greiman would see that and arrest Stu.

'You're not going anywhere,' Greiman said. 'Except to the station. All four of you.'

'Me, too?' Mario looked uneasy.

'Especially you,' Greiman said.

I stood protectively next to Mario. 'Angela, would you go with me?' he asked. 'I am feared I may not understand him.' Mario's normally excellent English had deteriorated. No doubt about it, he was upset.

'Yes,' I said. 'I'll be your representative.' Mario managed a tentative smile.

Stu wielded his cell phone like a weapon and said again, 'I want to call my lawyer.'

'Then make the call right here,' Greiman said.

Stu had his lawyer's number on speed dial. 'Hello, Danielle. It's Stu. I'm in a spot of trouble. Jessica died suddenly.'

Stu showed no more emotion than someone discussing a minor inconvenience. Stu had lost his wife. I've heard people who were more upset when their flight was canceled. After a pause, Stu said, 'Yes, yes, it's terribly sad. The police think she may have been murdered.'

Again, that matter-of-fact tone. What was wrong with this man? His wife had died in front of him, a violent, degrading death.

After another pause he said, 'I need you. I'm afraid I'm a suspect. The police want to talk to me. Can you fly out here to St Louis?'

More silence. This time, it seemed to stretch for a decade. Then an outraged Stu said, 'What? You can't come here? You want me to deal with a local yokel in Bumfuck, Missouri?'

I felt my temper rising at that last remark, and tried to tamp it down. I wondered what Reggie Du Pres would think, after he'd spent all that money on his lavish party to impress the Californians.

Stu was still whining to the lawyer. 'Are you sure you can't fly here? Yes, yes, I understand. You've called him and he'll be right over. OK, I won't say another word until he shows up. I'll be at the police station.'

He hung up and said, 'My lawyer's name is Montgomery Bryant. I'm told he lives here, and he's on his way. I've been instructed to say nothing until he arrives.'

I knew Monty, and he was damn good, but I wasn't going to say that to Stu. Monty's specialty was getting people out of tricky situations, and I was pleased his reputation was national. He was also dating my best friend, Katie.

'Come along,' Greiman said. 'All of you. You're riding in my car.'

Mario looked frightened. What had he been doing?

I told him, 'It's OK. I'll follow you to the station.'

I rolled my DI case to my car, loaded it into the trunk, and followed Greiman's car. The Chouteau Forest Police station looked like a boutique hotel on the outside, but inside it was a typical grungy cop shop: scuffed floors, wanted posters, and a miserable group of people waiting in the lobby.

When I joined Jessica's staff inside, Greiman turned on me. 'What the hell are you doing here?'

'I'm representing Mario Garcia. He sometimes has problems understanding English. I'm here to help him.'

'Oh, you are, are you? Let me remind you, you're involved in this case.' Greiman was in a nasty mood, and I wasn't having it. I drew myself to my full six feet – I was several inches taller than the detective – and said, 'I've already finished my death investigation. It's your choice. Either I stay here, or you wait while we get a Spanish interpreter. That could take hours.'

'All right, you can stay. But your job is to interpret. That's all.'

Good. I was betting he wouldn't want to wait.

My cell phone interrupted his tirade. I didn't recognize the caller ID. I started to take the call, and Greiman said, 'Put it

on speaker so we can all enjoy it, Mizz Richman.' He gave
the Ms a mocking buzz.

I didn't want to argue with the creep. I did as he said.

A woman's slurred voice said, 'Are you the death investigator
lady who was at the party?'

'Who's speaking, please?'

'This is Becky. I was one of the models at Jessica's stage
show.' I wondered about her slurred voice. Was Becky drinking?

'Oh, right. How did you find me?'

'I called the medical examiner and a lady gave me your
cell phone number.'

'Are you back in St Louis?'

'Yes, no thanks to Jessica. She left me high and dry. That
cheap bastard Reggie Du What's His Name said his man
would take me home if I took a shower. I told the old fart
to stuff it and hitch-hiked home.'

I tried not to laugh. 'Are you back on Olive Street, Becky?'

'No, I found a nice hotel downtown – the Hoffstedder.
That hundred dollars got me a whole week. And I have a
job prospect, too, from those ladies you told me to see.'

'That's good, Becky, but I'm kinda in a hurry. Why did you
call?'

'I saw something at the hospital when that woman was
there. I think it killed her.'

'What? This is about Jessica?'

'I'll tell you tomorrow. You can meet me for breakfast. Ten
o'clock at the pancake house on Jefferson.'

'Becky, don't play games. At least give me a clue.'

Becky chanted, *'Since you've been so dear, I'll make it
clear. It's not the red – it's the blue. Breakfast is on you.* Ten
o'clock. The St Louis Pancake House. You're buying.'

'No, wait! Becky, you have to tell the police what you
know.'

'Bye, sweetie.' There was a click.

'She hung up,' I said.

All five of them were crowded around me, listening – Mario,
Stu, Tawnee, Will and Greiman. Greiman's ears were positively
flapping, he was listening so hard. I knew he'd caught every
word.

'Don't bother having breakfast with her,' Greiman said. 'I'll bring her in for questioning before that.'

I bit back a smile at the thought of the fastidious Greiman cooped up in his unmarked car with the odiferous Becky. But maybe her hotel had a shower.

'All right, everyone, show's over,' Greiman said. He led Stu, Tawnee and Will down the dingy hall to separate interrogation rooms.

As soon as they were gone, Monty rushed through the door. The Forest lawyer was out of breath, and lugging a heavy black briefcase. I was pleased to see he wore a hand-tailored gray suit and blue-striped tie. Monty, a six-foot-two hunk with dark brown hair, looked impressive – no matter where you lived.

He seemed surprised to see me. Pleasantly surprised.

'Angela!' he said. 'What's going on?'

I told him briefly how I was mixed up in Jessica's death and what I knew. 'Your client Stu wants to go home to California,' I said, 'and Greiman wants to keep him here.'

Monty was too professional to make a face at the mention of Greiman's name, but the two had a long, unhappy history.

'Has he arrested Stu?'

'Not yet,' I said. 'We just found out Stu was secretly married to Jessica Gray. He didn't tell Greiman.'

Monty raised an eyebrow. 'Whoa. I bet Greiman hit the roof.'

'I've never seen him so mad. He threatened to arrest Stu for interfering with an investigation.'

'No way he can do that.'

'The whole entourage wants to go home. Can you help them?'

'I'm here to represent Stu,' Monty said, 'but I don't see why they can't leave as long as they're not under arrest. There's no way, absent an arrest or a court order, the police can force those people to stick around. The cops can ask them. They can suggest it would be better if they stayed, with all the publicity about Jessica's death, and having to get her body or ashes back to California. But even a court order could not keep them in town. It would just impose penalties and a mechanism to get them back if they left.'

'Oh. That's good news for them.'

'Thanks for the update, Angela. Now, I need to see my client.'

Monty straightened his blue tie and squared his shoulders. The Forest couldn't have a better person representing us.

'Good luck,' I said. Monty presented himself to the desk sergeant and was shown down the hall.

Mario shifted uneasily on his wobbly plastic chair. 'What's going to happen?' he asked. 'I'm a foreigner.'

'No, you're not. You're a US citizen. You have a thriving local business.'

'None of that matters. I'll be the Cuban outsider if there's trouble.'

He was right, and nothing I could say would make him feel better.

'I hope Tawnee will be OK now that Jessica is dead,' I said.

'And Will, too,' Mario said. 'He is very nice. And I get out to LA sometimes.'

I suspected Mario might have had a fling with Jessica's make-up artist, but he wouldn't dish. I tried to talk about his salon, Killer Cuts, but those conversations were stillborn. Mario had his styling case at his feet, crammed with his tools – scissors, brushes, blow dryers and more.

'Want to put your case in my car?' I asked.

'No, I'll keep it with me,' Mario said. 'I need to call my shop and tell Raquel I've been delayed.'

While he talked business with his assistant, I worked on my DI report and finished it nearly two hours later. I'd just emailed it in when Monty came down the hall with Stu. Jessica's husband looked like he'd been beaten with a rubber hose: his suit was rumpled and his oily hair stood up on end. Even his shirt was partly unbuttoned. I couldn't tell if Stu's disarray was from the shock of Jessica's death – or his own fears for himself.

'You're free to go,' Monty said.

'You've already been paid,' Stu told him. I thought he sounded cold to the man who'd just freed him. 'Do I owe you anything else?'

'No, that's it,' Monty said. Stu didn't thank him and there was no handshake. Monty left.

'I'll wait here until Will and Tawnee are free,' Stu said.

'Did the detective give you a hard time?'

'Not really. It was easy,' Stu said, and shrugged. He buttoned his shirt and tried to smooth the wrinkles in his jacket. He stank of vomit. 'The local man handled it. No big deal.'

At least he didn't call Monty a yokel.

'What's the best hotel here?'

'The Chouteau Forest Inn,' I said.

'Think I can get reservations?'

'In February, no problem. I thought you were anxious to go back to LA.'

'I need to stay with my wife.'

Why the sudden change of heart? An hour ago, Stu couldn't wait to leave. And why was he calling Jessica 'my wife'? He never used those words when she was alive.

Greiman charged down the hall and said to Mario, 'You! You're next.' The detective glared at Stu. I suspected Greiman was boiling with rage. Impotent rage. He'd wanted a quick arrest and his chief suspect was walking out the door.

Mario was trembling as he picked up his styling case. 'It will be OK,' I said. My words sounded unconvincing, even to me.

With that, Officer Blake Cameron came in with Rex, his K-9 partner. Rex was truly a king, a magnificent Belgian Malinois with huge dark ears. Rex was bigger than a German Shepherd and his eyes glowed with intelligence. He was a certified drug-sniffing dog, and Officer Cameron bragged Rex's nose was incredibly accurate. 'He can sniff out the tomato on a ham sandwich,' he liked to say.

'Hi, Blake,' I said. 'Hi, Rex.' I politely held out my fist for Rex to sniff, but the massive dog ignored me and went straight for Mario's case. He pawed it and whimpered.

'He's alerting,' Officer Cameron said. 'There are drugs in that case.'

'No!' Mario said, but the blood had drained from his face.

'Open it,' Greiman said.

'Do you have a warrant?' I asked.

'Since when did you turn into a lawyer?' Greiman said. 'You can get fired for hindering an investigation. Especially one that you're involved in. Open that case, Mario Garcia, or I'll file a complaint and Angela will get fired.'

'Don't do it, Mario,' I said. 'He's bluffing.'

Mario opened his case.

'Do I have your permission to search this?' Greiman asked. 'Remember what happens to Mizz Richman if you won't let me.'

'No!' I said.

'Yes!' Mario said. 'I give the permission.' His voice trembled with fear.

Inside, among the brushes and hair clips, Greiman found a black tube of lipstick. 'Chanel,' he said. 'Your color?' It was crammed with purple football-shaped Xanax tablets. An aspirin bottle held Percocet tablets. A lot of Percocet, maybe two hundred.

'You got a prescription for these?' Greiman asked.

Mario turned paler and said nothing.

Greiman read Mario his rights. The detective's next question was a hammer blow: 'Why did you give Jessica Gray Xanax and Percocet?'

'She was nervous,' Mario said. 'She needed to relax.' I kicked him in the leg to shut him up and said, 'Mario didn't understand your question.'

'The hell he didn't,' Greiman said. 'Your friend Will said you gave Jessica drugs.'

Will? The cute red-haired make-up artist Mario wanted to see on his next trip to LA?

Mario looked like he'd been punched. His good friend and maybe lover Will had betrayed him.

'Mario Garcia, you're under arrest for possession of two controlled substances with the intent to distribute both,' Greiman said. 'That's at least two felonies. And if the tox screen shows these killed Jessica Gray, the next charge will be murder one.

'Now, Angela, get the hell out of here.'

I left in defeat. Greiman got what he wanted – a quick arrest. He didn't care if Mario didn't have a motive to kill Jessica. Greiman would invent one.

TWELVE

Damn Greiman. I watched him snap metal handcuffs on Mario. Handcuffs! Mario was already inside the police station. Did Greiman think the hairstylist was going to overpower him with a curling iron?

Mario's handsome Latin face was distorted with terror. I figured he must be having flashbacks to his time in Castro's totalitarian Cuba, when homosexuals were hunted down and shot.

I fought to keep my temper. 'Greiman, there's no need for that. Mario is a businessman. He's not going to flee. He has a stake in the community.'

'He has the perfect business to sell drugs.' I hated Greiman's self-righteousness. 'As soon as I get a search warrant, I'm going to find them.'

Mario started to protest, then saw the warning shake of my head and shut up.

'Not a word, Mario,' I said. 'Not till your lawyer, Montgomery Bryant, arrives. I'll call Raquel and let her know what happened.'

'Thank you,' he said, as Greiman dragged him off.

I stormed through the station, silently damning Greiman for his theatrics. Outside, I heard Stu whining into his phone: 'I have to find some way to get her home. I'm not sure when they'll release her body or how I'm going to transport her, but I have to leave this freezing shit-hole.'

If he'd asked me, I could have told him which undertakers would do the best job of sending Jessica home, but the hell with him. He was the real killer, not Mario. Stu deserved to rot in jail – a Missouri jail.

I got into my car – my private phone booth – and called Monty Bryant. I was grateful when the lawyer answered on the second ring. He must have heard the tension in my voice.

'What's wrong, Angela?' he asked.

'It's Mario. He's been arrested for drugs. Possession and distribution.'

'That's ridiculous.'

I realized I was on a cell phone. 'Maybe I'd better come to your office.'

'Give me an hour,' Monty said. 'I'm with a client right now.'

Good, that gave me enough time to stop by Killer Cuts. I was in the parking lot ten minutes later. The salon's sleek black leather-and-chrome interior was quieter than usual: a stylist was blow-drying a customer at one station and a manicurist was gossiping quietly and painting a young woman's fingernails acid green.

Raquel, Mario's Cuban-American assistant, was booking an appointment at the reception desk. While I waited for her to get off the phone, I sat in a black leather chair and paged through *Vogue*. Finally, she hung up. I lowered my voice to almost a whisper and said, 'Mario's been arrested for possession of drugs.'

'No!' Raquel said. 'I told him he was getting careless. He's been making buys in the parking lot in daylight.'

'He had Percocet and Xanax in his styling case.'

'Oh, shit.' Raquel's red lips trembled and a tear threatened her perfect eye make-up. 'What are we gonna do?'

'I'm on my way to see Monty Bryant so we can get Mario out of jail. Meanwhile, does anyone have any, uh . . . drugs here?'

'Just aspirin in the break room.'

It was time to be blunt. 'I mean anything illegal like Xanax, opioids, pot?'

'The new manicurist keeps a joint in her station.'

'Flush it. I'll check Mario's station while you check the rest of the place.'

Mario had an alcove in the back with orchids and palm trees – a little bit of warm Cuba in cold Missouri. I was in a hurry – I couldn't get caught in the salon by Greiman. He'd know I'd tipped off Raquel. I pawed through the drawers and cases in Mario's station as fast as I could. Between a rack of brushes and a jar of sterilized combs, I found an unmarked vial of white tablets. I didn't know what they were, but I flushed them.

I met Raquel back at the desk. 'The place is clean,' she said. 'When do you think Greiman will show?'

'Any time now. Be careful. He's mad as a wet cat. I'm off to see Monty.'

'I'll handle that police officer,' she said. Her long black hair had been pulled into a stylish knot. She pulled out the pins and shook it free, then touched up her make-up. She was getting her weapons ready. Greiman was a notorious womanizer.

I wished her luck with the search. I still had time before my appointment with Monty. I stopped at a Best Buy and bought a new personal cell phone, and texted my new number to my friends. Then I dropped off the box and my broken phone at my house. I made it to Monty's office with two minutes to spare. I didn't have to wait long to see the lawyer. I'd barely sat down in one of his wing chairs in the reception area, when the lawyer came out to get me. I liked his office – it smelled of leather-bound books and had a stunning view of the winter woods. I turned down his offer of coffee and we got down to business.

'Can you rep Mario after you were called in to help Stu?' I asked.

'Stu made it very clear that once I got him out of the police station, he was no longer my client,' Monty said. 'He paid me on the spot, using his cell phone, and said if he had any other problems with the law, he'd bring in his own attorney. We're finished.' He didn't bother to hide his satisfaction.

'Good. Mario needs help. He carried his styling case into the police station, and Rex the K-9 "alerted" when he passed it. There were drugs inside the case. Greiman blackmailed Mario into opening it.'

'Tell me exactly what happened,' Monty said.

I did. Monty shook his head after I told him the story.

'This is not good. Missouri has some of the toughest drug laws in the country,' he said.

'What's the penalty?' I asked. 'Mario didn't sell the drugs to Jessica. He gave them to her.'

'He's looking at seven years. It's a Class C felony to possess or deliver those controlled substances – and it doesn't make any difference if he gave them or sold them to Jessica. "Delivery" is a crime whether the drugs are sold or given.'

'Can he get bail?'

'It depends. If Mario is cooperative and the prosecutor and the judge believe he'll show up for court, we can bond him out.'

'Of course he'll show,' I said. 'His whole life is tied up in his salon. He's not going back to Cuba. They hate gays.'

'I know, and those are points I'll make sure to tell the judge. We still have one other problem – if Jessica died of an opioid overdose, then there's nothing we can do. The judge will lock up Mario and throw away the key.'

'When will we know?'

'That information is supposed to be released any time now.'

There was a long silence. I finally figured out what Monty wanted.

'You can't call the ME's office,' I said. 'Not when you're dating the assistant medical examiner. At least, you can't leave a phone record. How about if I stop by to see my good friend Katie? It's part of my job.'

'Sounds good.' He stood up to show me out, politely sending me on my way. Dr Katie Kelly Stern's office was right down the road and I drove as fast as I could. I suspected Greiman was subjecting Mario to the full horrors of booking, including a strip search and delousing. We had to get him out of jail quickly.

Ten minutes later, I was at the medical examiner's office at the back of Sisters of Sorrow Hospital. I parked away from the funeral home vans picking up bodies, punched my code into the door, and made my way down the hall. Katie's closet-sized office had an autumn woodland scene on the main wall. She'd added a grinning plastic skull to the underbrush.

Katie was my age, forty-one, and a country girl who drove a pickup truck. She was brown-haired and practical as a pair of wool gloves. At first glance, she seemed plain, but Katie's wit and intelligence cast a spell. She'd definitely enchanted the Forest's most eligible bachelor, Montgomery Bryant.

Today, Katie was behind her desk, doing paperwork and drinking the bitter brew that passed as coffee at the ME's. 'I heard you caught the Jessica Gray investigation,' she said. 'I finished the post.'

'Why didn't Evarts do the slice and dice? I thought he'd want the glory.'

'No glory in this one,' Katie said. 'He was so upset he canceled his lunch at the club and kept moaning about what this would do to the reputation of the Forest. Whenever it's a dicey post, I get the honors.'

'What killed Jessica? Please don't say it was an opioid overdose.' I was holding my breath, waiting for her answer. Mario's life depended on it.

'No, she had those in her blood, but they didn't kill her. She died of nicotine poisoning.'

'Nicotine!' I was stunned. So many questions flooded my brain. 'How? Where did she get nicotine? She didn't smoke. I thought she had double pneumonia.'

'She did,' Katie said. 'And she should have followed her doctor's advice and stayed in the hospital.'

'She was hell-bent on leaving,' I said.

'She may be there now,' Katie said. 'She's in the morgue, the gateway to hell.'

'Explain how she died of nicotine poisoning. I've encountered all kinds of deaths, from overdoses to auto accidents, but this is my first nicotine poisoning.'

'Sit down,' Katie said. 'You're pacing around my room and there isn't room to think.'

There wasn't room to sit, either. Katie had traded her comfortable guest chair for a filing cabinet. Her current guest chair was a wire contraption that left me crippled. I perched on the edge of her desk and Katie explained what happened.

'Jessica wasn't young, she was way too thin, and she was run down from the pneumonia. But nicotine poisoning nailed her. She had a whopping dose – seventy milligrams. The Centers for Disease Control say sixty milligrams is enough to kill a 150-pound adult, and she didn't weigh even close to that.'

'How did she ingest that much nicotine?' I asked. 'And why? Was her so-called youth drink poisoned? Besides, wouldn't nicotine taste funny?'

'Yes, it would taste bad. But keep in mind, she had pneumonia, so her nose and taste buds weren't working right.'

'When she left the hospital this morning – jeez, did all this start this morning? – she was still peddling her Captivate line,' I said. 'She stopped in the lobby and gave a presentation for the press. Drank some weird health drink that had kale in it.'

'Kale – the devil's lettuce,' Katie said. 'Ever eat that shit in a salad? Tastes like spiky rubber. Amazing what people think is good for them. We see a lot of health drinks, but they usually don't kill people. Kale makes one nasty-ass drink, but it's safe enough.'

'I'll say this for Jessica,' I said. 'She's quite an actress. She downed that horrible green gunk with a smile.'

'Either that, or she was thinking of all the nice green money she'd be making,' Katie said. 'Anyone who can swallow kale with a smile must have no gag reflex. From the reports, it's clear that Jessica didn't have any bad reaction after she drank the kale cocktail.'

'And there were plenty of witnesses,' I said. 'The press taped it.'

'The best I can figure out,' Katie said, 'Jessica ingested the fatal nicotine dose in some kind of spray.'

'Spray? Like that throat spray she took all the time?'

'Exactly. Witnesses said she used the throat spray in the limo, and that's when she had the seizures and vomiting. We're not talking about some polite barfing when you're carsick – this was projectile vomiting.'

'You're telling me. Is vomiting one of the symptoms of nicotine poisoning?'

'Yes. It's a good thing nicotine deaths are rare, because they're ugly: a killer headache, dizziness, skyrocketing blood pressure, acute gut pain, and vomiting. Leads to seizures and death – within a few minutes to an hour.

'I think someone poured nicotine into her throat spray bottle and that's what killed her,' Katie said. 'A drop of agricultural nicotine on the skin can kill you. And she ingested more than enough to kill her.'

'Did the police find the throat spray bottle?'

'Sure did. It was under the seat in the limo. It's being tested. The bottle had Stu's fingerprints on it.'

'That makes sense. He's the one who found it in Tawnee's purse. Are you sure that she was killed by nicotine-laced throat spray?'

'Almost positive. All the killer would have to do was dump a bottle of vape juice into the spray bottle, and so long, Jessica. In the confusion surrounding her death throes, it would be easy for Jessica's killer to toss the bottle. Or hide it in a pocket and dispose of it at the hospital. I assume Greiman didn't search anyone who'd been in the limo.'

'Of course not. You know his methods – slipshod as ever. Greiman didn't even isolate the witnesses when he questioned them. He let them sit together in the hospital's waiting room. I do know that Will and Stu threw away their coats at the hospital because they had so much vomit on them.'

'They could have tossed the bottle with the nicotine there, too,' Katie said. 'I'm guessing Tawnee will have to get rid of her coat.'

'Yep. Tawnee wants to shop for a new one,' I said.

I groaned. 'I had the whole thing on video, thanks to Mario. He was in the limo and borrowed my personal cell phone to video himself working on Jessica's hair. Too bad he dropped my cell phone at the hospital and broke it.'

'How broken is it?' Katie asked.

'The screen has a big crack and the phone is dead.'

'Let me guess,' she said. 'You didn't buy a case to protect it, like I told you.'

'Didn't have time,' I said.

'Well, it may not be permanently dead,' she said. 'There are lots of forensic methods to recover the data. There's a program called Cellebrite that can work wonders. Did you try the old stand-by: taking the back off the phone and removing the battery and putting it back in?'

'No.'

'Where is it?'

'At home,' I said. 'I was afraid it would fall apart if I carried it around.' Katie offered me coffee but I declined the nasty brew and turned the conversation back to business. 'Listen, Katie, was there any way that Jessica could have been saved? She was so close to the hospital. As soon as she started flailing around, the limo driver turned around and roared back down the highway trying to save her. Maybe if she wasn't fashionably thin and gasping from pneumonia, she might have made it.'

'Not with that dose,' Katie said. 'Not even if she inhaled it at the hospital. Jessica didn't have a chance. Vape juice killed her. Vanilla flavor. Anyone around her vape?'

'All three members of her entourage,' I said. 'Tawnee, Will and Stu. That's her understudy, her make-up artist, and her assistant.

'All three smoked, and Jessica made them switch to vaping, and they weren't happy about it. I'm wondering if Tawnee's confusion in the limo – throwing everything out of her purse – was an act? What if she'd slipped vape juice into the spray last night at the hospital? She knew a desperate Jessica would grab the spray and never question it, once it was found.'

'Could be,' Katie said. 'But wouldn't she be too timid for a stunt like that?'

'Maybe Tawnee finally had enough,' I said. 'I heard her crying about Jessica's harsh treatment at Reggie's party. She hated Jessica.'

Then there was Becky, I thought, but didn't say. The homeless woman who hated Jessica – and with good reason. Becky had been on the edges of that drama, sneaking around the hospital suite last night, stealing from Jessica's entourage. Becky said being on stage with Jessica was like being raped, this time in front of witnesses.

I was meeting Becky tomorrow for breakfast. Meanwhile, I kept quiet about her. Becky had suffered enough and I wasn't doing anything to hurt her new start.

But I still remembered Becky's hard eyes when she asked 'Is she dead yet?'

Becky had stolen vape juice from Tawnee. And she would kill Jessica without a qualm, the way I'd step on a bug.

THIRTEEN

'Oh, wait! I forgot the best part,' I told Katie. 'Stu said he was secretly married to Jessica.'

'What?' Katie raised an eyebrow. 'She was married to her assistant? He's not listed as her husband on the hospital forms.'

'They were married in Vegas. He told Greiman, who had a fit.'

'Why keep the marriage a secret?' Katie said.

'Who knows? Maybe she was embarrassed. Why are you so surprised? Women can marry the young stuff, too.'

'Well, this youngster hit the jackpot,' Katie said. 'He gets her money and no more stud duty.'

I shuddered when I thought of Jessica's withered body. It was one thing if she and Stu had grown old together, but the studly Stu was a recent acquisition.

'So there's no chance Jessica died of Percocet and Xanax?' I asked.

'None. It was nicotine. Definitely.'

I relaxed. Now Mario had a chance of going free. 'Thank God. I need to call Monty ASAP. I'll explain as soon as I hang up.'

I called Monty with the good news on my new personal cell, then told Katie, 'Greiman hauled Mario into the station along with Jessica's whole crew. Rex the drug dog alerted in the lobby and the cops found Percocet and Xanax inside Mario's styling case.'

'Why the hell did Mario bring that case into the cop shop?'

'It's part of his identity,' I said.

'What? Drug dealer?' She took a sip of the ink-black coffee, made a face, and tossed the remains in her trash can.

'Before I could stop him, Mario admitted that he gave Jessica some Xanax and Percocet to help her "relax" – his word.'

'Oh, hell! Why didn't Mario keep his big mouth shut?' Katie said.

'Good question. Now that Monty knows Jessica didn't die of an opioid overdose, he can try to get Mario out on bail.'

'I'm glad you've got Monty on the case,' she said and gave me a starry-eyed smile.

I was, too, but if I didn't interrupt she'd spend the afternoon singing Monty's praises.

'At least Mario is off the hook for murder,' I said.

'Not really,' Katie said. 'Anyone can walk into a vape store and buy the juice.'

I got the bad news about Mario when Monty called at two-thirty that afternoon. I was driving back home when my new cell phone rang. I pulled into a shopping center to take his call.

As soon as the lawyer opened his mouth, I knew something was wrong. 'Mario didn't get bail. In fact, he's been charged with murder one.'

My stomach dropped like an elevator with the cables cut. 'What? Murder one? What happened?'

'Bad luck. Greiman searched Mario's styling case and found an empty vape juice bottle – vanilla flavor.'

'That's the kind that killed Jessica.'

'That's what the DA said.'

'Mario doesn't vape.'

'I know. Mario looked stunned.'

I had a vision of Mario's terrified face as he was being led off in handcuffs. Now his worst fears had come true.

Monty was still talking. 'I asked whose prints were on the bottle and Greiman said the bottle had been wiped.'

'That sounds fishy. Someone set him up.'

'Tell me about it. Worse, we had Lock 'Em Up LeMoine for a judge. Bail was denied. LeMoine said he was sending a message that murder and drugs will not be tolerated in Chouteau Forest. He wants the DA to go for the death penalty.'

'Oh, hell, Monty, I'm sorry. I can't believe this. Mario was so thrilled to do Jessica's hair. He thought it was an honor. Now he's looking at the big needle.'

'I know, I know. I agree with you – it's some kind of set-up.'

'Is he in jail? Can I go see him?'

'Not yet. I'm sorry, Angela. He'll be in the Chouteau County Jail. It's not a country club, but it's not bad.'

'They're all bad,' I said. 'What happens next?'

'He's been through the appearance, so he's already been told the charges and the judge set bail. Or in Mario's case, Judge LeMoine denied it.'

'So the preliminary hearing is next,' I said.

'Right. At the arraignment tomorrow, the judge may bind the poor guy over to another judge. If we're lucky, he'll be better than LeMoine.'

Monty did not sound hopeful, and I was feeling worse and worse. Monty must have realized it. 'Angela, I'll fight this every step of the way.'

'I know,' I said. 'If you can't get bail, will Mario be shut up in that godawful jail until the trial?'

'Unfortunately, yes.'

'And if Mario's found guilty and sentenced' – I was sure he would be, considering the Forest's dislike of outsiders – 'can he get anything besides the death penalty?'

'Life in prison,' Monty said. Those three words sounded ominous. For Mario, I knew that sentence would be worse than death.

I hung up, feeling dazed. This couldn't be happening. Saturday night, Mario was flying high, glowing under the stage lights at the Fabulous Lux while the city applauded him. Jessica was the toast of Chouteau Forest, in a glamorous black gown. Now Jessica was a raddled corpse, and Mario was in jail on drug and murder charges, his reputation in ruins and his life in danger. Missouri still had the death penalty. He could wind up on Death Row.

I wanted to escape to my home, but my work cell phone chimed. The ID said CHOUTEAU COUNTY PD.

Now what?

'Angela, it's Sergeant Bob Baker. I'm working the desk. You left your iPad when you were here earlier.'

Bob was one of the good guys at the Forest PD. 'Thanks. I'll be right there.'

I was only a few minutes away. I couldn't believe I'd forgotten my iPad – it was like an extension of my arm. I must have been really rattled over Mario's arrest. For a minute, I wondered if Stu had made it disappear, but dismissed that thought. It was my fault. I was distracted and left it behind. At least I'd filed my DI report.

Sgt Baker was behind the desk. He was a big, white-haired cop with high color and a nice smile. He smiled when he saw me and handed me my iPad in the black case. Then he looked around the lobby, checking to make sure it was empty, and lowered his voice. I leaned in to hear. 'Angela, a word to the wise. I know Mario Garcia is a friend of yours, but don't get caught helping him, or Greiman will have you up on charges of interfering with an investigation. He already thinks you let the staff at Killer Cuts know he had a search warrant.'

'He executed the warrant?'

'And didn't find so much as an aspirin.'

Raquel must have flushed those, too, I thought. She was taking no chances.

'Let me guess – he hit on Raquel and she turned him down.'

Bob smirked. 'That's what the uniform told me. Greiman is hopping mad and looking for trouble, Angela. Watch your back.'

'Thanks for the warning.' I slipped my iPad into my bag and was out the door, where I found the two remaining members of Jessica's entourage. Tawnee and Will were smoking real cigarettes, puffing like a couple of coal-fired chimneys. Both looked like they'd had a rough day. Tawnee looked worn and wrinkled, her blond hair flat. Will's hair seemed coated with 40-weight motor oil. He had an unfashionable five o'clock shadow.

Tawnee waved at me like I was a long-lost friend. 'Angela!'

'Are you going home to California?' I asked.

'No, Stu says we have to stay here.' She sounded angry. 'He's changed his mind. Now he says we can't go home until her body is released.'

'Her body.' Not Jessica.

'You looked surprised when Stu said he and Jessica were married,' I asked. 'Didn't you suspect something?'

'Hell, no. She ordered him around like a servant. You saw that. He couldn't smoke, just like the rest of us. I wonder if she ordered him to do the deed. Can you imagine Stu pumping away on that pile of bones?'

'Please,' Will said, covering his eyes. 'I can't unsee that.'

What was wrong with these people? The woman they'd worked with and traveled with was dead. Didn't they care? They'd witnessed her death – no, her murder – less than eight hours ago. And now they were joking about her sex life. I was too disgusted to say anything.

'Maybe he did it for the money,' Tawnee said. 'Married her, I mean.'

'What money?' Will said. 'She spent it all touring.'

'That can't be true. Every seat at her show was filled,' I said. 'She had to be selling out the theater.'

Will's laugh was nasty. 'And when the seats didn't sell, she papered the house. I heard about half of the St Louis shows were free tickets. Don't forget those free samples of her product. You should have seen how many of those were left behind in the theater. That last night, the leftovers could have filled a dumpster.'

'Don't people like her products?' The Forest dwellers sure snapped up her freebies at the party.

'Are you kidding? That health drink was kale, for gawd's sake. Nobody likes that stuff. You can get a kale smoothie for six bucks. She was charging sixty.'

'Stu kept the books,' Tawnee said. 'He would know if she had money, Will. You're just upset because she refused to back your new make-up line.'

'Am not,' Will said, sounding about six years old. 'I can get private financing. I plan to meet with my backers as soon as I'm in LA again.'

'What about you, Tawnee?' I asked. 'What will you be doing?'

'It's scary,' Tawnee said. 'But for the first time in years, I'm finally free.' She blew smoke like a happy dragon. 'Too bad I'm stuck in bumfuck nowhere.'

I tried to ignore this insult to my town.

Will was the only one of the entourage who hadn't given his opinion of the Forest, but Tawnee wasn't shy about sharing her feelings. 'I told Stu a week is my limit, and then I'm going home. And he's paying us double to stay, or I'm hopping on the first plane out of here.'

'Good luck prying money out of him,' Will said.

'I have a text confirming the terms,' Tawnee said. 'And he's paying for the Chouteau Forest Inn. He put our rooms on his credit card. I watched him.'

A black SUV pulled up and Tawnee checked her phone. 'That's our Uber to the inn,' she said. 'See you.'

I hoped not. I never wanted to encounter this heartless bunch again.

FOURTEEN

I fled to my car, anxious to get away from Jessica's nasty crew. I was still on call, but I could wait for my next assignment at home. Death investigators usually worked out of an office, but the ME, Evarts Evans, took my office space so he could have a fancy shower in his office. Fine with me. I liked my freedom.

Today, I didn't make it out of the parking lot when my work cell phone chimed, and I checked the ID – Butch Chetkin – a Chouteau Forest detective. Another good one.

'Angela,' he said. 'We've got a body on Shirley Circle. You know where that is?'

'Right off the interstate,' I said. 'Which house?'

'No house,' he said. 'It's in the vacant lot in the circle. He's a homeless man.'

Homeless? I hesitated, then said, 'We don't have homeless people in the Forest.'

'We have this one,' Butch said. 'Four days ago, the PD got reports that he was panhandling on the interstate exit, but when a car drove out there to check it out, he was gone. We thought he'd moved on. Turns out he was dead.'

'Exposure?' I asked.

'It doesn't look like natural causes,' Butch said. 'We need you here.'

'I'm at the cop shop. I'm on my way.' I hung up.

Shirley Circle was the closest Chouteau County had to a slum. It was in Toonerville, the Old Guard's sneery nickname for the blue-collar section of town. The circle was five rundown fifties shoeboxes next to a vacant lot bisected by a creek.

I parked on the circle behind three cop cars, and trundled my DI case over to the lot. An ambulance was parked at the edge, and a work-worn woman of about forty was inside, wrapped in blankets and sipping hot coffee. She was talking to Butch while two huge paramedics hovered protectively nearby. I paused and listened to her tell her story. She'd obviously recited it before.

'I got off at my usual bus stop on Gravois,' she said. 'I was walking home, checking out the specials at the super-market when the wind pulled the flyer right out of my hand. Took all my coupons. I ran after it, and that's when I found that poor old man, dead in the weeds.' Her voice was shaking and filled with tears.

'I dropped my purse, ran into the street, and flagged down my neighbor's car. She called you, and then I got the palpita-tions and passed out. But I'm fine now.'

I doubted that. She was shivering uncontrollably and her face was white as paper.

'Did you touch the deceased, Mrs Gordon?' Butch asked, his voice gentle.

'No. I was afraid to. He looked like he'd been real sick. He had blood everywhere. And other things, too. There was a package nearby. Something in foil. I didn't touch that, either.'

Butch patted her arm and said, 'You stay here and recover a bit, Mrs Gordon. I'll take your statement later.'

I met the detective on the street, out of earshot from the ambulance. 'I heard her talking, Butch. She must be really upset after finding that body.'

'Poor woman's in shock and has a dicey heart, but refuses to go to the hospital. Said she can't afford it. Works two jobs.' Butch shook his head.

The detective, a big, barrel-chested man, wore a dark police windbreaker, dark pants, and heavy boots. I eyed the weedy lot and wished I hadn't taken my boots out of the car to clean them. I needed them at this investigation.

'Can I carry your case?' he asked.

I brushed him off, then hoped I didn't sound too abrupt. I appreciated his offer, but I didn't want to seem like a helpless female. I dragged the case across the hard, cold ground, sticker plants pulling at my DI pantsuit.

'He's over there, by those maples,' Butch said. He pointed to a stand of winter-dead trees.

The old man had died hard. He was on a bed of brown leaves, curled up in the fetal position. Dried blood was in his nose and open mouth. He'd thrashed around in bloody feces and vomit. Near his right hand was a foil-wrapped package.

'What's that?' I asked.

Butch was wearing latex gloves, but he didn't touch the foil. 'Nitpicker is working the scene. I'll get her. She's working his campsite near the creek.'

'Why wasn't he at his campsite when he died?' I asked.

'My guess is when he started getting real sick, he didn't want to mess it up.' Butch left to find Nitpicker. Sarah 'Nitpicker' Byrne, the Forest's best CSI tech, was a sturdy woman of about thirty, and her hair color was her one flight of fancy. Today it was lime green. I'd gotten lucky with this case – a good detective and a good CSI tech.

Nitpicker handled the foil package as if it contained a bomb. She carefully opened it and we saw the remains of a sausage sandwich in a thick red sauce. 'I'll have the foil printed and the sandwich analyzed,' she said.

'Think he was poisoned?' I asked.

'That's my guess,' Butch said. 'But you'd have to have a heart of stone to kill an old man that way.'

I fired up my iPad, and was opening the 'Unidentified Persons' form, when Nitpicker came running up with a worn brown leather wallet. 'I found some ID,' she said. 'He hid it under his sleeping bag.'

We went through the wallet's contents – a used bus ticket from Chicago to St Louis, a McDonald's receipt for a 99-cent burger, and two wrinkled one-dollar bills. An expired Illinois driver's license had a name – Harold Galloway – a Chicago address, and a birth date, February 12, 1947, which made him seventy-two years old. He also had a VA card. 'He's a Vietnam vet, if this is his information,' Butch said. 'The driver's license photo looks like him.'

We both knew that wasn't enough for a formal ID. 'If Mr Galloway is really a veteran, he was fingerprinted when he enlisted,' Butch said. 'He'll be in the system.'

Fortunately, the body's hands could still be printed. They'd been preserved by the cold weather.

'How long do you think he's been dead?' I asked.

'One day,' Butch said. 'Two at the most.'

I switched to the 'Death Due to the Ingestion of Alcohol and/or Medications and/or Poisons' form, along with my usual 'Death Scene Investigation' form. After unzipping my DI case and putting on several pairs of latex gloves, I went to work. I noted the time – 2:17 p.m. – and the body's location, the northeast corner of the lot, 15 feet from the curb. The day was overcast and the ambient temperature was a chilly 22 degrees. I took the temperature on the ground by the body and it was one degree cooler. I was grateful for the cold weather – it kept the stink down.

I didn't find any poisons or prescription bottles on or near the body, and no alcoholic beverages. There were no corrosive substances nearby, such as antifreeze, pesticides, cleaning agents or other potential poisons.

I snapped my photos next. Mr Galloway had been tall and lean – six feet two inches. I estimated the decedent's weight at 180 pounds. His thin white hair was pulled into a greasy ponytail. His gray-white beard reached almost to his collarbone and was speckled with vomit, blood, and what looked like red sauce. He had a two-inch bruise (contusion) on his right cheek. He was missing three teeth – one front tooth (#8) and two in the upper right quadrant (#3 and #4). The remaining teeth were crooked and yellow. His face was red and roughened. He was not wearing a wedding ring or any jewelry.

He wore a stained and ragged green Army jacket. Brown wool gloves with holes in three fingers were jammed in his jacket pocket. He wore no belt. I turned down his waistband and found bruises in the waist area, possibly from contact with his pants. I wondered if he'd had some kind of Coumadin overdose. Blood thinners sometimes left bruises from contact with waistbands, watches, rings, even bra straps.

His hands were liver-spotted and callused. He had a three-inch bruise on his right hand and a half-inch cut-like defect near the thumb. I didn't see any signs of a struggle or skin under his fingernails, but I bagged his hands anyway. His scuffed black lace-up shoes were worn at the heels. The sole of the right shoe had come loose and was duct-taped to the upper. I lifted his pants legs and noticed a deep and very old twelve-inch scar on his right calf. I wondered if he'd walked with a limp.

I pulled up his sleeves to check for track marks or the tell-tale craters from skin popping. I found no signs of drug abuse on his arms, but he did have a faded tattoo on his right bicep: an angry eagle clutching a flag. Underneath it was this banner: Vietnam Vet 1968-1970.

'Butch,' I called. 'Come see this.'

I showed him further proof that decedent had been a veteran. 'What a country,' Butch said. 'This is how we treat the people who fight for us.' We sadly contemplated the old soldier, who'd spent his youth fighting an unpopular war in an unknown land. I felt a stab of pity – useless pity. The only way to help Harold Galloway now was to work this case and find his killer.

'I have a couple of leads,' Butch said. 'Four days ago, starting at 9:12 in the morning, there were six nine-one-one calls complaining about a panhandler at this highway exit. Three of them were made by Evelyn DuMont.'

'She's the head of the Forest Beautification Committee,' I said. An angry, imperious woman used to getting her way. 'She must have been in a real lather.'

'She was furious. She made the calls every ten minutes. Finally, the nine-one-one operator warned her to quit calling or she'd be arrested. Then we got calls from Liz Du Pres, Sloan Masters, and Deborah Smythe-Harris.'

'I know them,' I said. 'They're the other members of the committee. Known as the Flower Nazis. Hardly a corner of the county escapes their attention. They like to report home-owners who leave their garage doors open during the day.'

'Who cares?' Butch said.

'That's illegal in the Forest. So is parking a boat in your driveway. And leaving your trash containers in front of your house overnight. The committee makes sure these rules are rigidly enforced.'

'What a waste of the uniforms' time,' Butch said.

'Their latest crusade is demanding that the Forest "do something" about Shirley Circle.'

'Do what?' Butch looked puzzled.

'Get the homeowners to take better care of their lawns. Cite them for uncut grass and other violations. Better yet, have the city condemn the circle, deport the residents to St Louis, and raze the houses.'

'Those ladies have too much time on their hands,' Butch said, and laughed.

'It's not funny,' I said. 'They're fanatics. Did you find anything else?'

'A footprint in the mud by the creek. Looks like a thick-soled woman's shoe, possibly a nurse's shoe. We'll have to check it out. Also, the remains of a picnic lunch and a half-empty bottle of water at the campsite.

'A witness who lives on Shirley said she saw a Brenda Crandle in the lot four days ago,' he said.

'Miss Brenda? She's Evelyn DuMont's housekeeper,' I said. 'What was she doing here?'

'She was seen talking to the decedent,' Butch said. 'She gave him a brown paper shopping bag. How do you know her?'

'She was a friend of Mom's. Brenda used to make me chocolate swirl cupcakes when I was a kid. She must be close to eighty now. Brenda is a sweet old lady. She would never . . .'

As soon as I got halfway through the sentence, I realized I sounded like a typical Forest dweller, assuming my friends would never do anything wrong.

'I'm pretty sure this man died of poison,' Butch said. 'Sweet old ladies can poison someone just as easily as nasty young ones. I'll tell you what, since you know her, you can go with me when I talk to her. She may talk more around someone she knows.'

I finished the body inspection and the conveyance arrived to take the decedent to the morgue. When I signed off on the paperwork, it was almost five o'clock, and growing dark by the time I followed Butch to Brenda Crandle's apartment.

Brenda lived in a solid 1950s redbrick building. She answered the door wearing a flowered apron over her white housekeeper's uniform. She was a round, rosy-cheeked woman with blue eyes and crisply curled white hair.

She smiled when she saw me. 'Angela, dear, I haven't seen you in way too long. What brings you here?'

Butch identified himself, and Brenda said, 'I've never met a real detective before. I'm icing cupcakes in the kitchen for the church bake sale.' She showed no sign of fear or guilt. If I wanted to stop by her home with a detective, that was fine with Brenda.

'There's enough for both of you,' she said. 'Come join me.' We followed the path along the plastic runners that protected the pale green living room carpet into Brenda's kitchen, which smelled pleasantly of warm chocolate.

On the kitchen counter was a mixing bowl of chocolate icing. Six iced cupcakes were on a paper plate, and more were waiting to be iced.

'These are your favorite, Angela,' she said. 'Chocolate swirl. Would you like one, Detective?'

Butch declined, possibly because he thought she might be a poisoner, but I decided Brenda's cupcakes were to die for. I took one. We both turned down her offer of coffee.

Brenda stood at the sink and iced the cupcakes while Butch and I sat at her kitchen table.

'Did you take some food to a homeless man camping out in Shirley Circle?' he asked.

'Oh, yes, four days ago,' Brenda said, slathering a cupcake with icing and then adding it to the plate. 'I brought him a nice, big lunch. Late lunch, really. It was close to three o'clock when I got there.'

'Why did you do that?'

She iced another cupcake and licked icing off her thumb. 'Mrs DuMont – she's my employer – saw him panhandling by the interstate. She followed him, and learned he was camping in the lot. She said we should feed him – it would be Christian charity.'

Hm. Mrs D had never exhibited charity in any form, Christian, Buddhist or Muslim.

'What did you give him?' Butch asked.

'I wanted to fix him a nice pot roast sandwich, but Mrs DuMont said men liked spicy food, and she'd make him an Italian sausage sandwich, with lots of peppery red sauce. Fixed it with her own hands, she did, while I put together the rest of the food – four big oatmeal cookies, a bag of tangerines, a bag of potato chips, a nice slice of apple tart and a big bottle of water. I slipped in that pot roast sandwich, too.'

'Then what?' Butch asked.

Two more iced cupcakes joined the others on the plate. 'Mrs DuMont told me to go to the lot on Shirley Circle and give him the food. I was scared at first – I didn't know the man. What if he had mental problems or something? Mrs DuMont said he was perfectly harmless and I could have the rest of the day off. Shirley Circle is on my way home. I went, but I kept my pepper spray in my coat pocket, just in case, along with my cell phone.

'He turned out to be nice as pie. We chatted for a bit. His name is Harry Galloway. He's a Vietnam War veteran. He served eighteen months over there and got sent home when he was wounded in the leg. He was happy about the lunch. He was hungry and was looking forward to a good meal. He was trying to go south, where it was warmer. I gave him two dollars – that's all the cash I had with me – and then left. I didn't see him again, so I guess he got his ride. There. I'm all done.' Brenda had iced the last cupcake.

'I have an odd request, Miss Crandle,' Butch said. 'May I look at the shoes you wore that day?'

Brenda looked puzzled. 'My shoes? Yes, I suppose. They're in my closet. I haven't cleaned them yet – I do that on my day off. I have several pairs for work. They're all white Nurse Mates, like these.' She lifted her foot to show her thick-soled shoes.

'Is there a problem?' she asked.

'Just a little disturbance at the lot,' Butch said. 'Nothing serious. There are several footprints there, and we'd like to sort them out. If I could borrow your shoes for a day, it would really help me.'

'They're in my bedroom,' Brenda said. Butch followed her down the hall for the shoes.

I was quite sure that Evelyn DuMont – may she fry in hell – had used innocent Brenda to kill Harry. I figured Butch didn't want Brenda to tell Mrs DuMont that Harry Galloway had been murdered. We both knew the press wouldn't bother covering the homeless man's death.

While I waited, I eyed the icing bowl, tempted to lick the spoon. Instead, I ate another cupcake. After all, Brenda had offered it to Butch.

Butch came back with the shoes in a brown paper bag under his arm and a smile on his face.

FIFTEEN

After that horrible day, I sat in my kitchen for a while, too exhausted to move. My broken cell phone sat on my kitchen table like an accusation, but I was too tired to tackle it. Mario needed my full attention, and I could make a fatal mistake when I was this tired. I needed a fresh, rested brain for cyberwork.

About seven, my rumbling stomach reminded me that I hadn't eaten anything since breakfast, about a million years ago, except Brenda's cupcakes, and food eaten in the line of duty didn't count. I needed protein. I scrambled myself an egg, my go-to meal when I don't feel like cooking, which is most of the time. I never was much of a cook and after Donegan died, I gave it up for good.

I ate my sad, solitary egg and washed my dinner things. I was still hungry, but there was nothing else to eat. I was too tired to shop. I needed sleep.

As I was putting away the frying pan, I heard a car in my drive. A quick check out the window showed it was Clare Rappaport's beat-up green Land Rover. My mother's old friend was carrying a pink cake box from the Chouteau Forest Bakery. What luck. The Dessert Fairy had arrived.

Clare was smiling when I answered the door, so I assumed the crisis with her negligent children had been resolved. She cared too much about her son and daughter to look this happy if she had disinherited them.

I brushed aside her apologies for arriving without calling – Clare never called – and invited her in. 'You're sure it's not too late?'

'It's only seven-thirty,' I said. I didn't mention that I was thinking about going to bed before she arrived. 'I was just making some coffee. Come into the kitchen. Can I help you with that cake box?'

'Yes, yes. I hope you like Bavarian whipped cream.'

I opened the box on the kitchen table.

Oh, man. The sugar bomb supreme. Eight layers of chocolate cake with cherries and real whipped cream, topped by more whipped cream and semi-sweet chocolate shavings. Some women claimed the Bavarian whipped cream cake was better than sex. I wouldn't go that far, but it was darn good and definitely satisfying.

Clare propped her silver-headed cane against the wall and took a seat at my kitchen table. 'My problem is solved,' Clare said. No, she announced it. 'I have no doubts about my children anymore. I made the call, like I told you I would. I told Jemima and Trey they should come next Saturday for a family conference. I was having financial issues and wanted to discuss my problems with them. They didn't wait. They showed up this evening with this beautiful cake.'

Her eyes glowed. Tonight she wore a powder blue coat dress like the Queen of England, but white-haired Clare looked even more regal. I made admiring noises as I looked at the cake. I didn't have to fake those. My mouth was watering.

'First they whisked me off to dinner. They reserved a corner booth at Solange, my favorite French restaurant. She has the most divine sole – it's flown in from England.'

I brushed away a mental picture of a big fish reclining in an airplane seat and started making coffee.

'The booth was quiet,' she said, 'and we could talk in privacy. I explained that I would be completely broke by the end of the year and would have to sell the house. They were so sympathetic. My daughter patted my hand and said, "Don't worry, Mother, that's our job. We'll come up with a solution."

'Trey, who's the practical one, said, "We need facts, Mother, before we make any serious decisions. I'd like to bring in an accountant to look at your books for a professional opinion."'

'Are you going to let him do that?'

'I'll see what my daughter comes up with first. It was such a pleasant dinner.' Clare sounded wistful.

'Afterward, I invited the children back to my house for

coffee and cake. They both said they had to leave – Jemima had something with the children and Trey had a trip to Singapore early in the morning. I thought you might like to share the cake with me while it's still fresh.'

'I'm glad you stopped by,' I said. 'I've just finished dinner and was wishing I had some dessert when you appeared out of the blue with my favorite cake.'

'Angela, I can't tell you how happy I am that both children didn't wait until next Saturday to see me.' Her look of maternal satisfaction warmed my heart.

I set out my mother's flowered dessert plates and silver, as well as Mom's thinnest coffee cups, and linen napkins. I even brought out her silver cake server. By that time the coffee was ready.

'Cream or sugar with your coffee?' I asked.

'Black, please. This cake is going to be sweet enough.'

'Will you cut the cake while I pour the coffee?' I asked.

Clare cut the cake into quarters and gave us each one. She picked a chocolate shaving off her piece.

'Go ahead. Dig in,' I said, pouring her coffee.

'I can't resist,' she said. She was grinning like a little kid.

'I'll join you as soon as I pour my coffee.'

'Mm,' Clare said after her first bite. It was rather large for the ladylike woman and the second bite wasn't any smaller.

'I can't wait to taste that cake, Clare,' I said, as I poured my own cup and then set the pot back on the coffee maker. 'I'm so glad you stopped by.' That sounded crass. I added, 'I mean, I'm always glad when you stop by. You're a link to my mom, and I miss her. I know you do, too. I always enjoy your company.'

I heard a strange whistling noise, like a blocked tea kettle.

'Clare?'

I turned around and saw Clare's face was as white as her hair and she was clutching her throat.

'Clare! What's wrong?'

She couldn't tell me. Her lips and tongue were swollen, and she was turning blue.

I thought I saw the signs of anaphylactic shock.

'Clare!' I shouted, as the panicked woman wheezed and clawed at her throat for air. 'Do you have allergies?'

'Peanuts,' Clare gasped. She seemed on the verge of collapse. Now her face was flour white, her eyes were red, her tongue was so swollen she could hardly talk.

'Clare!' I had to get her attention. 'EpiPen! Where's your EpiPen?'

'Purse,' Clare gasped. That effort was almost too much for her.

I upended her Chanel bag on my kitchen table, and pawed through the lipsticks, tissues and mints until I found the EpiPen. I jammed it into her thigh, the best place for this kind of injection. In an emergency, you could inject someone through their clothes.

I called 911 and heard, 'Nine-one-one, what's your emergency?'

'Help!' I told the operator. 'I have an eighty-three-year-old woman who I think is in anaphylactic shock. I stuck her with her EpiPen. She's breathing a little easier, but she needs help fast. Yes, Angela Richman. I'm in the old guest house on the Du Pres estate. Hurry!'

Clare was breathing easier, but she was still wheezing. The crisis wasn't over. She tried to talk and I said, 'No talking, Clare. You need to save your breath.' She was still too pale and now she was shivering. I brought in the throw from my couch and wrapped her in it, then put her feet up on the other chair.

By the time I'd made her a little more comfortable, I heard the ambulance in my drive.

I ran out the front door and waved the four paramedics inside.

'It's Clare Rappaport. She was here for cake and coffee. She brought the cake, took two bites and started wheezing. She said she was allergic to peanuts. I injected her in the thigh with her EpiPen.'

The paramedics quickly loaded her on the stretcher. 'I'll follow you to the hospital,' I said, and squeezed Clare's hand. She looked terrified, and every day of her eighty-three years.

SOS was mercifully close, and for the second time that miserable day, I was back in the emergency room. I prayed that this visit would have a happier outcome.

Once in the ER, I found Clare Rappaport. I was relieved to see she wasn't in Room One, for the hopeless cases. She was in Room 2B, swallowed by a hospital bed. Now the dynamic woman seemed small and shrunken. Her snowy hair had come loose from its tight chignon and her blue coat dress was rumpled. Her skin was papery.

I smiled when I saw her. 'There you are.' She looked so fragile I was almost afraid to touch her, but I gently took her cold hand. She hung on like I was a lifeline. She was still wheezing. An ER doc who looked young enough to be Clare's granddaughter came in, listened to her chest, then gave her another epinephrine injection. A nurse and I helped Clare into an ugly hospital gown and the nurse started an IV.

The ER doc came back, looking serious. 'I'm ordering you a breathing treatment, Mrs Rappaport.' She spoke too loudly, the way younger people sometimes talked to the elderly.

'I'm old, not deaf,' Clare said, and I was glad to see this sign of spirit. Her color looked a little pinker. The nurse fitted the breathing treatment mask over Clare's face.

Clare fell asleep during the treatment. She was still asleep when the nurse gently removed the mask. I held the old woman's soft, veined hand and fell asleep myself.

When the ER doctor came back sometime around eleven, I woke up crusty-eyed and confused. Where was I? I heard the blare of televisions and the operator calling, 'Dr Daniels. Dr Daniels. Please call 7533.' I realized I was back in the ER, this time with Clare.

'I'd like to admit you overnight, Mrs Rappaport,' the ER doctor said. 'You're looking better, but we want to continue with the IV, the epinephrine, and the steroids.'

Clare didn't look too unhappy. In fact, she seemed relieved. After the doctor left, she said, 'Angela, honey, this was above and beyond. It's time for you to go home.'

'Do you want me to call your children?'

'No,' she said. 'There were peanuts in that cake. One – or both – of my children tried to kill me. I want you to have that cake tested. I'll pay, Angela, but promise me you'll do that.'

SIXTEEN

The next morning, Clare Rappaport was pounding her silver-headed cane on the tile floor of her hospital room.

'I'll disinherit both those fucking ingrates!' she said.

'Clare!' I was shocked at her language. She never talked like that. Clare was one of those women who said 'oh, sugar!' instead of 'oh, shit!'

She'd definitely recovered from the last night's near-fatal attack. Clare was sitting up in one of those high-backed chairs found only in hospital rooms, dressed and waiting for the final paperwork so she could leave. Her housekeeper had brought her fresh clothes early this morning. Clare's white hair was once more in an elegant chignon. Her color was good. As soon as I returned with her fur coat and her purse at eight-thirty this morning, she put on her light pink lipstick. Now she was ready for battle.

Clare began raging against both children. They were selfish, greedy and only interested in her money. They never bothered to call her. They didn't mean a word of those promises they'd made to help her last night. 'They want to kill me off now so there's still some estate left for them to inherit!'

She took a deep breath. This was the break in the tirade I'd been waiting for. 'Clare, let me check it out first,' I said. 'There must be some mistake.'

'There's no mistake,' she said, eyes narrowed. She pounded her cane on the tiled floor.

'I.' Pound.

'Nearly.' Pound.

'Died.' Pound.

'The Forest Bakery's Bavarian cream cake doesn't have peanuts,' I said. 'I should know. I've eaten enough of them.'

'This one did. When I get out of here, I want Mrs Holmesby to drive me straight to my lawyer so I can change my will.'

Pound. That cane again, coming down like a judge's gavel.

I couldn't let Clare do this. I didn't care about Jemima and Trey, but with this move, Clare would destroy her family ties permanently, even if she changed her will back. My mother would have stopped this. I had to, too. For her sake.

'At least let me investigate,' I said.

'Well . . .' Clare hesitated.

'Please, Clare. I'm not asking for any thanks because I went with you to the hospital, but let me check this out before you make any decisions.'

OK, I played the guilt card. But it was for a good cause. Clare took so long to answer, I could almost see the wheels turning in her brain. At last she said, 'All right, Angela. I'll give you three days. Then I'm going to see my lawyer and my money goes to the dogs!'

And the cats. Clare was determined to leave her millions to the Humane Society.

Three days wasn't much time, but it was something. I thanked Clare, and left for my ten o'clock breakfast with Becky, the 'street model' from Jessica's show, at the St Louis Pancake House. Greiman had threatened to interview her and 'lock her up' but I doubted he'd do that. He didn't need to now: He'd already arrested Mario for Jessica's murder. Greiman wouldn't make the forty-minute trip downtown for nothing. He was one detective who would never die of overwork.

On the drive to the pancake house on Jefferson Avenue, I thought about Becky's words: *I saw something at the hospital when Jessica was there. I think it killed her.*

And what did her odd little jingle mean: *Since you've been so dear, I'll make it clear. It's not the red – it's the blue.*

What did she see? Who did she see? Did one of Jessica's entourage pour vape juice into the star's throat spray? Was Becky trying to extort money for this information? Was she blackmailing one of the California crew? Or did Becky kill Jessica and now she was trying to deflect attention from herself?

Becky had a good reason to hate Jessica: The star had cruelly forced a destitute woman to strip in front of jeering strangers for a hundred bucks – and Becky had to beg to keep on her underwear. I was still embarrassed when I remembered her humiliation, and angry at myself that I'd stayed to watch it.

By the time I got to the St Louis Pancake House, the morning breakfast rush was over. The old pancake house was a forties-style relic with shining chrome and generous booths. Even the waitress had a forties name: Roxy. Her pink hair was a cheerful beacon in the restaurant's pale blue vinyl color scheme. Roxy gave me a wide booth near the window. I ordered coffee while I studied the menu and checked my watch. At ten past ten, there was no Becky.

Roxy kept coming back to refill my cup and ask, 'Ready to order now?' At ten-twenty, I ordered blueberry pancakes. I figured I could watch Becky eat when she finally showed up. At ten-thirty, there was still no sign of Becky.

I called the Hoffstedder. After ten rings, a woman with a whiskey-and-cigarettes voice answered the hotel's phone. I didn't know Becky's last name, but I said, 'Do you have a woman named Becky registered at your hotel?'

'You mean the one who was in Jessica's show? Yes, she's staying here, but she doesn't have a phone in her room.'

'She was supposed to meet me for breakfast at ten o'clock.'

'She isn't up yet, hon,' the clerk said. 'I haven't seen her this morning.'

I thanked the clerk, left the money for my bill and a tip, and drove two blocks to the Hoffstedder. The once-grand hotel was reduced to an SRO – single room only – home for people down on their luck. The limestone front was thickly crusted with pigeon droppings and the brown brick was dingy.

As I walked inside, the smell hit me first: mold and unwashed bodies with top notes of stale urine. The lobby was dingy: unmopped linoleum, a sagging orange plastic couch, a dusty silk plant and a single bulb in an overhead fixture. In the dim light, I could make out some of the late-nineteenth century ornamental plasterwork on the ceiling – wedding cake swags of flowers and swirls – now cracked and water-stained. Behind a Plexiglas barrier was the desk clerk, a seventy-something woman with her white hair in a cotton-candy beehive, puffing away on a Marlboro. She was fashionably dressed in a chic black-and-white suit.

'What can I do for you?' she asked. There it was, that same husky voice I'd heard on the phone.

'I called earlier,' I said. 'I'm looking for Becky.'

'Oh, right. She's still in her room, hon. Three-twelve. Take the elevator over there.' She pointed to it with a nicotine-stained finger.

Inside, the elevator looked like someone had beaten the walls with a baseball bat. It jounced and jerked up to the third floor. I was relieved when the doors opened into a small lobby with a cracked mirror and a gilt table piled with take-out menus.

I passed a housekeeping cart on the way to room three-twelve. Becky's room was at the end of the hall. Her door was thick, dark wood and had an actual transom at the top. I knocked and called Becky's name. No answer. I pounded on the door. Still no answer. Now I was worried. What if Becky was sick? Why else would she miss a free breakfast?

My pounding on the door attracted the attention of the housekeeper, an older woman in a turquoise uniform.

'Problem, miss?' she asked in heavily accented English.

'My friend in here' – I pointed at the door – 'may be sick. Can you open her door, please?'

'Sure, miss, sure.'

She took out a brass key and unlocked the door, then stepped back and watched me. The room was dark and the shade was down on the one window. I flipped on the overhead light and saw the room was a mess. The only chair had been overturned, along with a take-out cup of soda. Clothes were scattered about, and the covers were pulled off the narrow bed. I saw a shoe sticking out of the pile of bedding on the floor. A newish square-heeled black leather shoe.

Strange. Becky had been wearing a powder blue suit when I saw her in the hospital, and she didn't have shoes that expensive. There was a bit of hot pink wool near the shoe. I stepped carefully across the worn carpet and lifted the bedding. The pink wool was a pantsuit. Quite a good one, really.

I moved closer to examine the pantsuit. The arms were flung out, and a pink-and-blue flowered scarf was tied tightly around the neck.

Neck?

My fogged brain finally put the picture together: Becky was wearing the pantsuit, and she'd been strangled by the flowered scarf around her neck.

Now my death investigator senses kicked in: I saw the scratch marks she'd made around the neck as she tried to save her life. Her face was red and bloated, her eyes were popping and her lips were blue. Becky was dead.

That's when I screamed. Loud and long.

It was most unprofessional.

SEVENTEEN

I spent the morning with the St Louis police. I knew the routine. I showed them my Chouteau County death investigator ID, and they treated me like a pro. I told them the truth. Mostly.

I explained that I'd met Becky at Jessica Gray's show. I'd talked with her at the Du Pres party and encouraged her to get a job. I'd put Becky in touch with Women's Work, a group that helped homeless women, and she'd told me she'd had a job.

I didn't mention that Becky had information about Jessica's murder. Greiman had ignored Becky's information, but I wasn't going to let it die with her. I was determined to free Mario.

Before the cops showed up, while the housekeeper alerted the front desk, I recovered enough to wrap my hand in a towel and do a quick search of the apartment. I didn't find any alcohol, but there were two crisp one-hundred-dollar bills hidden under the mattress. One of the bills had a phone number with a Beverly Hills area code written on it. I photographed the bills and that number with my cell phone.

Where did Becky get that money? Was it seed money from Women's Work? Did she blackmail someone? Steal it? Or was she working somewhere for cash?

I didn't know. I heard footsteps in the hall, and dropped the towel where I'd found it on the dresser. I ran downstairs to wait for the police. The rest of the morning, and a good chunk of the afternoon, was spent with the detectives.

It was three o'clock by the time I signed a statement and the cops cut me loose. I was on call as a DI until six o'clock, and relieved that so far Chouteau County didn't need my services. I grabbed a burger and headed back to the Forest.

I'd just turned off I-55 into the Forest when my work cell phone chimed. By the ring tone, I knew it was the newest

Chouteau County detective, Jace Budewitz. I pulled into a parking lot to answer my phone.

'Angela,' he said, 'I need you. We have what looks like a drug overdose. Vera DePaul, age seventy-seven. Her daughter, Lydia, found her. She lives with her mother. The daughter's pretty shook.'

'Did Lydia find her mother in their house?'

'Yes. The victim died at her home. Thirty-nine Westminster Close. Off Gravois.'

'I know it. I'll be there in five.'

I liked working with Jace Budewitz. He was a complete professional. A Chicago transplant, he'd worked the worst neighborhoods in that city before he came to Chouteau County. Jace was often puzzled by the Forest's customs, until I explained the rich here were gangs in designer garb. Slowly, he was starting to understand the place.

The late Vera was the matriarch of the DePaul clan, with two sons and four daughters scattered across the country. She was a tall, horse-faced woman with iron-gray hair and an iron will. She'd decreed that her youngest daughter, Lydia, stay at home and take care of her, and in the finest nineteenth-century style, that's what Lydia did. Vera had enjoyed bad health for more than twenty years – she loved to discuss her symptoms – and Lydia was her willing servant. Only in the last year, when Vera had been diagnosed with cancer, had she been seriously sick.

The Westminster house was a gothic horror, with turrets, pinnacles and parapets, the perfect setting for a dead body. I parked my Charger in the circular drive and rolled my DI kit up the gray marble steps to a front door that belonged on a medieval castle.

I waved to Rick, the uniform on the porch. 'Detective Budewitz is in the front room,' Rick said, holding the door open. 'Go on in.'

The vast entrance hall was dismal: dark maroon rugs and thick heavy mahogany furniture. A Chinese vase with funereal calla lilies was on a round table big enough for a poker tournament.

I was relieved to see Jace's friendly, open face, a beacon

of life in this death house. Jace was six-two with one of those faces that stayed boyish forever. His buzzed blond hair was rapidly retreating.

'We're in the living room,' he said, and lowered his voice. 'Lydia is pretty upset. I made her tea.'

That kind gesture was pure Jace.

'I don't think she tried to clean up the scene. I saw a half-empty bottle of sherry and two pill bottles, for Percocet and zolpidem. Lydia says her mother doesn't drink and she doesn't take Percocet. The daughter swears her mother accidentally overdosed on zolpidem.' That was generic Ambien, a sleeping pill.

'It's possible,' I said, 'but I doubt it. Fortunately, it's the ME's job to decide if Mrs DePaul killed herself accidently or on purpose.'

'I didn't see any suicide note,' Jace said, 'and no copy of *Final Exit.*'

We saw that book by Derek Humphry at some suicide scenes. Final Exit deaths followed the precise instructions Humphry had laid out. We had to look for the plastic bag that was placed over the decedent's head, the pudding container for the pills, and the last will and testament. Readers of *Final Exit* made it clear that they were committing suicide. Many families, for cultural or religious reasons, try to cover up a suicide.

Was Mrs DePaul taking zolpidem? That drug had a lot of weird side effects, including depression.

'Lydia is calm enough to talk if you want to ask her some questions,' Jace said.

I parked my DI kit in the hall, took out my iPad and called up the form for 'Death Due to Ingestion of Alcohol and/or Medications and/or Poisons.' Thanks to the current opioid epidemic, I knew most of the questions.

The living room was as dark as the hall, with heavy red velvet and grim mahogany. Lydia was sitting on a camelback sofa upholstered in some slippery red fabric. A silver tea tray was in front of her on a dark table.

Lydia must have been a late-life baby. She was thirty-five and looked ten years older in her drab brown dress. Her long

hair was pulled into a bun. She had pale, even features, and
gray eyes with dark smudges beneath them. I itched to take
her to Mario for a makeover. She could have been a knockout.
But Mario was in jail, and Lydia was trapped in this gloomy
house.

She was drinking Earl Grey tea in a thin, flowered cup, and
offered to pour for me. I took the cup. Her thin hands trembled
slightly when she lifted the ornate silver teapot.

'Mother had stage three pancreatic cancer,' she said. 'She
was supposed to start another round of chemo on Monday at
the hospital.'

'How did your mother feel about that?' I asked.

'She hoped it would give her another four to six pain-free
months,' Lydia said.

'Was she in pain last night?' I asked.

'Some,' Lydia said. 'But Mother is – I mean, was – a fighter.'

'When was the last time you saw your mother alive?'

'About nine o'clock last night. She asked me to bring her
a glass of water. I offered to warm some milk, but she said
no, she didn't want to wait. She wanted to sleep.'

Lydia's voice wavered. 'She was in pain and she thought
a sleeping pill would help.' She wiped away a tear with her
hand.

'Did your mother take the pill while you were in the
room?'

'Yes. I kissed her goodnight, turned off the light, and went
to my own room, which is down the hall from Mother's. I
watched TV until about eleven o'clock. That's when I went
to sleep.'

'Did you hear your mother any time during the night? Did
she get up and move around? Did any strange noises wake
you up?'

'No, I'm a sound sleeper. I slept late – until well after ten
this morning. Then I found her.' Now Lydia was crying so
hard she couldn't talk. I sipped my tea and let her compose
herself. After she'd dried her eyes with a tissue, and sniffed
delicately, I asked, 'Did your mother take pain pills?'

'The doctor prescribed Percocet and OxyContin, but
Mother didn't like to take them. She said they muddled her

brain and she hated that she couldn't think straight. Mostly she took Aleve. Only if the pain got really bad would she take a Percocet.'

'Was she allergic to any medications?'

'Just penicillin.'

'What about foods or substances?'

'She was allergic to shrimp. We never ate shellfish.'

'Who was her internist?'

'Dr Carmen Bartlett.' Doc Bartlett saw most of the Forest families.

I took a deep breath before I asked the next question. 'Lydia, did your mother have a drinking problem?'

'Of course not!' Lydia looked offended.

'Did she enjoy a cocktail?'

'Mother would have a glass of sherry to be sociable, but that was all. Alcohol did not mix with the drugs she was taking for her cancer. Since she's been sick, she's rarely had a drink.'

'Has your mother been depressed?'

'No!' Lydia was agitated now. 'My sister Christine is expecting a baby next month. Mother was looking forward to this grandchild.'

I asked a soothing question next. 'How many grandchildren does your mother have?'

'Six, all girls. Christine was going to have a boy and Mother was very excited. She wanted to hold her first grandson.'

'What time did you find your mother this morning?'

'About ten-thirty. I dressed and went in to check on her, to see how she was feeling and what she wanted for breakfast. Our housekeeper is on vacation. As soon as I entered the room, I could see Mother was . . . gone.' Lydia suppressed a slight shudder.

'I dropped into the chair by her bed as if my strings had been cut. I could not move. It was nearly half an hour before I could call nine-one-one. The paramedics got here right away and they said it was too late. They did not try to revive Mother. The police came after that.'

'Did your mother leave any kind of note?' I steeled myself for the blast.

'Mother did not commit suicide!' As she said that, Lydia looked remarkably like her late mother at her most formidable. Her face was severe and her eyes were snapping with anger.

'But she did have stage three cancer. Did she give you any instructions about her final arrangements or her will?'

'Mother's lawyer has those,' Lydia said. 'She made her will after Father passed away and kept it updated.'

'Thank you, Lydia,' I said. 'I'll go up to see your mother now.'

'But I haven't had a chance to clean her up!' Lydia half-rose from the couch, as if to stop me. 'Mother was such a dignified person.'

'I know she was,' I said. 'The whole Forest admired your mother's elegance. But the medical examiner will have to see her the way she is.'

'You're going to cut up Mother? You can't do that! I'm calling our lawyer!' Lydia burst into fresh sobs.

EIGHTEEN

Lydia's tears finally stopped. I didn't think she was faking them. She was genuinely horrified by the thought of her mother being autopsied.

'Ms DePaul,' Jace said, 'you're welcome to call your lawyer, but he—'

'She!' Lydia said.

'She will tell you the same thing: Your mother's death was unattended and the medical examiner must conduct an investigation. Your mother died in an unusual manner. It may have been an accident or suicide.'

'Mother did not kill herself,' Lydia said. 'I told you that.'

'Yes, you did. But the medical examiner has to make that determination.'

'Mother had cancer,' Lydia said. 'When my father died of a heart attack at SOS there was no autopsy.'

'That's because he died in a hospital under a physician's care,' Jace said. 'There's a chance the ME's investigation may not include an autopsy.'

I doubted that, but kept my mouth shut. Jace was doing a good job of calming her.

'I'm still calling my lawyer,' Lydia said, her mouth set in a firm line. 'And I want to talk to her in privacy. I'll be in my study.'

Lydia stomped up the winding wood staircase. Jace looked at me and shrugged. I poured myself more tea and asked, 'Jace, if she's upstairs, can she go into her mother's room?'

'Nope, I have a uniform posted at the door. Matt won't let her even look inside.'

I should have known. I was too used to working with Greiman. Jace was careful.

Ten minutes later Lydia marched down the stairs, her

white face flushed with anger. She looked almost pretty in her fury. 'My attorney says you may proceed,' she said.

Of course she did, but Jace and I didn't rub salt into Lydia's wounds by commenting. 'Please stay down here,' Jace said. 'We'll call if we need you.'

Jace and I proceeded up the dark, steep stairs, watched by the leering gargoyles lining the staircase. I was grateful for the distraction of my heavy death investigator kit. I didn't want to damage the stairs by rolling the suitcase, so I carried it the whole way.

The scene in Vera's bedroom was grim. The poor woman did not have an easy death. The tangled sheets were covered with vomit and feces, and the chilly room had a sour, sickly smell. Someone – either her daughter or the paramedics – had rolled Vera onto her back. She wore a thin blue cotton nightgown, stained with fluids. Her head was nearly hairless, possibly a side effect of chemo, and her body was a skeleton wrapped in almost colorless skin. Vera didn't have many reserves left to fight the cancer attacking her. I was no friend of Vera's, but I felt sorry that the stately old woman had been reduced to this.

She looked lost in the massive mahogany four-poster bed draped in maroon velvet. I couldn't imagine a young Vera – or anyone, for that matter – frolicking in that bed. Especially under the disapproving gaze of the frowning, side-whiskered men in the gold-framed paintings. The room's maroon Oriental rug was the size of a parking lot and three tall windows were smothered with heavy velvet. The shades were down and the overhead light was on.

'Who turned on the light?' I asked. I needed to know if the decedent had left the lights on.

'The daughter,' Jace said. 'She says it was off when she came in the room this morning. So was the lamp on the bedside table.'

I opened my DI case, put on my latex gloves and photographed the death scene. Lydia had already given me her mother's demographic data – age, birth date, marital status, even her Social Security number. The paramedics had pronounced Vera dead at 11:17 that morning.

I noted my arrival time, and that the decedent was in the second-floor bedroom, face up in a double bed adjacent to the east wall. The furnace was rumbling, and the ambient temperature was sixty-one degrees. I got the same temperature on the bed. Vera kept her room cold. I photographed the thermostat in the hall. It had the same temperature.

I examined the body from head to toe. I checked her mouth for 'burns' or irritated areas, in case she'd swallowed a corrosive substance such as Drano.

Vera's arms and the backs of both hands were bruised from what appeared to be needle sticks. Her left hand had a livid purple contusion three inches long and two inches wide. Her right arm had a yellowing five-inch by three-inch contusion, and a small – one-inch by two-inch – bruise on the back of her right hand. She even had a two-inch needle-stick bruise on a big vein in her right ankle. The local phlebotomists must have used pitchforks on the poor woman. I wondered if Vera's veins were collapsing from the chemo and the constant blood tests.

Jace helped me roll her over. I lifted her gown and saw the large purple mark on her left side. That was livor mortis. Judging by the marks, Vera must have died in the fetal position. Jace and I left her face up on the bed.

I returned to my form. It wanted to know the 'location of medicine containers at the scene.'

An empty bottle that once held thirty Percocet tablets was on the nightstand by the bed. The label said these were five milligrams, and the decedent should take '1 or 2 tablets every 6 hours as needed for pain.' Next to the Percocet bottle was an empty bottle for zolpidem. The label said it had contained thirty '5 milligram tablets for insomnia.' Both medications were prescribed by Doc Bartlett. I logged them on my medications form.

Next to the nightstand lamp with swags of tasseled maroon silk was a nearly empty bottle of sherry – Fernando de Castilla Palo Cortado Antique. The good stuff, selling for sixty bucks a bottle. I wondered if Vera had kept the sherry upstairs, or if she had to go past those grinning gargoyles to get her last drink.

The pill bottles and the sherry were bagged. They'd go to the ME.

A glass half-full of a clear liquid that looked and smelled like water was also on the table. I poured the liquid into a Tupperware container and bagged the glass.

Between the bed and the table I caught a flash of powder blue, swathed in the bed's maroon velvet draperies.

'Jace, look at this,' I said, as I pulled out a vintage Kotex box, the blue one with the white rose on the side, with my gloved hands.

'Why would an old woman need Kotex?' Jace asked.

We pulled back the lid on the cardboard box. Inside, under yellowing white cotton pads, was a note on thick cream stationery engraved with Vera's name. The handwriting looked like a spider had crawled across the page. It said:

> My Darling Daughter,
>
> I cannot go on any longer. I know you want me to start another round of chemo, but I can't go through with it. The cancer has spread to my bones and the pain is unceasing. Not even the joy of holding my first grandson is enough to overcome it.
>
> I am so tired. I want to be with your father, my beloved Thomas. I hope God will forgive me for trying to escape this unbearable pain. You have been a kind and caring daughter, everything a mother could want in a child. I pray that you will forgive me for taking the easy way out.
>
> Your loving mother, Vera

'Poor woman sure didn't take the easy way out,' I said.

'But she is definitely a suicide,' Jace said. 'Her daughter's not going to like that.'

'That decision is up to the ME,' I said. 'Evarts Evans has been known to rule that obvious suicides were accidental deaths, out of consideration for the families.'

'And I bet he's especially considerate to the one percenters,' Jace said.

'You're catching on to the ways of the Forest,' I said. 'I'll bag her note and record that we found it.'

'Think the daughter hid it here?' Jace asked.

'I bet we'll find her prints on it. This note may be why she was so upset when we suggested her mother was a suicide.'

'Stupid hiding place,' Jace said. 'Did she think we'd be too embarrassed to look into a Kotex box?'

I couldn't answer that question. Personally, I thought Vera deserved the benefit of the doubt. Who knows? Maybe in the throes of her long, drawn-out death, she really did wish she hadn't committed suicide.

I answered the rest of the questions on the form. No substances in the room were 'out of place.' Those could be gasoline, pesticides, chemicals, cleaning agents and more. I once found a jug of antifreeze on a kitchen sink. The woman said she'd just bought it at the supermarket and forgot to take it to the garage. Turned out she'd poured a hefty shot of antifreeze into her husband's beer. Her late husband.

Jace and I didn't find much after that except for two gray wigs in Vera's habitual severe style. In her medicine chest was Pepto-Bismol, aspirin, corn plasters, Cortisone cream, and cancer-related medications. I logged them all and bagged everything, even the corn plasters.

Jace and I searched the drawers, tables, cabinets and waste baskets for prescription bottles, tablets, or parts of capsules. We found nothing. Vera had not been stockpiling medications or getting the same drug from more than one doctor, both signs of someone contemplating suicide.

At last the paperwork was finished and the body removal service arrived. Lydia wept in the hallway as her mother was carried out. I wondered if she was relieved that she was finally free.

It was three in the afternoon, and I'd dealt with death all day. Vera's death was sad, but she was a woman in unendurable pain. Butch was determined to find justice for the old soldier who died in the vacant lot. Becky's death bothered me the most. The homeless woman had been starting her life over when she was murdered.

Who killed her? And why? Where did she get those two hundred-dollar bills? What did she know about the murder of Jessica Gray? Why did Becky tell me: *It's not the red – it's the blue?*

NINETEEN

I slept until almost ten o'clock the next morning. I didn't have to work today, so I lingered over my toast and coffee. The local paper nearly ruined my morning. The *Chouteau Forest Gazette*'s front-page headline blared CUBAN HAIR STYLIST CHARGED WITH MURDER OF SUPERSTAR JESSICA GRAY.

Mario was an American citizen and a respected businessman, but you'd never guess it from the story. The paper made him sound like a Castro-planted assassin. Bail was denied. The Forest was up in arms that Jessica Gray, an international star, had been killed in their town by a Cuban. A gay one, too.

Naturally, Greiman took all the credit for the arrest. He was grinning on the front page, posed in front of the cop shop. Across from him was a glamorous photo of Jessica, smiling her approval. Mercifully, there was no photo of Mario or his salon.

I couldn't read any more. My broken cell phone was on the kitchen table, staring at me like a dead eye. I had a hard time prying open the back to take the battery out, but I finally did it, took out the battery, then put it back in, and tried to start it. Nothing. So much for Katie's tip. To make myself useful, I packed up the remains of Clare's Bavarian cream cake. I'd stop by to check on Clare and see if she still wanted me to take it to a lab for analysis. The layer cake, capped with white mounds of whipped cream and oozing cherry sauce, looked too luscious to waste. But I wasn't about to eat it. Not after what happened to Clare.

It was a chilly gray morning, with a weak sun trying to push through leaden clouds. I shivered in my heavy coat. My car door creaked in the cold and the car started reluctantly.

Clare lived in a white stone Edwardian mansion on an estate about two miles from the Du Pres spread where I lived. Her formal rooms were virtually unchanged since her grandmother's day. Clare and her husband had held soirees and musical evenings in her salon, and dinners for twelve in the dining room. Since his death, Clare rarely gave parties, except for her family.

Now Clare spent most of her time in the sunroom at the back of the house, an informal light-filled room comfortably furnished with overstuffed couches and needlepoint pillows, and lined with bookcases and clouds of white orchid plants.

Clare was sitting propped up on a fat navy-blue couch, wrapped in a red plaid blanket, watching TV. Her color was good and her snowy white hair was in its customary chignon. A Spode tea service was on a table next to the couch.

'Welcome, dear,' she said. 'Join me for a cup of tea. Cook made her famous lemon cookies.'

It was a command, and I obeyed. She used a silver bell to ring Cook for an extra cup and it was quickly delivered. The tea was a smoky lapsang souchong, and the tart, fresh-baked cookies were a good compliment.

Clare turned off the television with the remote, and poured me a cup. Then she said, 'I assume you're here to find out how I'm doing. I'm much better, dear.'

'I'm glad to hear that. You're looking better.'

'I am. The rash is nearly gone.'

I didn't remember seeing a rash. I said, 'Do you still want me to have your cake tested at the Forest lab?'

'Absolutely! I still get mad thinking about what happened. Those ingrates!' Her face darkened and a frown appeared on that papery white brow. She stopped for a sip of tea, then restarted her tirade.

'They *knew*. The whole family knows. I've been allergic to peanuts since I was a child. I was five when I nearly died at a birthday party because Aunt Cora scraped the peanut topping off a cupcake and gave it to me. She thought it wouldn't make any difference. I was lucky her husband was a doctor.

'I'm so sensitive I can have a bad reaction to peanut residue that an ordinary person cannot see, smell, or even taste. That's why I do not fly that nice airline that features peanut snacks. I know they won't serve peanuts to passengers if someone has allergies, but even a tiny crumb could kill me!'

She sat back on the couch, then said, 'As soon as I can get around on my own steam, I'm making an appointment to see my lawyer.'

'Don't you think that's a bit hasty?' I asked.

'HASTY! Trying to kill one's mother is hasty!' Clare gripped her fragile teacup so hard I was afraid it would shatter in her hand. I tried desperately to find a way to calm her. My mother used to be good at this.

'Clare, disinheriting your children could destroy your family,' I said.

'What family? What kind of children want to kill their mother? I've raised monsters, I tell you. A pair of monsters.'

I tried to remember the teenaged Trey and Jemima in school. Both had thick blond hair and enviably clear skin when the rest of us were spotted with zits. They had an inbred sense of entitlement and they collected all the honors the school could hand out. But neither one was mean. A little spoiled maybe, but not monsters. Not unless they'd changed dramatically since school.

'And why haven't they called me?' I heard the hurt in Clare's wail.

'Because they're busy with their lives,' I said. 'Jemima has a job and children, and Trey's in Singapore. The time difference alone would make calls difficult, especially if he's in meetings. I'm sure they're both working on a plan to help you.'

'Humph!' Clare said. 'More like a plan to help themselves to what's left of my money. I tell you, Angela, whenever I think about that trip to the hospital, I'm just furious. What a sneaky, humiliating way to kill me!'

Her eyes blazed with fury and I feared she'd call her lawyer right then. 'I don't understand why you're being so stubborn, Angela. My cake was poisoned, and that's that.'

Clare's insistence that her children were killers was something out of a fever dream – the paranoia of an old woman. I needed proof before I condemned Trey and Jemima, and the tests on the cake would be proof. I played my final card.

'Clare, promise me, in memory of your friendship with my mother, that you won't disinherit your children until I know more.'

There was a long, heavy silence. I listened to the old clock tick and sipped my tea. I crunched a cookie. Clare sipped her tea, lost in thought, then said, 'All right, my dear. Since you asked, I'll hold off until the end of this week. After that, I make no promises. I'm not getting any younger, you know. Have that cake analyzed and send me the bill.'

Relief washed over me. I stood up and said, 'Thank you, Clare. I'm off to the lab now.'

Clare let me squeeze her hand and said, 'I'm only delaying out of regard for your mother, Angela. For the life of me, I cannot understand why you're insisting on investigating this matter.'

I thanked her for the tea and cookies and left. As I walked to my car, I couldn't figure why I was so insistent, either. I just knew I had to do it. I'd lost both the husband I adored and my mother, but I had to save some part of my small world.

I dropped the cake off at the lab and ordered a full poisons test, including toxins, drugs, heavy metals, carcinogenic substances like asbestos, lead, and unknown substances. And peanuts. Especially peanuts. And because Clare was paying for this, I made it a rush order. The lab made me put down a hundred-dollar deposit and promised to have the results in three days.

TWENTY

About eleven o'clock, I stopped off at SOS to see my friend Katie. The assistant ME was in her office, drinking the bitter brew that passed for coffee there and eating a glazed doughnut. Detective Butch Chetkin was sitting on the edge of her desk, chomping another.

Katie's plain face lit with a smile when she saw me. 'Krispy Kremes,' she said, nodding at a grease-stained white box on her desk. 'Butch brought me a dozen. We're celebrating the take-down. Have one.'

I did. It was still warm, a tasty little sugar blast. I sat gingerly in the wire contraption that passed for her guest chair.

'What take-down?' I asked.

'Evelyn DuMont,' Butch said. 'We got her this morning. And all the neighbors were outside, too.' Butch smiled. It was not a nice smile. 'Led her out in handcuffs.'

I could see that mean old woman with her shellacked gray hair and thin slit of a mouth, being marched to the car.

'You got her for killing that poor homeless soldier. Good. I hope she dies of shame.'

'She better,' Katie said, her eyes flaring with rage. 'I did the post. If I get my hands on that bitch, I'll strangle her. That poor bastard died of rat poison! Rat poison. Vomiting and shitting blood. Alone in a field!'

The panhandler's awful death scene flashed in my mind, and I tried to block it.

'Harry Galloway was a hero,' Katie said, 'a decorated veteran with a purple heart and a bronze star. That shrapnel wound caused him pain every day of his life. And that dumb fuck Evelyn put him down like vermin.' She was shaking she was so angry.

'How do you know it was rat poison?' I asked. I knew it was too early for a tox report.

'The lab found the pellets in the sauce on that damned

sausage sandwich. Looks like d-Con. My guess is Galloway ate it four days ago.'

'That's when the sandwich was delivered, according to the housekeeper, Brenda Crandle,' Butch said.

Poor Brenda, I thought. She'll blame herself for that man's death, even though it wasn't her fault.

'How did you get Evelyn?' I asked, reaching for another doughnut.

'I talked with Brenda again,' Butch said. 'She told me that after her employer made that sandwich, she wiped the foil with a paper towel, which the housekeeper thought was odd. Brenda also said no poisons of any kind were kept in the kitchen. Those were stored in the garden shed, and Miss Crandle never went in there. Brenda said her employer bought rat poison at the Forest Garden Shop a month ago because a bag of dog food that was improperly stored in the garage had attracted rats.'

'So I served a warrant,' Butch said, and polished off another doughnut.

'Only Brenda's and the victim's prints were found on the foil sandwich wrapper, but I found the leftover sauce in the freezer and the d-Con on a shelf in the garden shed. And guess what? There was a big fat set of prints on the rat poison box – in red sauce. Evelyn's! And no one else's prints on the poison box but hers.'

'You got her!' I said. 'Did Evelyn confess?'

'Nope. She clammed up and demanded a lawyer.' While Butch demolished another celebratory doughnut, I questioned Katie. 'Did Harry Galloway die as soon as he ate the poisoned sandwich?'

'Looks like he died three days later,' Katie said. 'Best guess is he was dead about twenty-four hours when he was found.'

'Why the delay, if he ate poison four days ago?' I asked.

'Rat poison has a delayed reaction. The decedent probably didn't have any symptoms for two or three days after he ate the sandwich. He'd also eaten roast beef and other food – potato chips, tangerines and cookies. I've sent the contents of his stomach to be analyzed, but I'm betting they're OK and only the sausage sandwich was poisoned.'

'If Evelyn's smart, she'll plead out,' I said. 'A Forest jury will have people she's had fined and slapped with summonses, thanks to her stupid Beautification Committee.'

'They'll put her away for a long, long time,' Katie said.

Butch left to go back to work, and Katie and I settled for a talk over the rest of the doughnuts.

'I heard you brought Clare Rappaport into the ER the other night,' she said.

'The hospital gossip mill is amazing,' I said.

'Hey, you rarely come in with anyone who can walk out of the hospital again. That's news.'

I told her about Clare. She took a sip of her coffee and winced, probably at the taste.

'Angela, I know Clare is a family friend,' she said, 'but don't get involved with this fight to disinherit her kids. It's the law of the third dog. You don't come between a mother and her children.'

'I'm not trying to come between them,' I said. 'I want to help them.'

'There's major money involved, Angela. Millions. The kids will think you're cozying up to Mom to get a cut. You want my advice, stay out of this mess. I don't know why you're sticking your nose in it in the first place.'

'Because Clare is my mother's friend.'

'Your mother was a lovely woman and I know you were crazy about her. But she's long gone, Angela. And she and Clare weren't real friends. Your mom was a servant and Clare was Lady Bountiful. A lonely Lady Bountiful.'

'It's more than that,' I said and grabbed another doughnut. 'When Mom was in the hospital, Clare visited her. Mom had worked for Old Reggie Du Pres for years, but he never came to see her in SOS. Clare held Mom's hand and cried with her after her mastectomy. She sent flowers and food to feed my father and me when we were at the hospital every day. She came to Mom's funeral. Reggie sent a representative.'

I ate the doughnut in two bites, barely savoring its sweetness.

'OK, I admit that's above and beyond for a Forest bigwig,' Katie said. 'But I still say helping her is a risky business.'

She reached for another doughnut. So did I. I knew I had to help Clare, no matter what Katie thought. Clare was eighty-three. She needed her family. I finished the fourth doughnut and took the coward's way out. I changed the subject.

'Have you seen the morning paper with the story about Mario?'

'Couldn't miss it,' she said. 'That fish wrap went out of its way to ruin Mario's reputation. Greiman was grinning like a prize fool on the front page.

'And he pulled the evidence to arrest Mario out of his ass,' she said.

I blinked. Katie was always forthright.

'Mario admitted he gave Jessica Percocet and Xanax. Those are a bad mix,' Katie said, 'but they'd cause respiratory failure, not the violent reaction that killed Jessica in the limo.'

'Mario told me someone set him up,' I said. 'He doesn't vape. He smokes real cigarettes. He says someone planted that empty vape juice bottle in his case. I think it was one of Jessica's minions in that limo, either Tawnee, or the make-up artist, Will, or Jessica's husband, Stu. And of the three, Stu has the best motive. I think he married Jessica for her money.'

'No shit, Sherlock,' Katie said. 'No way he'd jump that bag of bones unless he was getting at least six figures.'

I reached for another doughnut to ward off the vision forming in my mind of Jessica and Stu in bed. Even a Krispy Kreme didn't help.

'How did you know so quickly that Jessica died of nicotine poisoning?' I asked.

'A process called WAG,' Katie said.

'WAG?'

'Wild-ass guess. The hospital suspected it because of her symptoms, though those could point to other things, and made a wild-ass guess it was nicotine poison. They checked her urine and blood and found increased levels of nicotine. They were right – it was nicotine poisoning. Made my job much easier.'

'Listen, Katie, I need a favor,' I said. 'Can you get an autopsy report from St Louis about a woman named Brenda, last name unknown, who was murdered in an SRO hotel?'

'And why would I want to do that?' she said.

'Because I think her death is connected to Jessica's and I want to get my friend Mario out of jail.'

'That's why he has Monty,' Katie said.

'Monty's good, but he's not infallible,' I said. 'And a not guilty verdict would still hurt Mario's reputation.'

'This is where I remind you that you can lose your job for interfering in a police investigation,' Katie said. 'Greiman is gunning for you, and you know it. You're not supposed to solve crimes. You just report the facts to the ME.'

'I know,' I said. 'But this is wrong. And I don't know where to get more information. I can't stand Jessica's crew. They're horrible.'

'You've got to talk to them,' Katie said. 'They were in the limo when Jessica died. One of them must have slipped that empty vape juice bottle into Mario's case. Which one is the least unpleasant?'

'Tawnee, I guess.'

'Take Tawnee to lunch. She's sitting at the Forest Inn, bored shitless. Call her now.'

I hesitated.

'The least you can do is eat lunch for Mario,' she said.

TWENTY-ONE

I didn't want to take any of Jessica's gang to my favorite restaurant, Gringo Daze. I liked the Mexican place too much to subject it to their rudeness.

Instead, I met Tawnee at Solange, a French restaurant. Forest matrons loved the place because it was designed to make women look more attractive. The decor was black lacquer and pale pink, with soft, pink-shaded lights. The mirrors made most of us look amazing. I never understood how, but their mercury-backed magic made stout matrons seem younger and slimmer.

Even these complexion flatterers couldn't help poor Tawnee. She looked tired and sallow. Her long blond hair was frizzy. She wore a soft gray cashmere sweater, black pants, black boots and a new black coat. I suspected she'd made an Uber trip to the mall.

'Thank you for inviting me,' she said. 'I'm going crazy watching trash TV. I mean, how many home renovations can you watch?'

'They do all start to look alike,' I said.

The lunch rush was over and only a few diners lingered. We had a coveted corner booth. The server, a brisk, forty-something woman in severe black, took our orders.

'I'll just have the house salad,' I said, thinking of those five Krispy Kremes at Katie's office, and Clare's lemon cookies.

'Oh, come on, don't go all virtuous on me,' Tawnee said. 'I'll have the sole almondine,' she told the server.

'Well, maybe I could use some protein,' I said. 'I'll have the sole, too.'

'That comes with the house salad with homemade ranch dressing,' the server said. 'Is that OK?'

'Certainly,' I said, abandoning all pretense of virtue.

'Would you ladies like wine?'

We both ordered white and she left.

'How's the Forest Inn?' I asked Tawnee.

'Very Midwestern,' she said.

'What's that mean?' My voice had an edge. I was hyper-alert for more insults to my community.

'Comfortable, but not chic. Very clean. Huge breakfasts with everything fried. The rest of the food is covered in gravy. Last night we had pot roast with carrots.' She sounded as if that was an exotic dish.

'Pot roast is pretty Midwestern,' I said.

She smiled tentatively. 'It was good. Very tender. Reminded me of my mother's cooking, and that's not a bad thing. I haven't had red meat in ages.'

Our salads arrived, along with a basket of crusty French bread, and we ate for a bit. The lettuce was crisp and lightly covered with creamy dressing. I patted myself on the back for avoiding the bread and watched Tawnee eat the whole basket full.

The server removed our salad plates and brought the sole. I was surprisingly hungry. After a few forkfuls, Tawnee said, 'This is some of the best food I've had since I came here.' She sounded surprised. 'Usually, sole is dry.'

'Mine's good, too,' I said. 'How are you doing? Jessica's death must have been a terrible shock.'

'I'm OK,' she said, and shrugged. Her tone told me that she wasn't OK. 'I keep seeing Jessica's death again and again in my mind. It's playing on an endless loop. We all tried so hard to save her, but by the time we got to the hospital it was too late. I keep wondering what we should have done.'

'From what the medical examiner told me, you couldn't have saved Jessica,' I said. 'She was doomed once she swallowed that vape juice.'

'That's what's funny,' she said, then stopped. 'Well, not funny. What's the right word? Ironic? She insisted we take up vaping, even though we all smoked three or four packs a day. We hated that vape shit. We were twitching for a cigarette, but we wanted our jobs.'

'I guess vaping is better for your health,' I said.

'Jessica didn't give a damn about us. Any of us. It was better for her health.' Tawnee was unexpectedly angry.

'Jessica was afraid she'd get cancer from our second-hand smoke. Turns out it wasn't smoke that killed her – it was vape juice.'

Tawnee seemed to savor that idea. I didn't like the look in her eyes. Did Tawnee kill Jessica? Suddenly, I could imagine her capable of murder. Jessica had ruined Tawnee's movie career and taunted her nightly from the stage, then forced her to vape. Tawnee had many reasons to kill Jessica.

'What are you going to do when you get back to California?' I asked.

'I have some money to live on,' she said. 'I have an agent. He's been after me to get on the nostalgia circuit and do some dinner theater.'

'I thought you told Stu you were trapped by the golden handcuffs,' I said.

'I'm not young anymore,' she said. 'Doing a nostalgia tour is risky. Working with Jessica was no fun, but she did pay, and pay well. I managed to save some money.'

I tried to imagine what roles would be available for Tawnee and couldn't. I suspected she couldn't, either. Her star power was dim.

We ate in silence until the server took our plates. We both turned down dessert but took black coffee. Mine was strong, dark and fragrant.

'Did you expect Jessica to die?' I knew it was a dumb question, but I couldn't think of how else to ask it.

Tawnee took a sip of coffee and then said, 'I never expected her to be murdered, that's for sure. But I was worried about Jessica when she came down with pneumonia on this trip. She hated cold weather and she was terribly sick. It hurt to listen to her cough. She'd be doubled over, coughing up her lungs. I don't know how she made it through the Saturday show. Sheer strength of will, I guess. I was relieved when she passed out at the party and was taken to the hospital. I knew it was a mistake for her to leave the hospital early.

'Sunday morning, we tried to talk her into staying at the hospital for at least another day.'

'You did?' I sipped my coffee.

'All of us. Stu, Will, and me. She was in no condition to

travel. We were glad when the doctor came. We hoped she'd talk some sense into Jessica, but she wouldn't listen. Jessica insisted if she had to be in the hospital, she wanted to be in Cedars-Sinai with her own doctors. She was determined to go home to California. Well, she's going home, all right. In a coffin.' She took another sip of her coffee. I could feel her grim satisfaction.

'What about Jessica's husband, Stu? Did she listen to him?' I took a drink, too.

'No. He was just another flunky like me.' I heard bitterness and self-contempt in her answer.

'Did you know they were married?'

'I had no idea,' she said. 'You could have knocked me down with a feather when Stu told that detective Jessica was his wife.'

'You never saw any signs of romance between them?'

'No. Jessica treated him like the rest of us. We were servants, and she chewed out our asses when we didn't do our jobs to her satisfaction. Stu got his share of shit, just like the rest of us. I never saw anything tender between them. He never kissed her or even held her hand around me. I thought their relationship was strictly business.'

'Why do you think she married him?'

Tawnee didn't hesitate. 'Sex. She told me it was good for her complexion. Said it gave her a glow and relaxed her. She called it "the ultimate beauty treatment." When she married Stu, she bought herself a young stud. Plain and simple. It was cheaper and safer to marry Stu than hire a hooker who could go running to the gossip columns later.'

'Do you think Stu killed her?'

'No. Why would he? He had an easy life. He was well paid. Like all of us, he learned to tune out her tirades.'

'Is it true she ruined Stu's career in Vegas?' I asked.

'There wasn't much of a career to ruin. Stu had visions of being another David Copperfield, but he was never that good a magician. I saw his lounge act. It was third-rate, and I'm being kind. He could make things disappear – "but not your bar bill," he'd joke – and he could pull a quarter out of a drunk's ear. Simple tricks like that and corny, outdated patter.

But he would have spent his life doing backyard gigs for kids if he hadn't gone to work for Jessica.'

I was shocked by her harsh assessment, but it seemed to fit Stu. It also seemed to give him a good motive for murder.

'Jessica may have put the final nail in his career's coffin with a word to the casino management, but he was going to get fired anyway.'

'What about Will?'

'What about him?' she said. She was checking her cell phone while she talked. I tried not to be annoyed.

'Will is a make-up artist,' Tawnee said. 'A real Rembrandt with the brushes. He is a much better illusionist than Stu ever was. You saw what Jessica looked like when you did her death investigation. You know all her tricks – the ass pads and the fake tits. She was old and scrawny. But turn Will loose with his make-up case, and she became a beautiful woman. His talent was the real magic.'

'Would she have bankrolled his cosmetics line?'

She shrugged. 'If it was convenient for her. She was good at stringing him along. Will undercharged her in the hope that she would live up to her promise, but she had him where she wanted him. He had no reason to kill her.'

She put down her coffee cup.

'And before you ask, it wasn't me, either. I didn't kill her. I had a good gig and I'll never find one to match it. Sure, I'll do all right on the tour circuit, but I've always preferred the safe choice. That's what's held me back all these years – being too scared to strike out on my own. I took Jessica's abuse night after night rather than launch out on my own. So now you know my secret: I'm a coward.'

'Who do you think killed Jessica?' I asked.

Tawnee's eyes flared with anger. 'You want to know who killed Jessica? She was murdered by that damned wetback.' She must have raised her voice because two diners at a nearby table stared at us.

I wasn't going to let her insult my friend. 'Mario's Cuban, not Mexican, and he's an American citizen. He wouldn't kill Jessica. He was honored to do her hair.'

'That just shows what a rube he was,' she said.

'Mario doesn't vape,' I said. 'He smokes real cigarettes. One of you planted the vape juice in his styling case.'

'That's ridiculous. As far as I'm concerned, Jessica's killer is in jail. I hope he gets the death penalty.'

Her cell phone pinged. She stood up. 'My Uber is here,' she said.

Tawnee marched out and stuck me with the bill.

TWENTY-TWO

'd eaten lunch with Tawnee for Mario, and paid the price
– $72.68 with tip. I hadn't learned anything useful, but I
intended to keep digging. Jessica's crew was still in town
and there were two more members to interview.

From my car, I called Stu at the Forest Inn and invited him
for a drink in the bar at Solange. He agreed to meet me at six
that night. I couldn't reach Will, but I left a message for the
make-up artist to call me.

Finally, I called Monty to check on Mario. His office
manager, Jinny Gender, said her boss was busy with a case,
but Monty insisted on taking my call. 'Mario's hanging in
there,' the lawyer said. 'But it's hard on him. The Choutcau
County Jail isn't as bad as some, but it's still a jail. It's taking
its toll on him.'

'Can I visit him?'

'Not yet. His visitors are limited and Raquel and Carlos
from the salon have both seen him. You can see him in two
days. I know you'll cheer him up. He needs that.'

'I'll try,' I said. 'Can I bring him anything? Like a cake
with a file in it?'

He laughed at my lame joke. 'You can deposit some money
in his cash account at the jail. That's it, I'm afraid. No food
and no gifts.'

Mario's current life sounded so bleak, I didn't want to think
about it. I needed to do something. I clicked off my phone
and stopped by Killer Cuts, his salon. The two cars in the
parking lot told me all I needed to know. Usually I had to
fight for room to beach my car.

Inside, I was hit by the silence. I heard the subdued roar of
a blow dryer. Carlos, the new stylist, was putting the finishing
touches on a blond woman, covering her short, sensible 'do
in a cloud of hair spray. The other three stylists' chairs were
empty, as well Mario's orchid-filled domain in the back. No

client was at the manicurist's station – the lone manicurist was painting her own nails pale blue. Raquel was at the reception desk, frowning at her computer. She looked ready for a fashion shoot: Her long, dark hair was smooth and shiny, her smoky eye make-up was perfect and her pink suit enhanced her curves. She greeted me with a smile.

'How's it going?' I asked.

'It's not,' she said, and now I saw the worry under the professional facade. 'Everyone is cancelling. We may have to let our stylists go, even though their only crimes are renting chairs here.'

'Carlos has a client,' I said.

'That's a fluke. That woman's regular hairstylist was booked and she has to go to a wedding. I talked with Mario, and told him the situation. If things don't pick up in the next two days, we're going to have to close the salon until he's free.' By her worried look, I heard the unspoken 'maybe for good.'

'When did you see Mario?'

'Yesterday. He's worried. Angry. Wondering how this could happen to him. He loves his adopted country, but he feels he's being railroaded because he's Cuban.'

'He is,' I said. 'Is he safe?'

'As safe as he's going to be in jail. He hasn't gotten in any fights. He keeps to himself. No one's tried to attack him. But he can't sleep. Jail is noisy. And the food is awful. He can't eat it.'

'I'm sorry to hear that,' I said. A useless comment and cold comfort.

'I know you are,' she said. 'You're a good friend.'

'I'm talking to Jessica's crew,' I said. 'Hoping to find out something.'

'Can you do that?' she said. 'Since the police have decided they have the right person?'

'I'm not supposed to,' I said. 'But I know they have the wrong person.'

I caught a glimpse of myself in a salon mirror. My dark hair was straggly. 'Would Carlos have time for a quick wash and blow dry?' I asked.

'I'm sure he'd be honored,' Raquel said. 'I'll go ask him right now.'

Two minutes later, I had my head tilted back in a wash basin while Carlos shampooed me. He was quick and efficient. I left Killer Cuts an hour and a half later, looking a lot better than when I arrived.

At home, I changed into a little black dress, and added some of my favorite gold jewelry. The chunky necklace and earrings were gifts from Donegan. When I put them on, I felt like I had him with me. His presence comforted me. I slid into black heels, something I rarely wore. I told myself I was enduring the pain for Mario. A quick glance in my bedroom mirror told me I looked good – sleek and long-legged. I had no idea whether that would cut any ice with Stu. I figured he'd be more interested in admiring my wallet, and that was anemic.

I headed to Solange's early and scored a quiet table in the bar.

The new widower showed up right at six o'clock, dressed in his version of West Coast cool: black Hugo Boss suit, black shirt, white tie and small sunglasses. Sunglasses! In a bar at night. I wondered why he needed to hide his eyes.

Stu greeted me as if I were an old friend and kissed me lightly on the cheek. Out of the corner of my eye, I saw old Mrs Rubelle watching this scene with avid eyes. The news would spread through the Forest like a California wildfire. By next week, the local gossips would have me married to Stu.

Stu sat down, and the server took our order – Chardonnay for me, single malt for Stu – and left us a bowl of salted cashews. Our drinks arrived quickly. Stu took off his glasses and his brown eyes were untroubled.

'How have you been?' I asked, my voice soft with sympathy.

'As well as can be expected,' he said. 'Jessica's death was a terrible shock.'

He seemed to need a sympathetic ear. 'I'm sure it was. And so sudden.'

'At least the police have the killer,' he said. 'I feel guilty that I hired the little son of a bitch to do her hair.'

I crunched a cashew to avoid answering. Finally, I said, 'Do you think Jessica's illness contributed to her death?'

'No. But I think she might still be alive if she'd listened to us,' he said. 'We all begged her to stay in the hospital one more day. I waited until Tawnee and Will were both out of the room and asked her to stay another day. For my sake. She said she hated the hospital. I said I'd get a suite at the Ritz in St Louis and she could recover there in comfort. We'd have a doctor in attendance if she needed one. Hell, I even wanted to fly in her doctor from California. But she wouldn't listen. She was determined to go home.'

There was a long pause, while we both thought the same thing: how Jessica was now going home.

I took a slug of Chardonnay for courage and asked my first rude question of the evening: 'Did Jessica have the money for that kind of care – a suite at the Ritz and flying in a specialist from California?'

Stu sat up straight, his body rigid with anger. 'Jessica was a highly successful businesswoman,' he said.

'I'm sure she was,' I said. 'But I heard stories that the Lux was papered, and half the audience had free tickets.'

'Ridiculous! I keep the books. And her Captivate line sells. Saks and Nordstrom both carry it.'

He finished most of his single malt and signaled the server for another. She brought it quickly. He threw it back and ordered another while I nursed my wine. When his third scotch arrived, I could see the rigid anger starting to leave him, almost like rigor mortis leaving a body.

'When did you and Jessica marry?' I asked.

'When the show was in Las Vegas in December,' he said. 'That's where we first met six years ago.'

And where she ruined what was left of your career, I thought.

'We married at one of those little wedding chapels. No press. No photos. We kept it quiet because people wouldn't understand the age difference.'

'Another double standard,' I said. 'It's OK for Picasso to marry someone forty years younger, but not for a woman celebrity.'

'Exactly,' Stu said and smiled at me. 'Although in our case it's only thirty-eight years. We were going to honeymoon in Hawaii after this show ended, then we'd meet with her public relations people and brainstorm on the best way to announce our marriage. In the meantime, we kept our marriage secret. I'm sure Tawnee and Will were shocked when I told that detective Jessica and I were married.'

'Tawnee said she didn't have a clue,' I said. 'And I thought I heard Jessica firing all of you the night of the party at Reggie Du Pres's house.'

'Oh, Jessica always did that,' Stu said, as if it were an endearing little quirk. 'It was her way of blowing off steam. Once she was back home and relaxed a bit, she'd be herself again. Tawnee knew that. I did, too.'

'Did Will?' I asked.

'Of course,' he said. 'Will was happy to have a gig as her make-up artist. He was good, I'll say that for him. He loved the publicity. He lived for those times when Jessica called us all on-stage and acknowledged us. He saw each on-stage appearance as an ad for his new make-up line and a way to impress potential backers.'

'Will was under the impression that Jessica would have bankrolled his make-up line,' I said.

'I doubt it.' Stu's laugh was harsh. 'Though Jessica might have insisted he put her name on it. But she wouldn't jump into any deal in a hurry. I told Will when he was hired to play it smart and work for her for at least two years. Then he could say that he was Jessica's make-up artist. He said he'd be able to get his own backing by then.'

'How is Jessica going home?' I said, 'Do you need the name of a good funeral home to embalm her?'

'No, as soon as the ME releases her body, she'll be cremated. I'll spread her ashes in Maui, where we planned to go for our honeymoon.'

'That's so sad,' I said.

'That's life,' he said. He tossed down the last of his scotch and signaled for the check. He threw down some bills and walked out without saying goodbye.

I shivered in the overheated room.

TWENTY-THREE

K atie called me at ten the next morning on my personal cell phone. I fumbled for my phone, then heard her say, 'I've got your information. Come on by my office.'

'Did you find Becky's autopsy report?' I said.

'That's right,' she said. Her voice sounded singsong and syrupy. 'I'll be in my office until noon.'

OK, she couldn't talk. I figured that much out. I was on call until six that night. I abandoned my coffee cup in the sink and quickly dressed in my DI outfit – black pantsuit, white blouse and lace-up shoes – and headed for the ME's office at SOS Hospital. On the way, I stopped by the chocolate shop and picked up some fat strawberries covered in dark chocolate as a thank you. Katie was a healthy eater, and I liked chocolate. This was my compromise.

I expected to be greeted with smiles as soon as she saw the box, but Katie met me with fire in her eyes. She dragged me into her office and shut the door. Her voice was a hissing whisper.

'Are you trying to get me fired?' she said. 'Evarts walked in here when I was calling you. I tried to be subtle, but no, Ms Sledgehammer. You have to yell into the phone, "Did you find Becky's autopsy report?"'

'Oh, God,' I said. 'He didn't hear me, did he?'

'If he did, I managed to convince him that your call was about Jessica Gray.'

'Well, it was,' I said. 'Sort of.'

'Explain.' Katie sat behind her desk, and I perched on the edge of it. 'And take a seat,' she said.

'If I sit in your chair and someone opens the door, they'll hit my knees,' I said.

I stayed on her desk, the chocolates in my lap. 'I was supposed to meet Becky the day she died. I talked to her on the phone in the lobby of the police station the day before.

Greiman was in one of his moods and made me put the call on speaker, so he heard it. So did Jessica's crew, along with Mario, who would shortly be arrested.

'Becky hinted that she had information about Jessica's murder. She gave me a clue. It was a poem. She was teasing me. She said: *Since you've been so dear, I'll make it clear. It's not the red – it's the blue. Breakfast is on you.*

'She said she was staying at the Hoffstedder Hotel, a rundown SRO, and she'd meet me for breakfast at ten the next morning. Except she didn't. I went to the hotel and discovered her body. She'd been strangled.'

'That's what her autopsy says.' Katie handed me a printout. I scanned the familiar form and read the details. Becky's name was Rebecca Henderson Barens, and she was divorced. There was no sign of sexual activity. She'd worn a pink pant-suit and she'd been strangled with her flowered scarf. The U-shaped hyoid bone in her neck was broken. Becky had clawed at her neck to stop the strangulation, but it didn't save her. The only DNA under her fingernails was her own.

'The cops think she knew her killer and admitted him to her room,' Katie said.

'Or her,' I said. 'Becky was streetwise and she'd already been raped once. She'd be careful who she let into her room. I'm convinced the killer was one of Jessica's crew. Mario is off the hook for her murder. He was in jail at the time.'

I carefully read the list of the clothes on Becky's body: one pair pink wool pants, one pink wool jacket with three buttons, one pink flowered blouse, all with Ellen Tracy labels. The flowered scarf was by Calvin Klein. The black heels were Aerosoles. A Victoria's Secret white lace bra and matching panties. All way too expensive for a homeless woman, even if she bought them at a resale shop.

I read the list four times. I knew something was missing on it. It niggled at my brain. What was it?

'I'm going to track down Suzy,' I said. 'She was another homeless woman at Jessica's wretched street fashion show.'

'I heard about that,' Katie said. Her face showed her disgust. 'What was that poor woman wearing when Jessica exhibited her?'

'Becky wore everything she owned: a shaggy gray coat with one button. Jessica made her strip on-stage. Under the coat was a man's plaid flannel shirt, a gray hoodie, a blue work shirt, a dingy white T-shirt, a blue blouse with the sleeves torn off and four pairs of pants. All of it was filthy and stained.

'Jessica made Becky strip to her ugly bra and granny panties, but Becky refused to take off any more clothes. The audience – a bunch of distinguished gray-hairs – acted like drunken frat boys, laughing and shouting "Take it off! Take it off!" and "More! More!" Jessica was stirring them up.'

'That freak Jessica made fun of Becky?' Katie was angry. 'She's got her nerve. Did the audience know about the star's ass pads, fake boobs, and wig? Not to mention the facelifts and enough make-up to paint the side of a barn!'

'Jessica was good at illusion,' I said. 'Much better than her magician husband, Stu. The audience adored her. Besides, if Jessica didn't age, then the gray-hairs in those plush seats could kid themselves that they hadn't gotten any older, either. They wanted her to look young.

'Jessica told Reggie that she was sending the "models" from the show to his party. He was expecting real babes and instead he got two bag ladies. Reggie called Jessica and raised hell. She said her street models would attend the party or she wouldn't go.'

'A real power play,' Katie said. 'I would have paid to see Reggie's face when those two staggered out of that limo.'

'Me, too. Jessica had a cruel streak, but Reggie was crafty. Reggie persuaded the one homeless woman, Suzy, to take a shower, eat, and rest in his pool house. Becky was defiant. She stayed at the party and I had dinner with her.'

'Good for you,' Katie said. 'Where does this Suzy live?'

'Nowhere. But she hangs out around the Lux. I'm going looking for her this afternoon. I hope Becky told her something in the limo.'

Katie repeated the jingle: '*It's not the red – it's the blue.* The only thing red I remember was the turtleneck that Jessica wore. The ER cut it off.'

'I saw that. In fact, I saw all her clothes,' I said. 'She

didn't have anything blue. Everything else was black, except for her white fake fur coat. I doubt it was something she wore.'

'Do you think Becky was pulling your leg?' Katie asked.

'No, she was grateful that I'd talked to her at the party,' I said. 'She told me about herself. She wanted to turn her life around. I gave her a lead on a group that helped homeless women and she promised to go there. She didn't blow the hundred dollars that Jessica gave her on booze. She spent it on a room at the Hoffstedder Hotel. She got those good clothes from somewhere – she wore an expensive pantsuit, blouse, scarf and shoes.'

'Do you think the homeless group gave them to her?'

'Maybe, but they looked too new,' I said. 'They were either from a high-end resale shop, or she stole them at the hospital, or she blackmailed someone for more money. And I'm thinking blackmail. I found two hundred dollars in crisp bills stashed between her mattress and box springs.'

'Funny, they're not on the list of her possessions,' Katie said.

'Do you think they were overlooked when her room was searched?' I asked.

'I doubt it. The city detectives are thorough.'

'Do you think the cops stole them?' I knew crime scene thefts happened, especially in the old days.

'Unlikely,' Katie said. 'Did you lunch with Jessica's crew, like I suggested?'

'I did. Tawnee stiffed me for seventy-two dollars at Solange and told me nothing. She called Mario a wetback and said he killed Jessica. I had drinks with Stu. He's as cold as Jessica. That pretty exterior hides an iceberg for a heart. Those two deserved each other. The only one left is Will, the make-up artist. I think Mario had a fling with him and Will sold him out to Greiman to save his own skin. I'll try to get him before they all leave town.'

'Did you ask them about Becky's clue?'

'No, I forgot.'

'See, that's why you shouldn't be investigating this,' Katie said. 'You're not trained for it.'

'I'll ask them again,' I said. 'And I can ask Will when I catch up with him.'

'Better hurry,' Katie said. 'They leave here as soon as Jessica's cremated. She surrounded herself with a freakin' snake pit. I'll be glad when that bunch leaves town.'

I wanted to forestall another lecture. She couldn't talk with her mouth full. I handed her the box of chocolate delights. 'Have a strawberry.'

'Thanks,' she said. She opened the box and took a fat berry in a thick dark coat. It was gone in three bites. 'Have one,' she said.

My work cell phone chimed before I could reach for one. I recognized Detective Jace Budewitz's voice immediately.

'Hi, Angela,' he said. 'We've got a case. A woman killed her husband on Ashby Road.'

'That's in Toonerville,' I said.

'If you say so. Looks like a nice neighborhood with lots of post-war ranch houses.'

Jace wasn't from here. Now I was ashamed of using the Forest's sneery nickname for the working side of town.

'What happened?' I asked.

'Mrs Tara Murphy's husband, Tom, came home drunk and she walloped him upside the head with a cast-iron skillet. Blood and grease all over the kitchen. Then she sat down and called nine-one-one. End of mystery.'

'Is she still there?'

'For now. You need to get here in a hurry.'

'On my way,' I said. I gathered my purse and said goodbye to Katie.

I didn't get to track down Suzy or Will.

Didn't get to eat a strawberry, either.

TWENTY-FOUR

T ara and Tom Murphy lived in a two-bedroom white ranch house with dark green trim and neatly clipped hedges. Two pots of ornamental purple cabbages flanked the door. By the time I arrived there were so many cop cars and official vehicles near the house I had to park two blocks away. I pulled my long, dark hair back into a ponytail.

The day was warm for February, about forty degrees, and curious neighbors had drifted out on their porches to watch the show.

I greeted Rick Samuels, the Chouteau County uniform who was posted at the house's front door, and he reminded me to put on shoe covers. I rolled my DI case inside.

Tara Murphy was in the cramped living room, swallowed by a massive beige recliner. She looked to be in her late fifties, and they'd been hard years. Tara's face and thin lips were slashed with wrinkles. She was built like a teenage boy, and just as skinny. Her sparse gray hair was tightly permed, and her hands were yellow with nicotine stains. She was wrapped in a brown plaid throw and trembling so hard her teeth chattered.

Shock?

She stubbed out her cigarette in a hubcap-size ashtray on a table next to the recliner. The ashtray was ringed by six empty beer bottles.

Jace Budewitz nodded at me, and said, 'Excuse me, Mrs Murphy. I'll be right back.'

We walked down the narrow hall to the master bedroom. 'The victim, Thomas Murphy, is on the kitchen floor,' Jace said. 'The paramedics pronounced him dead at 10:37 a.m. I'm still questioning his wife. He was about as tall as she is, but definitely outweighed her. She says he was drunk and trying to beat her, and she hit him with a cast-iron frying pan to save her life.'

'Typical domestic abuse case,' I said. 'Except Mrs Murphy looks pretty small. Could she whack her husband hard enough to kill him?'

'She told me she works as a cleaning lady, scrubbing floors six days a week. He's an unemployed construction worker. She was wearing a T-shirt and jeans. Her arms are scrawny, but corded with muscle. I think she hit him more than once. That kitchen looks like a slaughterhouse.'

'Was the decedent taking aspirin or blood thinners?' I asked. 'That could account for the blood.'

'Don't know.'

'I'll check his medications,' I said.

'We had Mrs Murphy change clothes so we could bag what she was wearing. We swabbed the blood on her to find out if it was his or hers. She was barefoot and there are bloody footprints everywhere. After we swabbed and photographed her, we let her wash her feet and put on socks.'

'Any signs of violence to her?' I said.

'No bruises or black eyes that I could see,' Jace said. 'Mrs Murphy said her husband was going to punch her in the face when she hit him with the frying pan. Nitpicker is about finished in the kitchen.' Our top CSI expert was on the case. I felt better already.

Jace went back into the living room and sat on the over-stuffed couch across from Tara Murphy. His voice was soft and respectful. 'Would you repeat what happened, please, from the time your husband came into the kitchen this morning, Mrs Murphy?'

'I just told you,' she said with a resentful whine.

'I know,' Jace said. 'But I need to hear it again. We'll ask you these questions many times.'

'He got up about five a.m. – said his sciatica was bothering him – and started taking pain killers and drinking beer.'

'What kind of painkillers?' Jace asked.

'Oxy,' she said. 'You can see he drank a whole six-pack by the time I got up, and he was mean as a rattlesnake. This was my morning to sleep in – I don't have to clean the Millers' house until noon – and he wanted breakfast. He was mad that I slept until 9:30 and he demanded food. I started frying up home fries. I was gonna make him bacon and eggs, the same breakfast he always has, when he started mouthing off. He said he was tired of my greasy cooking. He wanted Belgian waffles.

'I said, "I ain't no short order cook. I'll have to get the waffle maker out of the top cabinet."

'He called me a lazy bitch, cussed up a blue streak, and tried to punch me in the face. I ducked. He ran to pick up the kitchen chair – and I knew he could really hurt me with that. I grabbed that skillet and swung hard. Grease is splattered all over my new wallpaper. I meant to stop him, not kill him. But I'm afraid of him, Detective. He weighs one-eighty-two and I'm ninety-seven pounds.'

'How many times did you hit him with the skillet?' Jace asked.

'Once.'

'Just once?' Jace said.

'Maybe more.' She looked confused. 'I can't remember. I was so scared. He was gonna kill me.' Great tears ran down her wrinkled face. 'It was self-defense.

'We've been married twenty-seven years and he never used to be like this. After he broke his arm and couldn't work, he got hooked on pain pills and started drinking heavy. That's what changed him.' She was sobbing too hard to talk now. I knew opioid abuse did not respect any class. I'd found it in the rich and poor.

I opened my iPad, called up the 'Scene Information' form, and wrote down the case number Jace had given me. Tara's beige carpet was protected by heavy plastic runners, which made it easy to roll my DI case. 'Have you photographed these footprints on the runner?' I asked. Jace nodded, and I followed the bloody footprints to the kitchen.

I'd braced myself for an ugly scene, but this was worse than I'd imagined. The kitchen looked like someone had tossed a gallon of dark red paint at it.

The decedent was supine – face-up – on the beige linoleum kitchen floor, his battered head facing the east wall. Bunched-up beige throw rugs exposed the worn spots in the linoleum near the stove and sink areas. The rugs were thick with drying blood. There was even blood on the ceiling. Head wounds bleed like crazy, and this one was no exception.

Dark red had spattered the kitchen wall next to the stove as if someone had hosed it down with blood. Mrs Murphy must have really clobbered her husband with her frying pan. More blood dripped down the stove like spilled paint. It appeared to be alongside an oily substance that I guessed was cooking fat, and sliced fried potatoes.

The kitchen wallpaper – an old-fashioned pattern of grapes, cherries, pears and apples – was spattered with blood and grease. A bloody fried potato was stuck to a ripe red wallpaper apple near the stove.

My stomach turned.

It would be a long time before I would eat fried potatoes.

The cast-iron skillet, upside-down and painted with blood, was on the floor next to Mr Murphy's right arm. Small bloody footprints crisscrossed the floor.

Sarah 'Nitpicker' Byrne was dusting a heavy wooden captain's chair that had been overturned near the table. Her hair was blueberry and she wore a white hazmat suit for protection.

'I'm finished over there,' she said, her voice low.

'Did you find his shoe prints in the blood?' I asked.

'No. I'm guessing she hit him once or twice, then cold-cocked him and beat the crap out of him while he was out. Check out the low spatter and cast-off on the stove and kitchen cabinets. I bet once the body is moved, I'll find more blood under the cabinets. Once he was out cold, she pounded this poor dude to hamburger.'

We both knew the ME would have to confirm Nitpicker's theory, but she knew her business.

I took the ambient temperature. The room was fairly warm – seventy-five degrees. I took the temperature again on the floor near the body, then photographed the hall thermostat. They were all within a degree or two.

I photographed the scene with my point-and-shoot camera – wide shots, medium, and then close-ups. I was ready to begin the body inspection.

I measured the decedent's height at five feet, five inches

and estimated his weight at one-eighty. I started my examination at the top of the body. Examining the head was the worst part. It looked like Mrs Murphy had hit him once or twice, then felled him with a mighty swing to his left temporal bone, just above his ear. I guessed that he'd fallen, and there appeared to be repeated blows to the left side of his head while he was out cold. At least two other bones on the left side of his head – the frontal (forehead), parietal (the top) – were battered, and there was blood leaking out of his nose and mouth.

The repeated blows caused his blood to transfer to the skillet and become spatter on the walls, stove, fridge, table and just about every other surface – including a drip down an open can of Crisco.

There were burns on the decedent's face, neck, and hands. He had fried potatoes in his short gray hair and on his thick neck.

He was wearing a white sleeveless undershirt, the kind called a wifebeater, and blue-patterned boxer shorts. His undershirt was hitched up and I saw an enormous bruise on his abdomen from his collarbone down past his navel. The yellow-green bruise measured fourteen inches long and ten inches wide. It disappeared around to his back and into the waistband of his boxers. I pulled the waistband out and saw the bruise was another three inches to the top of his graying pubic hair. His only jewelry was a plain yellow-metal ring on his burned, blood-spattered left hand. I saw what looked like defensive wounds on his hands and wondered if he'd put up his hands to cover his face when she'd swung that hot skillet at him.

Murphy's right arm had a healed surgical scar one inch above his elbow. There were fading yellow bruises two inches wide on the undersides of both arms. Both arms had bright red burns, probably from the grease. The burn on his right arm was three inches long and half an inch wide, and six red grease spatters striped his forearm, along with pieces of fried potato.

I checked and then photographed the bottoms of his bare feet. There was no blood on the soles. More proof that he had not walked around during this so-called fight.

I took a clean, sterilized sheet from a plastic bag in my kit and spread it out on the floor, then said, 'Nitpicker, help me turn him over, please.'

We rolled the heavy body onto the sheet and one strap on the man's undershirt slipped down. 'Holy shit, what's that on his back?' Nitpicker said.

'Looks like a burn mark in the shape of an iron,' I said. 'It's scabbed over and covered with some kind of cream. Jace needs to see this.'

I called the detective into the kitchen and showed him the burn on Murphy's back.

'Jeez, that poor guy,' he said.

'He's got a huge, healing bruise on his chest,' I said, 'two on his arms, and one on his shin.'

'That corroborates what the neighbors told the uniforms,' Jace said. 'They described Thomas Murphy as "a big old teddy bear" and said his tiny wife beat him up. He refused to fight back. At Thanksgiving, the fight was so loud the next-door neighbors called the police.'

There was a commotion at the front door, followed by a man shouting, 'Let me in! That witch killed my son. I know she did.'

I followed Jace into the living room as a short, stocky man tried to force his way past Rick, using his black cane. His bald, liver-spotted head was flaming with fury.

Jace hurried into the front room. 'Are you in charge here?' the old man demanded when he saw Jace.

'Yes, I am, sir,' Jace said. 'And you are?'

'Nick Murphy. Thomas is my son. A neighbor called and told me she finally killed him.'

'I did not!' Tara screamed. 'He was high on oxy and tried to kill me!' She leaped out of the recliner and ran straight for Nick Murphy, her bony fists clenched. Jace caught her. 'Whoa, Mrs Murphy,' he said. 'Settle down.'

She struggled in his arms and screeched, 'That old bastard has hated me since the day I married Tom. He's ruined our marriage.'

'I told Tom not to marry her,' Nick shouted. 'I was right.'

'Quiet!' Jace said.

Nick shut up, but Tara screamed louder. 'I will not be quiet! He's the cause of all our trouble.' She struggled in Jace's arms, trying to hit Jace and attack her father-in-law.

'Officer Samuels,' Jace called, and Rick appeared. 'Please escort Mrs Murphy to a patrol car. If she gives you any trouble, cuff her.'

Tara went quietly outside, but her glare singed Nick Murphy.

'Sit down on the couch, Mr Murphy,' Jace said. 'I'm sorry about your son.'

'I knew she was beating up on him,' he said. 'She'd attack him with anything she had in her hand. He got that broken arm when she hit him with a vacuum cleaner at Thanksgiving. The neighbors heard the fight and called the cops.

'Tom refused to testify against her. He said he loved his wife and it was his fault and they'd both been drinking. Missouri's got some good domestic abuse laws and the prosecutor is the one who files charges – even if the battered spouse won't testify. The prosecutor had a talk with Tom and the responding cop and Tom begged them not to charge her. He said they'd get counseling and work it out. My son broke down and cried.'

Now Angela could hear the tears in the older man's voice.

'The prosecutor said he'd hold off, but if there was another incident, he'd have her arrested and charged. Those two were lovey-dovey for a month and then she started up with her mean ways. That big bruise on his chest was a Christmas present. She hit him with a floor polisher. When he was asleep, she burned his shoulder with an iron. She kicked and tormented that poor man and he did nothing. I should have had the guts to kidnap him and take him to a shrink.

'But I didn't, and now I've lost my only son.' His voice was thick with tears. 'Well, that prosecutor's going to get to file those charges after all, but this time it's murder.'

Now the old man put his big head on his cane and wept hard, harsh tears.

TWENTY-FIVE

Nick Murphy's tears turned to anger when he saw a uniform carefully prying the cloth front off a black speaker.

'Why are you monkeying with my son's stereo speakers?' he asked. No, Nick wasn't asking. He was demanding an answer. He pounded the coffee table in the living room so hard I jumped. All Nick's frustrated grief and anger was poured into protecting his son's prized sound equipment.

'We're looking for his oxy supply,' Jace said.

'Did that liar say my son took oxy? He quit,' Nick said. 'He was going into rehab in Oakville on Monday. He—'

Nick stopped in mid-sentence as the uniform pulled out a Ziploc bag filled with round yellow and red tablets. Oxy. The yellow tablets were stamped '40' and the red ones were '60' – the highest dosages available.

'She planted those!' Nick said. 'My son swore he'd quit taking oxy. That's why he was going into rehab.'

'Tests will show us if he'd quit, Mr Murphy,' Jace said.

The transport van had arrived to take Tom Murphy's body to the medical examiner's office.

'Would you like to step outside, Mr Murphy?' Jace asked.

'No, I want to see my son.' He shook his liver-spotted head, but his entire body was shaking with grief and anger. He leaned on his heavy black cane.

'I'm sorry, sir, but the kitchen is a crime scene.'

'I have to see my son.'

'It's better to remember him the way he was.'

'I want to remember him the way he is now! I want to hunt down that bitch and kill her!' he shouted. 'She'll pay! She'll pay!'

'If she's guilty, I promise she'll pay,' Jace said. 'Please let us do our job.'

He managed to steer Nick to the door. The old man was

outside when the attendants brought out his son's black body bag on a stretcher. The metal stretcher clanked on the suburban concrete porch with a terrible finality.

The old man's howl of grief made the hair stand up on my neck. Jace shifted uncomfortably. Nitpicker, head down in the kitchen cabinet under the sink, stopped taking apart the plumbing down there, just for a moment.

Nick's haunting cry stopped and I began packing up my DI case. 'Are you going to arrest the wife?' I asked Jace.

'The victim is dead on the scene and she admits to hitting her husband, so I could arrest her,' he said. 'But she claims his death was self-defense: He went nuts on oxy and attacked her first. And we did find a big stash of it.'

'Do you think the father's right and Tara Murphy planted the stash?' I asked.

'I had the bag printed. It had been wiped. So were the six empty beer bottles by the chair. No prints on any of them.'

'Someone wiped the prints on six beer bottles? You gotta be kidding. Nobody's that clean.' I couldn't keep the disbelief out of my voice.

'I couldn't believe it, either,' Jace said. 'That's why Nitpicker is taking apart the sink trap. Tara Murphy might have poured the beer down the sink. I think she tried to set the scene to support her defense that he was drunk and high and attacked her.'

'But won't the beer be gone by now?' I asked.

'I hope Tara Murphy didn't do a load of dishes or decide to clean the sink. If she poured a six-pack of beer down the sink it would remain in the trap until such time as a sufficient quantity of something else was poured down the drain to flush it. I'm thinking that the trap probably holds about five or six ounces of fluid. Nitpicker will know.'

Nitpicker appeared on cue. She looked tired and flushed and her blue hair was wilted. 'Here's your beer, Jace, just as you suspected.' She showed him a large Tupperware bowl filled with pale gold liquid. I smelled the sour stink of beer. A light skim of grease and a few grayish hairs floated on top the beer.

'Nobody throws out that much beer,' she said. 'The sink wasn't flushed with something else, so we found it.'

'Amazing,' I said.

'Works for toilets, too,' she said, and grinned. 'It takes at least three flushes to completely get rid of a stash.'

Thank God Greiman was too lazy to check the toilet traps when he searched Mario's salon, or he would have found drugs for sure.

'The wife can still claim her husband threw out the beer when he was crazy-mad,' Jace said.

'Can the autopsy be done today?' I asked.

'Katie said she'd do it as soon as the body arrives. I'm gonna keep the wife pigeonholed at the station until the assistant ME rules, then arrest her if he's clean for drugs. I don't want Tara Murphy claiming her husband was high on oxy and that made him go crazy. I'm playing it safe.'

I was glad. I was used to Detective Ray Greiman, who held the world record for jumping to conclusions. I still remembered the case where Greiman found the husband dead in bed and decided the wife had killed him. He had her cuffed and booked, and was preening for the press an hour later. She sued the city for false arrest after the ME ruled that her husband had died of natural causes. Jace would never do that. I was glad he was making sure the suspect was guilty.

I was ready to roll. As I left the sad little house, I saw Nick being comforted by a next-door neighbor, a gray-haired woman in her sixties, wearing a pale blue warm-up suit. Tom's father was weeping on her shoulder. Poor man. He would spend the rest of his life blaming himself because he couldn't tear his son away from his killer. Scrawny Tara Murphy was no femme fatale, but she'd had a deadly hold on her husband.

Now the neighbor was leading a broken Nick Murphy inside her home. I heard the words 'coffee' and 'cake.' Maybe those would help him through this terrible day. To outlive one's children is a curse. Nick Murphy had been doubly cursed – his son was dead and Nick believed he could have saved him.

*   *   *

At home, I finished my DI report about two o'clock. Then I found the photo I'd taken of that pair of one-hundred-dollar bills under the dead Becky's mattress, and dialed the Beverly Hills phone number on the one. A woman answered the phone with 'Jorge Cantata Salon, hairstylist to the stars.' That wasn't hype. Jorge Cantata and his stylists did the hair of the rich and famous in Beverly Hills. But why would Becky need the name of a salon that had five-hundred-dollar haircuts?

I finally decided she didn't. Someone connected with Jessica gave her that money and scribbled that phone number on it. The question was, why?

I felt the walls closing in on me. Restless and hungry, I left home and stopped at a local lunch spot for a quick chicken sandwich, and nearly lost my appetite when the waitress said, 'That comes with a side of fried potatoes.' She didn't understand my vehement refusal, but reassured me I could have fresh fruit instead.

It was about four o'clock when I finished lunch. I wandered over to the ME's office at SOS. Katie was writing up Thomas Murphy's autopsy report, angrily pounding the keys on her computer.

'Finished with Tom Murphy?' I asked.

She nodded. She had on a fresh lab coat over one of her practical brown suits. A cup of coffee that looked like crankcase oil was next to her.

'What did you find?' I asked.

'That poor bastard.' She shook her head. 'His wife nearly pounded his head flat with that frying pan.'

I winced, and a picture of Tom Murphy's battered, blood-stained head flashed in my mind. It would be a long time before I forgot his death.

'She must have hit him at least twenty times with that cast-iron skillet,' Katie said. 'He put up his hands to protect himself, and she burned them with hot grease, then she cold-cocked him and kept hitting him. Nearly crushed his head. He bled out. It was overkill, plain and simple.'

'He had other bruises, too,' I said. 'Old ones.'

'I saw. She tortured that poor man. He was burned and bruised front and back. That big bruise you noted in your report injured his liver.'

'Tara Murphy claimed he was high on oxycodone,' I said.

'The hell he was!' Katie said, fire in her eyes. 'We checked his urine. Oxy is detectable in a urine test for three to four days, and his was clean. Clean! So was his blood – oxy stays in the blood for about twenty-four hours. Not a trace.'

'What about his hair?' I asked.

'Oxy can be detected with a hair follicle drug test for up to ninety days. We don't have those results back on that test yet, but his blood and urine were negative, so he was clean for three days. She can't use that excuse.'

'His wife said he was addicted.'

'If he was, he had a good excuse – whoever did the surgery on his broken arm botched the job. He must have been in constant pain, along with having the wife from hell. What a life.'

'Is Jace going to arrest her?'

'Already has. I hope they throw the book at her.'

'I've never come across a man's domestic violence death before,' I said.

'I have,' she said. 'Happens more than you think. About 830,000 men a year are victims of domestic violence. Women are almost twice as likely as men to get beat up, but men are more afraid to admit it. They're ashamed.'

'Of being hit?' I said.

'Society expects a man to control his wife,' Katie said. 'Men are wimps if their wives beat them up. And this guy was what – a construction worker?'

'Yep.'

'I rest my case. He tried to take it like a man. That's what guys do.' Katie took a sip of the coffee, winced and tossed it in her trash can. 'So what's going on with the case you're not supposed to be investigating, Angela?' she asked.

'I'm stalled. I'm trying to have lunch with Will, Jessica's make-up artist. And I want to track down Suzy, the homeless woman who was at the Du Pres's party that night.'

'Ever figure out what Becky's jingle meant: *It's not the red – it's the blue?*'

'No,' I said. And I couldn't get the thought out of my mind that I was overlooking something.

Something that was the key to the whole case.

TWENTY-SIX

The next morning was frighteningly warm for February. The temperature shot up to almost eighty degrees. I was in St Louis searching the hot concrete canyons around the Lux Theater. I checked smelly alleys, stinking dumpsters, and any cardboard container bigger than a breadbox. I was hunting for Suzy, the homeless woman who'd been on-stage with Becky the night of Jessica's last performance.

Panhandling was increasing in the city, mostly because that's where the homeless shelters are. Beggars are slowly spreading out west toward the rich county areas, panhandling at the highway exits. So far, Harold Galloway was the only one who'd reached the enchanted environs of Chouteau County, and he paid for that with his life.

Near the Lux Theater, I saw lots of homeless people with their hands out, but none were Suzy.

I wondered how she'd felt after she'd been mocked on-stage that awful night at the Lux. Suzy looked dazed as she was pushed out into the limelight in her ragged clothes. She wore two dresses – a once-white summer dress over a dirty beige wool number with a dragging hem, and a gray Salvation Army blanket for a coat. Suzy was toothless, with urine stains on her clothes. She paraded around, carrying a bottle of Rosie O'Grady wine, while the crowd laughed and hooted. Then she flopped down and swigged the wine on-stage. The well-dressed, well-fed audience applauded, damn their shriveled souls.

Suzy didn't seem as tough as Becky. Suzy was easy to bully. At Reggie Du Pres's party, Suzy had let the old man talk her into having a hot dinner and a shower in his pool house. He hid that smelly, unwanted guest, and Suzy never complained. Becky was tougher. She'd refused Reggie's 'kind offer' to stash her in the pool house. She'd defied the formidable old man and paraded her unwashed self around the Forest's upper crust, eating choice delicacies from the buffet.

Now Becky was dead and I had to find Suzy. I needed to solve Jessica's murder and free my friend Mario. Suzy might know what Becky's odd, taunting jingle meant: *It's not the red – it's the blue. Breakfast is on you.*

The red what? Why was Becky killed before I could buy her breakfast? What did she know? Why didn't she just tell me?

Now Suzy had disappeared. Was she hiding after Becky's sudden death? Was she afraid someone was stalking the bedraggled stars of Jessica's show?

By noon, there were hordes of panhandlers out on this unseasonably warm day, trying to shake down wary workers. Most of the suits kept their eyes fixed on the sidewalk. They'd all been warned not to give money to panhandlers. Some office types crossed the street to avoid the more aggressive panhandlers.

A block from the Lux, a disheveled black woman in a long gray dress and black winter coat stopped a fifty-something white man in a dark suit. She was drinking a bottle of something in a brown paper bag, and from the way she was weaving down the sidewalk, I didn't think it was water.

'Change, mistah?' she asked. Actually, it was an angry demand.

Her target kept his eyes down and mumbled, 'Sorry,' as he sidled by her.

The woman roared at him, 'You're a racist!'

He took two more steps, then whirled around and blasted the woman. 'I don't care what color you are!' he shouted. 'I don't give money to inappropriate users! How dare you call me a racist! You don't even know me!'

'Bastard!' she said. But quietly, under her breath. The man stomped down Olive Street, his pale face red with fury.

Too bad. They were both right. The businessman probably wasn't racist – he just wanted to walk down the street without being accosted. And the woman was probably trapped. Nearby St Louis University was growing like a cancer, but when the school tore down or took over the old buildings to expand, no provisions were made for the homeless people who haunted the area. There weren't enough beds in the shelters – or programs to help the homeless. Panhandling was dangerous work, especially for the homeless. They were robbed, beaten, even set on fire. People shook their heads when they read the news stories about their deaths, but too many secretly thought, 'One less. Maybe now they'll go away.'

I was about to wrap up my search and come back tonight when I saw a woman rolling a shopping cart down the sidewalk. The cart zigzagged and nearly sideswiped a lamp post. The woman looked familiar. I recognized the baseball cap, black hoodie and green army jacket. Where had I seen her?

I hoped she was Suzy, but as I got closer, I saw those haunted eyes. Then I knew: this wasn't Suzy. It was Jessica's third 'model,' the one who'd warily circled the stage with her cart, as if she feared Jessica would steal her trash-bagged treasures. She'd been too afraid to abandon her shopping cart to go to the Du Pres party that night. What was her name? Diana? Debbie? No, Denise. That was it.

I called, 'Denise! Denise!'

She stared at me, then made a U-ee with her cart and took off in the other direction.

I fished a twenty out of my purse and called 'Denise!' again, waving the twenty-dollar bill. 'Denise, wait!' She glanced over her shoulder, as if the devil were pursuing her, then saw the money and slowed down. Meanwhile, the other panhandlers were closing in on me, grabbing for the twenty. I shoved it in my pocket and tried to outpace the hungry horde.

'Denise!' I called again. Now she turned around and came my way.

'Is that for me?' she asked, her voice tentative, her eyes lit with a strange fire. 'Can I have the money?'

'If you'll answer some questions,' I said, dodging a large woman in an orange muumuu.

'Can't talk here,' Denise said. 'Follow me.'

She turned off into an alley near a parking lot. The panhandlers stayed on North Grand Boulevard, where the prospects were better.

I followed Denise down the alley for about a block. We passed a dumpster and she parked the shopping cart next to it, then took a seat on the rusty iron stairs at the back of a tall redbrick building. I was going to sit next to her, but as I got closer, her unwashed odor was overpowering. I leaned against the cart. She eyed me uneasily. I backed away from her belongings.

'What do you want?' she asked. Her face was gaunt and yellow, her body lean and ropy, her eyes bright with suspicion.

'I'm looking for Suzy.'

Denise crooked her pinkie, mimicking a piss-elegant woman. 'Her ladyship don't bother with the likes of us no more.'

'Where is she?'

'She has a room at the Hoffstedder,' Denise said in a mock-English voice. 'She's too good to panhandle. Now she's an entrepreneur.'

'What's she do?'

'She sells cold water to the afternoon rush hour traffic. Buys herself a case of bottled water at the liquor store for six bucks. Humph! The likes of her buying water! Never touched the stuff before. Fills a bucket with ice, and hauls it all down to the Highway 40 exit. Sells each bottle for a buck apiece between four and six every afternoon. Sells out the whole case nearly every day.'

'And she makes money that way?'

'Fifteen to twenty dollars a day. Now that she's making money, she says she's going to expand to the Lux crowd on warm nights. Or so I've heard. She's too good to associate with us now. I asked her for five dollars for food and she told me no.'

'Where did Suzy get a bucket for the ice?'

'Found it in the alley. Next thing we know, she's living at the Hoffstedder. Wearing nice clothes, too. And don't ask me where she got that money. All I know is she suddenly has plenty of money, got herself a hotel room and began selling water. She doesn't have a permit, either. The police are going to put a stop to that.' I could hear the satisfaction in her voice.

I gave Denise the twenty, thanked her, and headed for my car. Suzy had almost four hours before she started her next round of sales near the highway exit. Maybe I could catch her at the Hoffstedder.

I found a parking spot near the old hotel, and noticed a new trendy farm-to-table restaurant across the street. It wouldn't be long before this SRO hotel would be gentrified, and then where would the marginal people like Suzy live?

Inside, the elegant woman behind the Hoffstedder's front desk said Suzy was in 512, a suite on the fifth floor.

A suite? She did have money.

I took the stairs rather than brave the slow, groaning elevator, and tried to ignore the stink of disinfectant and urine in the staircase. Suite 512 still had its original brass plaque on the door. I knocked, and thought that I saw a shadow at the peephole.

'Suzy, it's me,' I said. 'Angela Richman, from Chouteau Forest.'

She opened the door with a smile.

I was stunned. Suzy was a changed woman: she was clean, her mousy hair was washed and permed, and she wore a freshly washed purple polyester pantsuit and a necklace. Her shoes were new black Nikes. Suzy bore no resemblance to the drunk who'd paraded across the stage.

'I remember you,' she said. 'You were at the party with Jessica.'

'Yes. You look terrific.'

She gave me a toothless smile. 'What do you think of my room?'

Her pride was obvious. The sagging bed had a puffy new blue spread and pillow shams, the chest of drawers was polished, and the curtains opened onto the midtown cityscape. I saw fresh flowers on the coffee table, along with two new hardback mysteries and the latest *Vanity Fair*. The room's worn gray carpet was covered with a large flowered area rug. To the left was a small galley kitchen. A loaf of bread and half a sliced ham were on the counter, along with a basket of fruit. Suzy had come into money. Major money.

'It's beautiful,' I said. 'I love your view.'

'I'm working now. I sell water.'

'Congratulations,' I said.

'I go to AA meetings at the church,' she said. 'I'm going to turn my life around.'

'I can tell you're on your way. I'm hoping you can help me. It's about Becky.'

'She's dead,' Suzy said, and instantly looked sad.

'Yes, I know,' I said. 'I was supposed to meet her for breakfast. I'm the one who discovered her body. The day before she died, Becky told me, "*It's not the red – it's the blue. Breakfast is on you. Ten o'clock. The St Louis Pancake House. You're buying.*" Do you know what that means?'

Suzy looked thoughtful. 'Becky really, really liked the Pancake House.'

Was Suzy being deliberately obtuse? 'What did she mean by "*It's not the red – it's the blue*"? I feel that's a clue,' I said.

'You're rhyming, too,' Suzy said, and giggled.

'I know that, but I'm serious, Suzy. Please help me.'

She looked at her watch, a square-faced Kate Spade. Where did she get the money for a designer watch?

'Oops. Time for me to go to work,' she said. 'I have to leave.'

'Then you won't help me?'

'I'm sorry about Becky,' she said. 'We all are – but I don't know anything.'

She stood up, and I followed her to the door. She turned for a moment, and I caught a glimpse of her necklace, before it disappeared inside her purple pantsuit.

It looked familiar. I wished I knew why.

I left knowing nothing new – except that for some reason, Suzy was lying.

TWENTY-SEVEN

Mario looked awful. I saw him at the Chouteau County jail, after my useless interview with Suzy. Either Mario was wearing an orange jumpsuit three sizes too big, or he'd lost weight in the last few days. His normally thick, shiny black hair looked thin and dirty. Worse, he had a black eye going from sunset purple to sickly yellow-green. If his eye hurt as bad as it looked, he was in serious pain.

Men awaiting trial were kept at the Chouteau County jail. The building was fairly new, and on the outside it looked like a junior college, if students went to school behind razor wire. Inside, the building scared the heck out of me – the foul air, the inmates' weird cries, and the grim gray walls.

I stashed my purse and cell phone in a locker and was directed to a small booth with a Plexiglas barrier and a phone. Mario and I both picked up our phones. I was the first to talk.

'Mario! What happened to your eye?'

'Some idiot thought I was Mexican and told me to go back to my own country,' he said. 'I told him this was my country – I'm a US citizen. Then I said, "You're so stupid you don't know the difference between a Cuban and a Mexican." After that, things got nasty.'

'Your eye looks painful,' I said.

He shrugged. 'It is nothing. You should see him.' He tried a wobbly smile.

I didn't smile back. 'Did you get in trouble for fighting?'

'No. At least everyone leaves me alone now.'

'I'm sorry,' I said.

'Don't be. It is not your fault.'

He switched topics so quickly I nearly had whiplash. 'What have you done to your hair, Angela?' Despite his badly injured eye, his disapproval was obvious.

'My hair?' I patted a hunk hanging over my forehead.

'Nothing. Why are we talking about my hair?' It was a bit flat and frizzy after my morning search for Suzy.

'It looks terrible,' he said.

'Not as bad as your eye.'

I felt a little better. If Mario was fussing about my hair, he was OK. Right now, he looked like he wanted to rip out the Plexiglas barrier and start styling my hair.

'Mario, I know you don't like my hair, but we have more important things to worry about.'

'Your appearance is always important. Always. Promise me if you go anywhere while I am in here, you'll call Carlos at the salon. He is new, but he shows promise.'

'Mario, I'm not going anywhere.'

'Promise me anyway.'

'OK.'

He knew I wasn't serious. 'For real.'

I put my hand on the Plexiglas and said, 'I solemnly swear that I will see Carlos at Killer Cuts if I go anywhere before Mario gets out of here.'

He looked happier at that. At least he managed another smile. 'I know you are trying to help. Any progress?'

'I'm working on it.' I kept my response as vague as possible. I didn't want to discuss my failures, especially after my disastrous search this morning. That would only discourage him.

'Did you find out anything at all?'

I couldn't kill that hope on his face. 'I have a clue,' I said. 'Do you know what this jingle means? *It's not the red – it's the blue. Breakfast is on you.*'

He looked puzzled. 'No. Why would someone worry about breakfast?'

'I don't think that jingle was about breakfast,' I said. 'Becky, the homeless woman who was on-stage that night at the Lux, told me.'

'Why not ask her?'

'I can't. She's dead.'

His eyes widened – even the beat-up one. 'Dead! That is terrible. Was she attacked on the street?'

'No, she was turning her life around. She'd sobered up and had a job. She was killed in her hotel room.'

'Oh. I am sorry.' Mario had had a difficult time when he first came to the US from Cuba during the 1980 Mariel Boatlift. That's when Castro threw out homosexuals, criminals, and other 'undesirables.' Mario left with nothing, so he had some idea how hard Becky had to struggle for her achievements.

'Who killed her?'

'I don't know, but I suspect it was the same person who killed Jessica. Becky knew something. I asked her friends about that jingle and they don't know what it means, either. But I think it was about something red or blue that was in the limo when Jessica was killed.'

'I saw Will holding a red lipstick,' Mario said. 'He was brushing it on Jessica's lips when she had that coughing fit. She collapsed and died before he could finish.'

'Anything blue you remember? Maybe some eye shadow?'

'Blue? Will would never use blue on Jessica.' Mario sounded as if everyone knew that. Everyone but me, the woman who had to swear that she'd have her hair done before she went anywhere.

'There must have been something blue in that limo,' I said. I could visualize the interior as it roared up to the ER – sleek, black, speeding to deliver Jessica to her horrible death.

'Becky wasn't in the limo.'

'She was at the hospital, and she told me she went through everyone's belongings when Jessica's staff spent the night at the hospital. I'm sure Becky helped herself to some of their money.'

'So? They should have paid her more. I want to help, but I don't remember anything blue in the limo. Maybe it was on the video I took on your phone the day Jessica died. Have you been able to watch it?'

'No, I tried to start the phone up last night, but it didn't work. But Katie says there are lots of programs to get it going.'

'I am so sorry.' Mario's apology was cut off when a guard signaled our time was up. I pressed my hand to the Plexiglas and Mario pressed his, and I said goodbye. It was as close as we could get.

When I got to my locker and recovered my phones, I saw a message from Will, Jessica's make-up artist. 'Hey, Francesca,' he'd texted. 'Want to have a goodbye drink tonight at Solange? I leave for LA tomorrow evening at 6:30.'

I'd been trying for days to reach that man. I quickly texted back that I'd meet him in the bar. I had just enough time for Carlos to do my hair. I am a woman of my word. Besides, the Forest is so small Mario would find out if I'd disobeyed him.

When I called Killer Cuts, Raquel the receptionist told me Carlos could see me immediately. That was not a good sign.

The salon was ominously quiet. Not a single stylist was working. Even the manicurist wasn't reading magazines or painting her nails at her station – she was gone.

Raquel was still beautiful, but the strain was showing. Small dark strands escaped her normally perfect chignon and her face was pale and drawn. 'Change into a robe,' she told me. I quickly changed. All the dressing rooms were empty.

'Carlos will be here momentarily,' Raquel said when I came back out.

'You had to call him in?'

'Yes, but he wanted the work. You're our only client today. Even our regulars have canceled their standing appointments. I may have to close the salon by the end of the week if business doesn't improve.'

'Oh, no.' I felt as if I was hearing about a death. The salon was Mario's life's work.

'I just talked with Mario,' I said. 'He didn't mention anything about that. He seemed to be doing fine.'

'Really.' Raquel's voice was flat with disbelief. The empty salon chairs mocked my words.

'OK, Mario was as well as can be expected,' I said, 'but we didn't talk business – except he made me promise to get my hair done before I went anywhere.'

Raquel managed a small smile. 'Now I know you're telling the truth. That sounds like Mario.'

'I'm working on the case,' I said. 'I tracked down another witness this morning. Monty is doing his best, too.'

'I know,' she said, and gave me another smile – a tired one. 'You're all working hard. But we're running out of time.'

Fortunately, Carlos came bursting through the salon door,

lugging his styling case, and ended that discouraging discussion. Carlos is in his mid-twenties, with sharply cut features like a fine cameo, and long raven hair, which he'd tied back. I envied him his thick eyelashes, and many women mourned the fact that he was gay.

'Angela!' he said, and sat me down in a leather-and-chrome chair. 'We'll have you fixed up in a minute.' By the time Carlos finished washing and blowing out my hair, it was more like ninety minutes, but my hair did look better. Carlos was almost as good as Mario.

I hurried home to change into my little black dress and heels to meet Will. When I arrived at Solange at 6:37 that evening, Jessica's make-up artist was impatiently checking his watch. The bar was packed with suits. By day, Solange was a ladies' lunch spot, but at night the Forest's movers and shakers took over the restaurant and bar. They didn't mind its pink-and-black decor, and they admired themselves in its amazing mirrors.

'Sorry,' I said, taking a seat at the bar next to Will. He had a neat scotch in front of him, and judging by his breath, it wasn't his first.

'You're worth waiting for,' he said. The soft pink lights of the bar really were flattering to everyone.

'A gallant answer,' I said.

His hair was combed straight back and he wore a black sweater with a distinctive rust design that brought out his dramatic red hair.

'Dynamite sweater. Did I see that on an actor somewhere?'

Will looked pleased. 'You did. Ethan Hawke, in *GQ*.

'I hope you don't mind, but I'm meeting Stu here at seven o'clock,' he said. 'We want to discuss some of the details of winding down Jessica's show and taking her back home to California. Personal things.'

There was a long silence, until it suddenly dawned on me, 'And you want to discuss them here without me.'

'Yes. If you wouldn't mind.' He looked so charming, I couldn't be angry. No wonder Mario had fallen for him.

'Of course,' I said. 'No need to apologize.'

I saw the bartender hovering nearby. 'Where are my manners?' Will said. 'I forgot to ask. Would you like a drink?'

'A Cosmo,' I said, almost defiantly. I didn't care if it was a cliché. I liked that drink.

'We should order some appetizers.' Will picked up the small menu. 'What's toasted ravioli?'

'It's a local specialty. The ravioli is deep-fat fried. You dunk them in a tomato-based sauce.'

'No, thanks,' he said. 'I've had enough grease and gravy here. No offense.'

'None taken,' I said, and shrugged. 'I don't cook.'

He signaled the bartender and said, 'I'll have the pork belly sliders, and the lady will have a Cosmo. An appetizer for you, Angela?'

'No, thanks.'

'Another drink, sir?' the bartender asked.

'Make it a double,' Will said.

'So you're leaving tomorrow?' I asked.

'Yes, all of us. Jessica is being cremated at a private ceremony at nine tomorrow, and Stu will take her ashes back home tomorrow night.'

'Is Stu going to have a memorial service?'

'Definitely, a big bash when we're back in LA,' Will said. 'He's already hired an event planner and he's having a studio prepare a slide show. He says Jessica wanted to be cremated. At the memorial service Stu can use her favorite photos and everyone will remember how glamorous she was.'

My mind flashed back to her body in the hospital room – a scrawny, shriveled woman with thin hair, fake boobs and a flat, flabby rear end.

'She'll go out in style,' I said. 'What will you be doing when you get back home?'

'I have two offers, including one in Beverly Hills, and there's some interest in my make-up line. I'm taking a meeting with investors next week.'

'Congratulations,' I said.

He'd downed his scotch and ordered another double. I nursed my Cosmo.

'I'm glad the cops caught Jessica's killer so we can leave,' he said.

'I'm happy you can go home, but I don't believe that

Mario killed her. It makes no sense. He was thrilled to be her stylist.'

'He shouldn't have given her the drugs,' Will said.

I wanted to slap his treacherous face. 'Percocet and Xanax didn't kill her.' I tried to cool the anger in my voice. 'Maybe you can help me with something, Will. Becky, the homeless woman who was on-stage at Jessica's last show, told me: *It's not the red – it's the blue. Breakfast is on you.* Do you know what that means?'

Will frowned, and swallowed his scotch in one gulp. 'Uh, no. Ask her to explain it.'

'Can't,' I said. 'She was killed before I could meet her.'

'She was?' Will's eyebrows shot up, but I didn't know him well enough to tell if he was really surprised or faking it.

'You don't remember anything red or blue in the limo, Will?'

'I was brushing on Jessica's red lipstick before she got sick and she wore a red sweater, but I can't think of anything blue.'

Will was sweating now. He said, 'Bartender! Another double! Would you like another drink, Angela?'

'No, thanks,' I said. 'I found Becky's body.'

'That must have been terrible,' Will said. The bartender set down his double and the pork sliders.

'It was terribly sad,' I said. 'She was turning her life around.'

I let that sentence hang there before I finally said, 'I also found two crisp one-hundred-dollar bills squirreled away under her mattress.'

'She definitely must have been doing well.' Will took a long drink.

'One of those bills had a Beverly Hills salon's number scribbled on it: the Jorge Cantata Salon.'

Will's eyes darted around the room. 'I saw some well-dressed women at the Du Pres party. Maybe one of them was going there for a makeover.'

'I doubt it,' I said. 'They can get a good makeover here in the Forest for a lot less. A haircut by Jorge is five hundred dollars. Besides, that Beverly Hills salon is looking for a make-up artist.'

'So? They want to talk to me about a job, now that I'm free.'

'Why did you give Becky two hundred dollars, Will? And don't deny it. The cops have printed those bills.'

He bit into his pork belly slider. For a man tired of grease, I saw a big lump of grilled fat on his tiny sandwich. 'OK, I gave her the money, but it wasn't two hundred. It was five hundred dollars, actually. I felt sorry for her. Jessica only gave her a hundred and the poor woman was humiliated.'

'Did you give money to Suzy and Denise, the other two women? They were also laughed off the stage. And don't lie. I've already asked them.'

'No. I couldn't find Suzy and Denise is bat-shit crazy.'

Fair enough, I thought. Poor Denise was terrified of everyone, and it took me half a day to track down Suzy in her new digs.

I noticed Will never said that Becky could have stolen the money. 'Give me the real reason you gave Becky five hundred bucks,' I said. 'Or I'll tell the detectives on her case your connection to the phone number on the bill.'

Will sighed. 'OK, Becky was blackmailing me. She said I groped her.'

'You groped Becky?'

He gave a mirthless laugh. 'She claimed it happened at the hospital, the night Jessica stayed. Yes, I'm gay and she's a mess – she doesn't even bathe – but because of the #MeToo movement I couldn't risk it. Not now, when I'm trying to line up investors for my make-up company. It was easier to pay her off, and five hundred was a fortune to her. Would you like another drink?'

Sweat was running down his forehead. 'It's hot in here. I need some air.' Will called for the check and handed the bartender his credit card. He used a paper cocktail napkin to wipe the sweat off his brow. He looked toward the door and waved someone over.

'It was nice talking with you, Angela, but Stu is here. We need to talk.'

'May I ask him about Becky's jingle?'

He looked doubtful, but I hurried to crush any objections. 'It will just take a second of his time. I promise.'

He relaxed slightly. 'OK. Just make it quick. Please.' That please was definitely an afterthought.

Stu was all smiles tonight as he pushed through the crowd to us. Once again, he was totally dressed in black – from his well-cut jacket to his T-shirt and pants. I thought he was trying to look hip rather than mourning for his wife. Stu wore his sunglasses, though it was pitch-black outside. He greeted me with a kiss on the cheek, and ordered a double bourbon, neat.

'Angela,' he said, his smile fixed. 'Will told me he was meeting you for a drink. I'm sorry I can't ask you to join us.'

'I understand,' I said.

The bartender swiftly set the bourbon on the bar top next to Stu. 'Becky, the homeless woman who was in Jessica's show, wanted to meet me for breakfast. She recited an odd little jingle.' I quickly told him, then said, 'And before you ask me why I didn't ask her, I couldn't. She was dead – murdered in her hotel room.'

Stu looked shocked. At least, I thought so. His eyes were hidden by those dark glasses.

'Really? She was the one who took off her clothes on-stage, right? That's too bad,' he said. 'Have the police connected her death to Jessica's?' He downed his double in one gulp.

'I don't know,' I said. 'The cops think Jessica's killer is in jail.'

Stu looked at Will. 'I think it's too crowded in this place to have our discussion,' he said. 'Let's go back to the Forest Inn. We can talk in my room.'

Will nodded. Stu grabbed the check off the bar, and presented his card to the bartender. Before I knew it, I was being hustled out of the bar between both men.

'Thanks for the drink, Will,' I said.

We walked to the door and he handed the valet his ticket. So did Stu.

'Where are you parked?' Stu asked.

'I'm the black Charger by the back wall,' I said.

'The one under the light?' Will asked.

'That's it.' Will's anonymous silver rental car had arrived and I was hoping he'd give me a ride to my car. I was regretting my killer heels.

'Goodbye,' Will said, tipping the valet and getting into his car.

Stu's car was next, and it was an exact copy of Will's rental. I lingered a moment, hoping he'd offer me a ride, but he tipped the valet, and was adjusting the seat when I set off for my car.

I didn't realize how far away I'd parked. By the time I was past the first row, my stiletto heels were torturing my toes. By the second row, I was hobbling, with a blister on my heel. That's when I saw headlights coming down the aisle. They were aimed straight for me. Couldn't the driver see me?

Of course not. I was wearing black. The silver car revved up, as if it were aiming for me. I limped quickly across the aisle, but the car seemed to follow me. It speeded up as it neared me, and I threw myself over the boxy trunk of a faded gold Mercury. I held on, as the silver car peeled off the Mercury's bumper, then roared out of the lot.

I was gasping for breath. The valet came running.

'Ma'am! Are you OK?'

I finally caught my breath, 'Yes, I'm fine.'

'Some crazy fucker tried to kill you.'

TWENTY-EIGHT

'Damn, woman, are you lucky,' the valet said. His face was even paler than most Forest dwellers'. Even in the parking lot's dim light, I could see that – and the dark roots in his blond hair.

'Lucky!' I said, my voice shaking. 'My dress is ruined.' I had a long rip, almost to my hip, on the side of my favorite cocktail dress.

'And look at my shoe!'

When I'd leaped onto the trunk of the Mercury, I'd lost a high heel. The killer car had run over one of my black Stuart Weitzmans. The heel was broken and the sleek black satin was torn off. This was a double loss: my late husband had admired those sexy shoes.

'That could have been you,' the valet said, pointing at my crushed shoe.

I presented a scraped, dirty hand for an introduction. 'I'm Angela.'

'Garrett,' he said.

Now I heard sirens approaching the restaurant. 'I called the police,' he said. 'I'm glad you're OK.' Despite a bloody scrape on my right knee, Garrett was checking out my legs.

'Did you see the car that nearly hit me?' I was shivering so hard my teeth were chattering.

The valet's eyes were wide and he was talking too fast. 'It was silver, but I didn't get any license number and I couldn't see the make. I'd just brought back three silver cars in a row: a Toyota, and two silver Chevy Malibus. Those last two were rental cars. A fourth silver car that was too cheap to valet was leaving the lot. I have no idea which car it was that tried to run you down.' Garrett talked like he'd watched a lot of cop shows. Maybe he had.

I heard a car screech into the lot. A CFPD patrol car parked at the end of the aisle and a young, crew-cut cop swaggered over. As he got closer, I recognized the new Chouteau Forest hire, Officer Christopher Ferretti.

Garrett the valet ran over and filled in the officer on the violent near-miss. By the time they'd reached my perch on the trunk, Ferretti had some idea of what had happened.

'You OK, miss?' the officer asked. That was his first question.

'Fine,' I said. 'Just cold.'

'You're probably in shock.' His concern seemed sincere. His brown eyes looked troubled. 'I'll call an ambulance.'

'No! I'll be fine,' I said. 'I'm Angela Richman, a death investigator for Chouteau County. I have a blanket in my trunk.'

'So do I,' Officer Ferretti said. He turned to the valet. 'Can you get Angela a shot of whiskey?'

'No alcohol,' I said. 'I had a cocktail in the bar.'

'Get her some hot coffee then,' he said. 'Lots of cream and sugar.'

Garrett ran off to get the coffee. Officer Ferretti sprinted back to his patrol car, rummaged in the trunk and came back with a silver survival blanket. He helped me down off the Mercury's trunk and wrapped me in the blanket. I felt like a Thanksgiving leftover in the shiny silver, but the blanket worked. So did the hot coffee Garrett brought. I leaned against the Mercury and studied Officer Ferretti. On second look, he wasn't quite so young, but he definitely worked out. He had lines around his eyes and some gray in his close-cropped hair. He must be closer to my age.

He asked me what had happened, and I gave him my version, starting with my meeting with Will London, the make-up artist for Jessica Gray, and ending with Stu Milano.

When I finished, he asked, 'Do either of you know the owner of the damaged vehicle?' I saw the bumper had been nearly peeled off.

'No,' Garrett said, 'but when I went back for the coffee, I told the restaurant manager. She's looking for the owner. She'll have him out here shortly.'

'Good work,' Ferretti said. 'It looks like what we have here is a hit-and-run with property damage. The speeding car hit this Mercury and left the scene of an accident.'

'Don't forget attempted murder,' I added.

'What murder?' he said.

'Me. Someone tried to run me down and nearly killed me.'

'Who was that?'

'I think it was either Will London or Stu Milano.'

'And why would they want to kill you?' Ferretti asked.

Because I'm looking into the death of Jessica Gray, I almost said. But I clamped my mouth shut just in time. I wasn't supposed to be looking into Jessica's death. Mario had already been arrested for her murder, and I was the DI on the star's case. Her closed case.

'I don't know,' I said. I knew I sounded like an idiot.

'Do you have any injuries, ma'am?' the cop asked. 'Did you hit your head?'

At least he was giving me the benefit of the doubt. 'Just a skinned knee and a scraped hand.' I felt ridiculous pointing out those scratches.

'Can you testify that you were the intended target?' he asked.

'Uh, no.' Not unless I wanted to get fired for meddling in a police investigation.

'Then I think what we have just might be a reckless driving hit-and-run with property damage. I can put out a BOLO for a hit-and-run reckless, possible DUI.'

'Stu was a good tipper,' the valet said. 'That Will guy was awfully drunk. I had to pour him into his car. But he wasn't the only drunk who left here tonight in a silver car.'

'We can try to get him for a DUI,' Ferretti said. 'Do either of you know his license plate number?' He turned to Garrett, 'What about Will's or Stu's plates? Did you write down that information?'

'No, it's not on the tickets,' Garrett said. 'We're a small operation.'

'I didn't get it either,' I said. 'I was too busy jumping out of the way.' I took another sip of coffee. It was sweet and hot.

'Would you like to warm up in my car?' Ferretti asked me.

'Thanks, but I'm feeling better now.' I was, too, especially about this new hire on the Forest force.

'If we catch the driver with a BOLO,' Ferretti said, 'he

could be arrested for DUI, reckless driving, and leaving the scene of an accident with property damage. If you want to include an assault complaint, Ms Richman, you can.'

I looked at the scratch on my knee. It had stopped bleeding. 'I'd feel ridiculous.'

He studied the bumper of the damaged car. 'I do see some paint transfer from the hit-and-run,' he said. 'It looks like silver. I'll get CSI out here.'

At that point, a tall, thin older woman in a black silk pantsuit and stylish silver jewelry hurried over to us.

'My car!' she wailed. 'My car! Who hurt my car?'

'I'm sorry, ma'am,' Officer Ferretti said. 'Your car was damaged in a hit-and-run. But it can be fixed.'

'Fixed! That car belonged to my late husband. There wasn't a mark on it.'

There wasn't. The pale gold car was old, but well-kept. Not a single ding or dent until tonight. It looked like a late nineties model, with its square front end and trunk. Thank God that trunk was big enough for me to leap on.

The woman burst into tears.

Ferretti looked puzzled and uncomfortable. 'I'm so sorry,' he said, 'but it will soon be good as new.'

'Never!' she said. 'It's not the same.'

I understood her tears. I walked over to her barefoot, and picked up my mangled shoe to show her.

'Your car saved my life,' I told her. 'Someone tried to run me down and I jumped on its trunk. All he killed was my shoe.'

'Then I'm happy that Sherman has an honorable war wound,' she said, and gave me a tentative smile.

She saw our blank stares. 'My husband and I name our cars. This one is Sherman, because he's a tank. And now he's performed well in battle.' She patted her damaged car's fender affectionately. 'Good job, boy. I'm Holly Barteau. My late husband's name is Charles.' We introduced ourselves.

'Wait till my children hear this,' Holly said. 'They've been after me to trade in Sherm for a boring Beemer. But now he's saved a life. Is Sherm drivable, Officer? Can I go home? I live nearby.'

'I'd have the car towed to the repair shop and get it checked first, if it was mine,' Ferretti said. 'As soon as I finish my report, I can take you home, Mrs Barteau. What about you, Angela? Can I give you a ride?'

Could he? He'd dropped the formal 'Ms Richman' for the friendlier 'Angela.' The invitation was tempting, but I wasn't ready for even a mild flirtation. 'I'm OK. May I leave now?' I asked.

'As soon as you give me a statement.'

It was eleven o'clock by the time I got to my house. I was too jittery to sleep. I tossed my dress in the trash, but I couldn't bring myself to throw away my heels. I put them tenderly in their box, wrapping the battered heel in tissue as if tucking it in, and told myself I'd try to get the shoe repaired, even though I knew that was impossible. I showered and put Neosporin on my scrapes. I was too angry and restless to sleep. Someone in Jessica's entourage had tried to kill me tonight, and tomorrow they'd be on a plane to LA and Mario would be doing time for their crime. I had to see Mario's video or else. I was even ready try Cellebrite, the Israeli company that offered to help the FBI unlock the iPhone of the San Bernardino shooter, though it was fabulously expensive.

I went into the kitchen, made myself some coffee, and tried to start the phone, but the cracked, dead screen stared blindly at me, mocking my effort. I took out the battery – again – and put it back in. Nothing. Then I remembered how I made my balky desktop computer work. My cell phone screen was already broken, so I had nothing to lose. I whapped the phone smartly on the table. At last! It opened. I quickly found the video, transferred it to my iPad and sat down to watch it.

Most of it was as I remembered: I saw the inside of Jessica's long black Mercedes stretch limo, with a black leather bench seat, a bar fully stocked with drinks, and a TV. The sound system played the late sixties music of Johnny Grimes, Jessica's lover. Knowing Johnny was long dead, the music sounded eerie, as if he was welcoming her home. Did Jessica feel any guilt for giving the man she loved that fatal overdose?

'Turn that shit off,' Jessica yelled, and the music evaporated. With only minutes left to live, Jessica was bursting with malicious life, a cursed queen returning to her throne. She piled on the insults against the Forest dwellers while Stu, Tawnee, Will and Mario sat mutely.

We were coming to the crucial part. After Jessica shrieked insults and the driver tried to reassure her the delay was minor, she commanded her staff to fix her up. Will applied fresh red lipstick.

Was that the red that Becky was talking about? Where was the blue?

I watched Tawnee's frantic, futile efforts to find the spray bottle in her purse as she angrily accused Stu of deliberately making it disappear.

Wait! Was that something in Stu's hand? I paused the video and examined the frame. I swore I saw something, but it might have been a shadow in the dark limo. I studied the frame until my eyes watered, but I couldn't make out what – if anything – Stu held. I resumed the video.

Will, cool as a fighter pilot in an emergency, offered to help look. He reached into his make-up kit and put the lipstick into a slot. The brush stuck straight up. Now it looked like Will had something hidden in his right hand, and it wasn't a tube of lipstick. What was it?

Will took the huge purse from Tawnee, rummaged around and came up with nothing, while Jessica struggled with her racking coughs. Stu impatiently pushed Will out of the way and found the blue spray bottle, claiming it had been in a fold of the purse.

Yeah, right.

The rest of the drama unfolded as I remembered, ending with the mad race to the hospital while Mario, Will, Stu and Tawnee tried to stop Jessica from hurling her body around. This was the part I hadn't seen before.

Will backed away from Jessica and her three helpers momentarily. He was holding something in his hand, I was sure of it. I couldn't see the color, but he disappeared into the far corner of the limo, out of the camera range. Mario, Stu and Tawnee were still trying to restrain Jessica as the limo rocked and swerved. Then Will was back, helping them.

As the limo rolled to a stop, Stu slipped something into his coat pocket. Next it looked like he was shoving it between the seatback and the cushion, but then the limo door was flung open by a nurse. We all knew what happened next.

I rewound and watched the video three times. Each viewing seemed to confirm that Stu handed Jessica the blue bottle of throat spray, then hid something in the far corner of the limo. I couldn't see what or exactly where. Stu was too good at sleight-of-hand. It also showed Will concealing something out of camera range.

Was homeless Becky's riddle solved? *It's not the red – it's the blue.* Did Will kill Becky? Is that why he tried to kill me? Or was it sly Stu, and he hid the evidence in the limo seat? Was he the one who tried to run me down in the parking lot? My money was on Stu. He had the best reason for killing his old, rich wife.

Now that we had this video, did we finally have a chance of freeing Mario? I didn't want to wait until tomorrow to call Monty, his lawyer.

TWENTY-NINE

'Angela, what's wrong? Why are you calling at one a.m.?' Katie sounded amazingly alert for that hour. She'd moonlighted as an ER doctor to pay off her school loans, and still had the ability to wake up instantly. The man's voice I heard in the background did not.

'Who's that?' he asked, his words slurred with sleep.

'I'm fine, Katie,' I said. 'I need to speak to Monty. He's not home, so I figured he'd be with you.'

'You'd better have a good reason for getting us up in the middle of the night.' Katie wasn't letting go of the phone yet, and now she sounded annoyed.

'I do! I think I have the evidence to free Mario.'

'You think? And you didn't think this could wait until morning?'

'No! We may be able to get him out before breakfast. Katie, you were right about how to fix my broken cell phone. I got it working. I have the video Mario took inside the limo. It shows someone else killing Jessica.'

'I wanna see it,' I heard Monty mumble. 'Now.'

'OK, bring it over to my house.' Katie said. 'I'll make us coffee.'

I still didn't get to talk to Monty, but I'd see him at Katie's home.

Outside, the moon was shining an eerie white, and the night sky was lit with stars. The air was chilly. The early morning had a fresh, do-over feel: it made me feel that this would be a better day.

It was a ten-minute drive to Katie's home, a two-story white Victorian farmhouse with a gingerbread porch. The lights in the kitchen had a welcoming glow. I parked my car, knocked on the side door, and heard, 'Come in!'

The farmhouse kitchen was warm and welcoming. Katie, dressed in jeans and a plaid shirt, greeted me. A sleepy-eyed

Monty was wearing the same thing, except he was barefoot and had a serious case of bed head. The kitchen was scented with coffee and the sweet, sugary lure of a warm pecan ring on the oak round table.

'I don't know why this couldn't wait another five hours until I have to get up,' Katie said, but she wasn't really grumbling. She poured three mugs of coffee and sliced three generous portions of the coffee cake. I joined them at the table and set up my iPad. We ignored the food while we sat down to view Mario's video on my iPad screen.

Katie and Monty watched in silent fascination. After the first time through, Katie said, 'Damn, Stu was bold. It looks like he poisoned Jessica in front of three people, and while she's having seizures, he pulled off the switch and nobody noticed.'

'I'm not sure the killer is Stu,' Monty said. 'Looks to me like it could have been Will. He's definitely hiding something. Let's watch that video again.'

And so we did, each of us silent, searching for details.

At the end of the video, I said, 'See. Stu murdered Jessica.'

'It looks that way to you,' Monty said, 'But there's no way we can prove it. We maybe see Stu slip something between the limo seats . . . maybe. We also see Will with something but we can't prove what it is. He couldn't even find the bottle. The police found the red bottle on the floor, and it was harmless throat spray. The blue bottle hasn't been found.'

My heart sank.

'Then the bottle that killed Jessica still has to be in the limo,' I said.

'Not necessarily,' Monty said. 'You said Stu got rid of his coat at the hospital, and so did Will. If Will had the bottle, he could have stashed it in the seat cushion and then stuck it in his coat pocket until he dumped the poison bottle – and the coat – in the hospital trash, where they will both be gone for good.'

'I think it's Will. He tried to kill me, too,' I said, 'after I mentioned Becky's jingle.'

That got their attention. Katie sat down her coffee mug.

Monty's hovered in the air, lost between the table and his mouth.

'I met Will at Solange for a drink. Stu joined him. I told them both about Becky's jingle. The two were going to stay and talk in the bar after I left, but suddenly Stu announced it was too noisy and he wanted to go back to the Forest Inn. They both got their cars – identical silver rentals – and someone tried to run me down in the parking lot. I barely escaped by jumping on a car trunk.'

'Who was driving the car that nearly hit you?' Monty asked. 'Will or Stu?'

'I don't know. I didn't see the driver.' Now I was feeling foolish.

'Did you file a police report?' Monty asked.

'Yes, definitely. The car that saved me was damaged.'

'So we have nothing,' Katie said. 'Just a lot of suspicion.'

'There's still the limo,' I said. 'It's our only hope. If we find the bottle in it, we'll have solid evidence. Has the limo been released back to the company?'

'Not yet,' Monty said. 'The police impounded it and they still have it. We can have it searched, but if the police didn't find the bottle the first time, why would they find it now?'

'Who searched it?'

'Nitpicker Byrne.'

'Oh. She's the best.' I felt worse. The evidence against both Stu and Will had vanished and Mario would be trapped in jail. He'd lose his freedom, his beloved salon – and maybe his life.

'I'll ask the police if we can examine the limo again under their supervision,' Monty said, 'first thing in the morning.'

'It is morning,' Katie said.

'When their offices open,' he said. 'Thank you, Angela, for bringing this now. I have time to prepare my argument.'

'Are you working today, Angela?' Katie asked.

I had a big mouthful of that luscious pecan coffee cake, and felt like an idiot while they both watched me chew. Finally I said, 'I'm not on call today.'

'Then you can stay here with Monty. I have to go to work. I'm going back to bed for a few hours of shut-eye. If you want, you can sleep in the guest room. The sheets are clean.'

With that, Katie left us. 'I'm going to study this,' Monty said, patting my iPad with the video. 'You go get some sleep. Good work, Angela. We'll free Mario yet.'

'What's the evidence against him?'

'It's very slim: He was in the limo and he had drugs in his styling case, even though those drugs didn't contribute to Jessica's death. There's the empty bottle of vanilla vape juice – the same flavor that poisoned Jessica – but the bottle has been wiped clean. Also, he has a criminal record.'

I was stunned. 'He does?'

'Yes, in Cuba. He was part of the Mariel Boatlift, remember? That's when Castro was throwing out the trash – that was his attitude toward the refugees. He opened the jails and told people he considered "undesirables" that they could leave the island. People grabbed anything that floated and headed for the US. Mario's crime was that he was gay.'

'That's a crime?'

'In Cuba, it was. He could have been killed.'

'Horrible. But it doesn't count here, does it? It's not illegal to be gay in the US.'

'He should be OK. If they try to use it against him, I'll get it thrown out.'

Should, could, may – those terms were not reassuring. But there was nothing I could do right now.

I glanced at the Kit-Cat clock on the kitchen wall – two-thirty. 'I'll get a couple of hours' sleep,' I said. 'See you about eight.'

Katie's guest room was upstairs at the end of the hall, a narrow room with a sloping ceiling. The pale blue walls and patchwork quilt were soothing, but I couldn't sleep. I tossed and turned and . . . and woke up with the sun in my eyes. What time was it? The little alarm clock by the bed said 9:32. I put on my clothes, stumbled out of bed to the bathroom down the hall, where I washed my face, combed my hair, and brushed my teeth with an extra toothbrush Katie had thoughtfully left for me. By the time I walked downstairs, I was almost awake.

Monty was sitting at the kitchen table, a nearly empty coffee cup by his laptop. He was dressed for the office in a fresh blue shirt and gray suit, his jacket on the chair back. He was running his fingers through his thick brown hair, a sure sign he was worried.

'What happened?' I asked.

'The cops refused my request for a second search,' he said. 'I'm filing a two-part emergency petition with the court asking that the limo be first, preserved, and second, that the cops be ordered to allow us, as the defense, to examine the limo.'

'Will you do the search yourself?'

'I've lined up Duncan to do it, and I'm lucky he's available on short notice.'

I knew Duncan da Silva was a PI Monty sometimes hired. I wished I could do the search, but it wasn't a good idea to be seen working this case at the cop shop. Greiman would haul me in on charges of interfering with an investigation.

'I'm faxing the petition now,' Monty said. 'We should hear back in about an hour. Come have coffee. Katie has eggs if you want. Help yourself.'

I was too nervous to eat. I sipped coffee and picked the pecans off a piece of coffee cake while Monty talked on the phone to his office manager, the ever-efficient Jinny Gender. He issued orders and suggestions while he ran his fingers through his hair, making it wilder at each pass.

I paced the kitchen until Monty begged me to stop. Then I sat in a kitchen chair and fidgeted for another fifteen minutes until his computer pinged. He read the message and quit tormenting his hair. He even smiled as he said, 'Well, well, the judge granted our request. The examination has to be videoed, which is fine with me. Duncan has to consent to a search to refute any claim that he planted any evidence, but he'll do that.'

'When is he going to do the search?'

'As soon as I call him, which is right now. This search will take another hour or so. Do you want to wait?'

Of course I did. My life was on hold until I knew if we could prove Mario's innocence. This time, I went for a walk down the country road, admiring the trees and flowers that were starting to bud into life. This happened often during a stretch of unseasonably warm weather – the springlike temperatures would bring out the trees and flowers, and then an unexpected ice storm would turn the display into dead brown mush. I hoped it wouldn't happen this year.

I felt better after the walk, and went back to the kitchen to whip up some eggs. Monty didn't want any food, but two scrambled eggs settled my stomach. I'd finished cleaning up when the call came from Duncan.

The disappointment in Monty's voice told me all I wanted to know. 'You searched everywhere and found what? A locket?' he said. There was a long pause, then, 'It's inscribed "To my darling Tawnee" and has a photo of a woman with an old-fashioned hairdo. Send it to me, will you? I have an idea who that belongs to. Nothing else? I guess that's it. OK, thanks for trying. Send me a bill.'

He rang off and said, 'You heard that?'

I nodded. I was too upset to speak.

'This is just a small setback,' Monty said. 'We'll get Mario out.'

I didn't share his confidence. I managed a nod, but something about Mario's video nagged at me. I opened my iPad and looked at the video again, studying Mario's sweep of the interior, before Jessica's death: the long leather seat, the bar crystal glittering like diamonds, the huge TV and the sound system. Why did that remind me of something? It niggled in my mind. Maybe if I saw the limo in person, it would jar the memory loose.

'Where's the limo now?' I asked.

'It's being towed to the limo company, even as we speak. They want to start the repairs so they can rent it again.'

'What if we looked at it at the limo company?' I asked. 'Could we search it there? Could I search it there?'

'I can call – but why?'

'I have an idea. I'll know it when I see it. Call Duncan. He can meet us there. And tell him to bring his camcorder.'

Monty looked puzzled, but he humored me. He made a couple of calls and said, 'The limo company agreed, if we go now. Duncan will meet us there. I'll let you take a look inside. See if anything jogs your memory. Then Duncan can go in and search. I can't be on tape and neither can you.

'I hope you know what you're doing, Angela,' he said. 'I've called Harper Jackson, the Chouteau County prosecutor, to be there, in case we find something. Harper will preserve the chain of custody. I had to call in a major favor to get him there.'

Harper Jackson, known to his (many) enemies as Harper Jackass, was a by-the-book type. Whatever I thought of him – which wasn't much – he wouldn't tolerate any slipshod behavior.

The limo company was near the St Louis airport, and huge passenger planes roared overhead. Duncan was waiting for us near the entrance. The PI was almost scarily anonymous. A round face with not a single distinguishing feature, brownish – or was it blond? – hair, average height. He could blend into almost any crowd.

Harper Jackson showed up in a dark gray three-piece suit. The prosecutor was skinny as a fence post and had about as much personality, but we needed him. I knew there would be law and order when Jackson was there.

The limo was parked in the back of the lot. It had lost its shine and was spattered with white bird lime. We were escorted by Earl, a skinny guy with jailhouse tats who cleaned the limos. He stayed well away from Jackson, as if he expected the prosecuting attorney to nab him.

'Glad it's you and not me going into that thing again,' Earl said. 'I'm lucky I don't have to clean it.'

'Better wear a mask, Angela,' Duncan said.

I don't wear masks, smear Vicks under my nose, or use anything to block even the worst decomposition odors. After the first few wretched breaths, my nose shorted out and I didn't smell anything. Like when you go to a movie theater – at first all you smell is the popcorn. Then you don't notice it. Well, sort of.

I didn't say anything to Duncan, but the PI was going back inside that limo. He had to officially find that bottle. As soon as my memory was jogged and I figured out where the spray bottle was.

I gloved up, and Earl opened the driver's door with a flourish. I sat in the driver's seat and surveyed the chaos behind me. The stink was horrific – vomit and feces had simmered in the hot sun. The interior was a shambles: Long slashes of vomit on the leather seats and carpet, the shattered TV screen, tiny flecks of a broken crystal glass on the floor, after the police had removed the broken glass. I tried to ignore the horrors and concentrate. What did this remind me of?

I stared at the long back seat, and remembered the driver playing the haunting music of Johnny Grimes, Jessica's long-lost lover. Gossip said he'd died a rock god's death, collapsing in a fog of alcohol and drugs. Pain pills. That was it! Where had I seen pain pills recently? At Tom Murphy's bloody death scene. His wife, Tara, had showed us where he'd supposedly hidden them.

'The speaker!' I cried. 'It's in the speaker in the far corner of the limo!'

I emerged gratefully into the fresh air. Monty said, 'Duncan, you have to search the speaker at the end of the seat. Pop the speaker's cover and see if the bottle is in there.'

'Me?' Duncan did not look happy.

'I can't do it and neither can Angela. I'll ask Jackson to pat you down and then Earl will tape you finding it.'

'Whoa,' Earl said. 'That's not my job.'

I found my purse, pulled out a twenty and put it on his palm. Earl looked at it like it was a used Kleenex. Monty added another twenty. Earl brightened slightly. Two more twenties, and we had ourselves a videographer.

Monty pulled Duncan aside and said, 'I need you to make another search.'

'It's foul in there,' Duncan said.

'I know. There will be a bonus. If you go right to the speaker and find the evidence, it might raise questions. Search the limo thoroughly.'

Earl was ready to begin. Duncan pulled his pants' pockets inside out to show there was nothing in them, and Harper Jackson briskly patted him down while Earl videoed them.

Finally, Duncan put on a face mask and a pair of latex gloves, and crawled into the back of the limo. He searched the seats, checked the carpet, and looked in the now-empty bar. Finally, he popped the speaker top with a house key. Nestled inside was a blue plastic spray bottle.

'You're a genius!' Monty said. He warned Duncan to handle the bottle carefully. The camera rolled while they gingerly put the bottle in a plastic evidence bag and Jackson watched.

'I'll take this bottle and have it printed,' Jackson said.

'Better hurry,' I said. 'It's noon – and Will and Stu leave at six tonight for California.'

'They won't get away,' Monty promised.

But they had so far.

THIRTY

Mario wasn't freed by breakfast – or lunch, for that matter. Monty and Harper Jackson decided to wait until the prosecuting attorney had the fingerprints on the spray bottle. 'I'll take custody of it,' Jackson said. 'That way, the chain of custody is secure.'

Monty made sure the prosecuting attorney had access to Mario's prints and we waited tensely for the verdict. Was the solution inside the bottle harmless, or did it contain deadly nicotine? Were there any prints? If so, who did they belong to? Was Stu or Will the killer?

The spray bottle was ready at two-fifteen, which was amazingly fast. But the prosecuting attorney wanted this case out of his hair – and a hair turned out to be an important find. He announced that he'd found a short piece of hair wound around the cap.

'We found a two-inch red hair on the inside of the cap,' he said.

'That means it's Will,' I said.

Both men ignored me. Jackson continued, 'We're having the hair tested for DNA. The solution in the bottle contains a lethal amount of nicotine. We also found a fingerprint inside the bottle, as if someone had grasped the open bottle by the top. The prints are not Mario Garcia's.' Monty and I cheered.

'The three sets of prints belong to Ms Gray and Ms Tawnee Simms, which would be consistent with Ms Simms' account. The third set belongs to Mr William London.'

Definitely Will! So the red bottle had held a harmless throat spray. The lethal mixture was in the blue one. Now Becky's jingle made sense: *It's not the red – it's the blue.*

The two of them went straight to see Detective Ray Greiman at the Chouteau County Police Department. I tagged along in my car, inventing an excuse to be at the cop shop. I stayed well in the background.

As they entered, Monty looked cool and ready for a fight – his blue shirt was crisp and his gray suit unwrinkled. Jackson's suit pants had knife-edge creases.

Greiman met the two men in the lobby, angry and defensive. His black Hugo Boss shirt and pants could have used a pressing. I knew he was rattled before Monty even said a word.

'You've arrested the wrong man for Jessica Gray's murder,' Monty said.

The detective sputtered like an old car. 'That faggot hairdresser killed Ms Gray.' Greiman crossed his arms over his chest, prepared to stonewall.

'Then why aren't his prints on the murder weapon?' Jackson asked. 'And what's someone else's hair doing on the bottle? Red hair, I should add.'

He showed Greiman the bagged, tagged and fingerprinted bottle and Monty gave him a private viewing of the limo video. Greiman still hesitated, and Jackson threatened to take the case away. He knew that Greiman was territorial and the murder of Jessica Gray, an international celebrity, was a once-in-lifetime prize.

That's when Officer Christopher Ferretti, Chouteau County's new hire, burst into the CHPD and announced, 'I found an abandoned rental car registered to Will London of Los Angeles.'

'That's Jessica's make-up artist,' Monty said. I edged myself around the corner of the waiting room for a better view. Will was looking more like our killer every minute.

'A rental car under his name was left in a ditch a quarter-mile from the Forest Inn,' Ferretti said.

'Then Will could have dumped the car and walked to the Forest Inn,' Monty said.

'Staggered, is more like it,' Officer Ferretti said, 'if he was as drunk as the witnesses say.'

'Was that the car in the parking lot collision?' Monty asked.

'Looks like it,' Ferretti said, then slipped into officialese. 'The 2018 silver Chevy Malibu appeared to have been in a collision before it was abandoned. I photographed the vehicle and determined that the damaged front end had traces of gold paint on it. That's when I called CSI's Sarah Byrne to see if the gold paint was a match for Mrs Holly Barteau's 1997 Mercury, which was damaged in the Solange parking lot by a hit-and-run driver.'

'What about Stu Milano's car?' Monty asked.

'It was in the Forest Inn's lot. The security cameras showed he arrived back at the inn at 7:41 p.m. last night, and the car wasn't removed until 8:15 this morning.'

'I bet that's when he went to Jessica's nine o'clock cremation service,' I said.

'I haven't confirmed that yet,' Ferretti said. 'But Tawnee Simms and Will London drove off with him in the car.'

Ferretti's cell phone rang – it was Nitpicker, confirming that the paint on Will's abandoned car was from Holly Barteau's beloved bashed Mercury.

'We've got the hit-and-run driver,' the young officer said. 'It's Will London.'

'He's staying at the Forest Inn,' Monty said. 'Better arrest him now, before he leaves for the airport. He's flying home to California at six tonight.'

'I'm on my way to the inn now,' the officer said.

Ferretti nabbed Will while the make-up artist was waiting at the inn for his Uber ride to the airport. Will tried to claim that his silver rental car had been stolen and he was too shaken (i.e., drunk) to call the police, but there was no evidence to support that. Only Will's prints were found in and on the abandoned Chevy, and he still had the keys in his pocket. The car had not been tampered with.

Ferretti brought Will back to the station with his hands cuffed behind his back – the most uncomfortable position. Will could have used his own cosmetic artistry – his eyes were bloodshot, his red hair was flat and greasy, and his skin had a greenish-gray tinge. He must have had the mother of all hangovers.

Ferretti charged Will with everything he could think of, including leaving the scene of an accident and a hit-and-run with property damage. Ferretti saw me in the waiting room and said, 'I can press charges for attempted vehicular homicide.'

'Do you have enough to hold Will until he can be arrested for Jessica's murder?' I asked.

'You bet,' Ferretti said. I liked his enthusiasm.

'I can't swear I saw Will behind the wheel last night, and I'm afraid my scabbed knee won't impress a jury.'

By now, I'd figured out that the crafty Detective Greiman knew which way the wind was blowing. I could see he was eager to nail Will for Jessica's murder. He knew it was a good career move. If Greiman could prove the beloved celebrity wasn't killed by a local – even a Cuban-American transplant – but an outsider from Los Angeles, the Forest's shame would be erased. Mario's arrest would be quickly forgotten.

Ferretti let Monty, Jackson, and me into the observation room connected to the interrogation room. Through the mirror, I watched Greiman grilling Will relentlessly. When he showed him the video with the switched spray bottles, Will looked like an animated corpse. The final touch was the bagged and tagged blue spray bottle, retrieved from the limo, and the red hair. The detective told Will that his finger-prints were on the bottle and there was a lethal amount of doctored spray in it.

Will barely managed to say: 'I want a lawyer. A real one from LA.' He endeared himself to all of us by saying, 'I don't want some local hick.' It must have cost Will a fortune to fly defense attorney Ethan Heller to Missouri first class from Los Angeles.

The hit-and-run charges were enough to keep Will in jail overnight. Ethan Heller arrived at six the next morning, after a night on the red-eye flight from LAX, and once again, I got to observe Will's questioning. The high-powered attorney showed up at the Chouteau County jail. His suit was as shiny as a mobster's, and his hair was gelled. Ethan was one slick lawyer. He looked around at his surroundings as if a tornado had dropped him in a pigsty.

During Greiman's grilling that morning, Ethan constantly cautioned his client with, 'Don't answer that!'

Will obeyed. Except one time. When Greiman asked if Will had murdered Rebecca Barens – Becky, the homeless woman – the make-up artist blurted, 'I didn't shoot her!'

Where did he get that idea? Becky wasn't shot – she was strangled. The news of her death had been buried in the local papers, and never made the TV news. Maybe, since he was from LA, he assumed all murders were shootings. That outburst helped convince me that Will didn't kill Becky, even though her death would be convenient for him. In my experience, people under pressure gave themselves away in little blurts like that.

Will's expensive attorney was no more effective than a local yokel. The make-up artist was arrested and charged with the first-degree murder of Jessica Gray, and the Forest still wanted the death penalty.

Later, Detective Greiman would be commended for the arrest.

Mario was freed by dinnertime on the second day. Monty got the drug charges dropped in exchange for Mario's promise not to sue for false arrest.

Monty and I met Mario at the jail. Mario came running out. He was thin as a scarecrow, and his black eye was now an evil yellow-green. His dark clothes hung on him. Mario threw his arms around me and kissed me, then said, 'Your hair is a disaster.'

'All the good stylists were in jail,' I said.

He demanded a brush and comb. I forced myself to sit patiently in the backseat of Monty's car while Mario fixed my hair. I knew it made him happy.

'Where can we take you, Mario?' Monty asked. 'Would you like dinner? Do you want to go home?'

'I want to go home and take a long, hot shower,' Mario said. 'Tomorrow I want to check on my salon. Thank you, thank you, my friends.' His voice was husky with emotion. 'When this settles down, I will hold a big party at my salon to celebrate.'

We promised to be there.

After Monty dropped Mario off at his home, he said, 'Good work, Angela. I'm going home.'

'You did the real work,' I said.

On the drive home, I felt strangely empty after my so-called triumph. At home, I was too lazy to fix real food. I scrambled a couple of eggs, warmed up some frozen banana bread and made coffee. I slathered the banana bread with butter, poured more coffee and sat down to think.

Who killed Becky?

Will had the best reason, but I believed his blurted denial. At least, I thought I did. Stu and Tawnee had no reason I could think of, now that Will was arrested for Jessica's murder.

I'd admired Becky for her toughness. The theater crowd at the Lux had laughed at her, but she didn't run off the stage. Becky had been bribed and bullied into taking off most of her clothes in front of the audience. Finally, she was shivering with cold and fear on-stage, down to her grimy gray circle-stitch bra and granny panties. Her glittering gold G – her lucky piece – was on a ribbon around her neck. Becky said she never took that necklace off.

Even though she had been humiliated at the Lux, Becky refused to back down to old Reggie Du Pres when she showed up at his house. She wasn't going to be hidden in the pool house like Suzy, with promises of a bath and a nap. Becky stalked into his mansion and sat at a table, dirty and defiant. She had guts. That night, she told me she was determined to turn her life around. And she did – for the short time she had left.

I also remembered finding her body – and the two crisp one-hundred-dollar bills she'd squirreled away under her mattress. Will admitted he'd given her five hundred-dollar bills because he feared the backlash from the #MeToo movement. And yes, he'd written the Beverly Hills phone number on one of them. When I confronted Will at Solange, he'd tried to run me down later in the parking lot.

My last view of Becky flashed in my mind, and I tried to push it away. I'd seen her on the floor of her hotel room in a pink wool pantsuit. Her arms were flung out, and a pink-and-blue flowered scarf was tied tightly around her neck.

She'd been strangled by the scarf. I saw the blood-streaked wounds, where she'd clawed her own neck in a hopeless attempt to stop the strangulation. When she'd lived on the streets, Becky told me she'd been raped. There was no way she'd admit strangers to her room. She was killed by someone she knew. And her killer had taken a souvenir. I was sure something was missing from her body.

Maybe the answer was in her autopsy report.

I carefully read the list of the clothes Becky had worn: 'one pair pink wool pants, one three-button pink wool suit jacket, one pink-and-blue-flowered blouse, all with Ellen Tracy labels.' The flowered scarf was by Calvin Klein. She'd ditched her ugly underwear for a Victoria's Secret white lace bra and matching panties.

The report said she'd been strangled with her flowered scarf. The U-shaped hyoid bone in her neck was broken.

Neck. Wait! Now I knew what was missing. Where was her lucky charm, the sparkly rhinestone G? Becky said she never took it off. Did her killer steal it? Why?

It wasn't anywhere in the inventory of the room, either. Neither was the money. Crooked cops were known to help themselves to cash at a crime scene, but I'd watched these officers during the investigation. They were professionals. They wouldn't take anything. I'd searched the scene, then left it for about ten minutes, when I ran downstairs to the front desk and waited for the police. I couldn't bear to be alone in that room any more with Becky's body.

Maybe Suzy knew if someone had been preying on homeless people around the Lux. I'd visit her again at the Hoffstedder.

I was surprised that toothless Suzy had become an entrepreneur, trading her bottle of Rosie O'Grady for bottled water. Better yet, she was doing so well peddling water to the rush-hour crowd that she'd moved into a fifth-floor suite.

About nine that morning, I bought a gooey butter coffee cake at the Chouteau Forest Bakery. Gooey butter was a local specialty that lived up to its name – one small coffee cake had at least a stick of butter and a whole box of confectioners' sugar. It should be easy for Suzy to eat.

It was nearly ten o'clock by the time I knocked on the door of her suite. Once again, Suzy was well-dressed. She wore a blue pantsuit with a pink-and-blue checked scarf.

She greeted me with a toothless smile. I admired the newest improvements she'd made to her hotel suite. 'Beautiful orchid on your coffee table.'

'Thank you. I've never had a live plant before.' Her pride was childlike.

On the dinette table, a delicate glass-covered cake stand protected half a chocolate cake. I'd guessed right that she loved sweets.

Suzy spotted my bakery box and said, 'Oh, you brought me something from the fancy bakery.'

Opening the box, she said, 'Gooey butter! My favorite! I have coffee made. Have some cake with me.'

I was hoping she'd say that.

I sat at the white metal dinette set with the two basket chairs, while Suzy buzzed around, playing hostess. She served us two generous pieces of cake on new blue plates, and poured coffee into matching mugs. She took the chair closest to the wall, and sat down to enjoy her treat. As Suzy spooned sugar into her coffee she said, 'Now that I'm going to the AA meetings, I live on coffee.'

She ate her cake in small, precise bites while she talked about her water-selling business – 'One man gave me five dollars and told me to keep the change.'

I mentally added up the price of the suite's improvements, including the new bedspread, the new rug, the dishes, books and flowers. She had to be spending more than she could possibly make – even if everyone gave her four-dollar tips. She must have had a stake to start redecorating this room. As I calculated the price of these luxuries, I thought of the two crisp bills stashed under Becky's mattress. I also recognized the blue-and-pink checked scarf that Suzy had on. Becky had worn one like it at the hospital.

It was time to end the pleasant chitchat. 'Do you know if there's going to be a funeral for Becky?'

'Uh, I don't know.' Suzy looked uncomfortable. Her eyes shifted away from me. 'That would depend on whether her ex-husband claims her body. She doesn't have anyone else.' Suzy pulled at her scarf, as if it were choking her. It slid off and I saw the ribbon around her neck. Suzy was wearing Becky's sparkly G.

'Where did you get Becky's necklace?'

Suzy looked frightened. 'I don't know what you're talking

about,' she said, scooting back in her seat. She tried to get up, but I pushed the dinette set against the wall, trapping her. Coffee slopped out of her mug and Suzy mopped it absently with her scarf.

'My scarf!' she said. 'Look what you made me do!'

'That isn't your scarf, Suzy. You stole it from Becky. Just like you took her necklace.'

'She gave it to me!'

'No, she'd never do that. She told me she never took it off. It was her lucky piece.'

'She changed her mind.'

'Why did you kill her, Suzy? She was your friend. You stole her money, too.'

'She didn't need it anymore,' Suzy said.

'Then you did kill her.'

Suzy pushed at the table, but I pushed harder. The table tipped and the cake holder slid to the floor with a crash.

Suzy wailed as it smashed to pieces. 'You broke it! You broke it!' She crouched over the remains, rocking back and forth in grief.

'You killed your friend.'

'She wouldn't share,' Suzy said. 'When she got all that money, I asked if I could sleep in her room, and she said no, she wanted to be alone. I asked for enough money for one night. One lousy night out of the cold. She still said no. She laughed at me. It was bad enough when all those people laughed at me at the theater, but when Becky did it, I'd had enough. I grabbed the ends of her designer scarf and . . .'

With that, Suzy stood up, a long dagger of glass in her hand, and swiped it at me. I ducked, picked up a chair, and pinned her against the wall with the legs. Suzy screamed and struggled. A lamp shattered. I was having a hard time holding her there when I heard pounding on the door.

'What's going on in there?' a man's voice demanded.

'Help!' I cried. 'Call the police. I've caught a killer.'

THIRTY-ONE

When the city detectives hustled Suzy out of her suite, she wailed like a mother ripped from her child. Fat tears fell like raindrops, spattering her new carpet, and Suzy couldn't wipe them away. Her hands were cuffed.

Was Suzy crying for her lost friend or her lost luxury? I didn't know, but I suspected those tears were for her new suite-life.

I stayed there several hours longer, downplaying my part in this drama, claiming it was an accident that I asked Suzy about Becky's funeral. 'I thought they were old friends,' I said. 'I had no idea it would trigger such a backlash.'

I made sure the homicide detectives gave themselves credit for finding Becky's killer. 'It must be difficult to solve the murder of a woman who until recently was homeless,' I said. They agreed, and happily claimed the shopworn glory for this arrest.

The detectives, meanwhile, found things in Suzy's suite that connected her to Becky. In addition to Becky's checked scarf, Suzy had also helped herself to Becky's blue Crocs, though she didn't wipe off the coffee stain. The Crocs would be tested for Becky's DNA. They also found a crisp hundred-dollar bill hidden in the medicine cabinet. It turned out to have Becky's fingerprints on it. I told them Suzy may have spent the other stolen hundreds on her new luxuries.

If Suzy got a good lawyer, he could argue that Becky had given her those things, but I suspected she'd wind up with an overworked court-appointed attorney.

After about three hours, I signed a statement that was mostly true, and fled back to the Forest, where I went to see my old friend, Katie, at SOS. It was four o'clock and her day was nearly done. She greeted me with, 'You look like recycled shit,' and I instantly felt better.

'I found Becky's killer,' I said, perching on the edge of her desk. 'She tried to kill me.'

'You always know how to grab my attention,' Katie said. 'Let me ditch this lab coat and we can get some coffee at the hospital's new café. Their coffee is several cuts above the dishwater they serve in the cafeteria.'

The To Your Health café was in an alcove that was the former staff smoking lounge. SOS had been declared a smoke-free campus, and the smokers had to sneak into the dumpster enclosures now, where they risked their lives even further for a cigarette.

The hospital café was made to resemble a French sidewalk café with metal bistro chairs and small marble-top tables. Most of the tables were taken by doctors in surgical scrubs, but Katie found a table near the cash register.

She bought two coffees and two pain au chocolat. The buttery chocolate croissants were just what I needed, and the coffee was strong as an amazon. The sugar and caffeine revived me and I told Katie the whole story. 'It was so touching when Suzy told me she'd never had a "real plant" before.'

'And how touching was it when she strangled Becky?' Katie said, fury in her eyes. 'It took at least two or three minutes for that woman to die. That's an eternity. Becky was ripping at her own neck with her nails, trying to breathe. Strangling is a long, ugly death.'

'Personally, I blame Jessica Gray for Becky's murder,' I said.

'Hard to do. She was dead, sliced and diced by then,' Katie said, sipping her coffee.

I took another bite of my croissant. 'But her brutality lived on,' I said. 'I watched what she did to those homeless women on-stage, to my everlasting shame. I should have walked out. They were totally exposed up there – naked in front of that fat, fed audience. All three women were humiliated, and in Suzy's case, the experience unhinged her.'

'What about the other one, with the grocery cart?' Katie said.

'Denise. That poor woman was already over the edge, so it's hard to measure the damage Jessica did to her. But Suzy struck me as more fragile than Becky, and she'd been easily bullied by Jessica and Reggie Du Pres. Suzy felt entitled to some of Becky's money after what she suffered. When Becky refused to give it to her, Suzy snapped and killed her.'

'Maybe,' Katie said. 'But don't forget that Becky was denied her second chance at a new life, thanks to Suzy.' Katie finished her croissant and delicately patted her lips with a paper napkin. 'Well, Jessica is answering for her evil deeds now, wherever she is.'

'Some place hot,' I said, 'and I'm not talking about Florida.'

From there, the conversation shifted to Monty and his slick move to free Mario. Katie was always happy to praise her lover, and so was I.

We ended our conversation on a serious note. 'Now listen here, Angela,' Katie said. 'You got lucky this time. Greiman's been so busy taking credit for arresting Jessica's killer that he didn't complain about you interfering with his case. But you're not always going to have that luck.'

'I know that,' I said, using my fork to scrape up the last smears of chocolate on my plate.

'Promise me you won't do it again,' Katie said.

'I promise I won't try to solve any more murders,' I said, and solemnly raised my right hand.

I did have one more mystery to solve. It didn't involve murder. In the Forest, it was a fate far worse than that.

THIRTY-TWO

Clare Rappaport still blamed her children for trying to kill her. She was determined to disinherit them. I had to stop this. Not for the kids' sake – I was barely a blip on their radar – but for Clare's. She needed her family. Most of all, she needed to know that her son and daughter hadn't tried to poison her. My last task was to prove Trey and Jemima were innocent: I knew they wouldn't give their hyper-allergic mother a killer cake laced with peanuts. Now I had to prove it.

The lab report on the cake was in my email. Translated into plain English, the test results showed no poisons, and no whole or chopped peanuts in the Bavarian cream cake. However, the tests did find 'peanut particles about the size of a grain of sand and microscopic traces' of peanuts in the cake.

I still had the pink cake box from the Chouteau Forest Bakery. The label described the contents as a 'Bavarian whipped cream 8-layer cake.' The store's slogan, in curly white script, proclaimed the bakery as 'The Sweetest Place in the Forest.' The cake's ingredients were listed, and I read them all. No nuts. And no label warning that the cake was 'made in a facility that processes peanuts, ground nuts and tree nuts.'

Clare said she couldn't even ride on a plane where people had been eating peanuts without risking an allergic attack. Maybe the problem had started at the Chouteau Bakery.

I remembered Katie's warning: 'Don't get involved with this fight to disinherit her kids. It's the law of the third dog. You don't want to come between a mother and her children.'

But what if I wanted to bring the family together? I was willing to risk a few barks and nips if I could help reunite Clare with her children. I had no interest in Clare's money and didn't belong to her social circle. She'd been kind to my mother when Mom was dying and I was grateful for that.

Mom had worked for Reggie Du Pres for years, but when she was diagnosed with breast cancer, the old man acted as if cancer was catching. He'd docked her pay on those days when chemo left her too weak to work. Many a morning, Mom dragged herself to his house, nearly too sick to stand up.

On the morning after Mario was freed, I finished my toast and coffee about ten o'clock and drove to the Chouteau Forest Bakery. The weather was starting to turn cold again – low, dirty-gray clouds frowned over the Forest – and I wore a winter coat for the first time in days.

The bakery's green-and-white striped awnings – Forest green, of course – were a local landmark. In the big plate-glass window, fancy iced cakes were displayed on silver stands like fine jewelry, and cost almost as much.

I saw signs celebrating Valentine's Day, and tried to avoid them. Now that my husband Donegan was dead, I couldn't bear the holiday. I averted my eyes. The brass bell on the door jingled cheerily, announcing my entrance. I inhaled the sweet scents of sugar and butter.

Amy, a fresh-faced young woman in a pink uniform, was behind the sparkling counter. She greeted me cheerfully, and looked concerned when I told her what had happened to Clare. 'I'm so sorry Mrs Rappaport had a problem. She's a nice lady and a good customer. But we never put peanuts in our Bavarian cream cake. That cake has no nuts in it at all.'

'Do you still have her order?' I asked.

'We should have it in the back. The slips aren't processed until the end of the month.'

Thank goodness the bakery hadn't entered the computer age. Amy disappeared into the back room and came back several minutes later with a handwritten order to show me. 'See,' she said. 'This notation means that her daughter, Jemima, called in the order and this one means that her son, Trey, picked up the cake and paid for it in cash.'

'The order says, "NO PEANUTS" – underlined three times,' Amy said. 'Jemima was very worried about peanuts. I told Jemima what I told you, we don't put nuts in our Bavarian cream cakes. Never ever.'

'But there were traces of peanuts in it,' I said. 'Enough to send Mrs Rappaport to the ER. And I have a lab report that proves it.'

'I don't know how that happened.' Amy looked distressed.

The shop doorbell jingled again and another customer came in, a Forest lady in a navy boiled wool coat with brass buttons. She asked, 'Do you have any more of that peanut butter cheesecake? My husband loves it.'

'Oh, yes, Mrs Sullivan,' Amy said. 'It's made right here on the premises.'

I pricked up my ears. Peanut butter cheesecake. Made right here at the shop. That's where the peanut traces could have come from.

'Sixty-five dollars is a good price for a whole cheesecake,' Mrs Sullivan said, as Amy boxed up the cake.

'It's our peanut lovers' special this month,' Amy said. 'We also have peanut chocolate chip cookies, chocolate-peanut butter pie, and our bittersweet chocolate peanut butter cups. Those are my favorites. They're all made right here.'

Now I saw a flyer by the cash register, sprinkled with red hearts and pink flowers: 'February is for lovers!' it said. 'Peanut lovers! Treat your true love to peanut chocolate chip cookies. Chocolate-peanut butter pie. Bittersweet peanut butter cups. We promise the pea-nuttiest treats ever!'

At the very bottom the flyer said, 'Proudly baked in our shop for extra freshness!'

I thought of the standard warning label: 'made in a facility that uses peanuts, ground nuts and tree nuts' that appeared on so many baked goods.

The Forest Bakery didn't use it, but they did produce peanut desserts. Lots of them, made on the premises. That's how Clare Rappaport's cake picked up those near-fatal traces of peanuts. And she didn't get any warning.

Once Mrs Sullivan had paid for her cheesecake, Amy asked me, 'Is there anything else I can do for you, Angela?'

'May I have a copy of that cake receipt to show Mrs Rappaport? It would ease her mind.'

'Of course,' Amy said. She came back with a copy in about two minutes.

'Anything else I can help you with?' she asked.

'No, thanks,' I said. 'You've been a big help.' I took two peanut lovers' flyers and left.

Back in my car, I called Clare. She answered on the second ring. 'Angela,' she said, and I heard the wariness in her voice. 'Do you have news for me?'

'I do. Very good news. When may I come see you? Or would you rather see me at my place?'

Her wariness changed to pure pleasure. 'I'd love to talk to you as soon as possible. Could you come over in half an hour, if you're free? Cook just made the most delicious caramel-apple tart, and we should both enjoy it. We'll have some with tea.'

'Coffee for me,' I reminded her.

'Yes, of course.'

Thirty minutes later, I was in Clare's morning room, a sunny alcove that looked out on the south lawn. Clare – or her housekeeper – had prepared a handsome round table with a snowy, perfectly ironed linen cloth, two lace trimmed napkins, and as a centerpiece, a round apple tart, drizzled with caramel. The table was set with Sèvres china.

Clare fit perfectly into this comfortable domestic scene: Her white hair was freshly coiffed, and she wore pearls and a pale blue twinset the same color as her eyes. There was no sign of her recent hospital battle. Clare greeted me with a warm smile and I sat across from her.

Millie, her housekeeper, served coffee for me, and English breakfast tea for Clare, then left both pots on the table. Clare cut us two generous slices of apple tart. My mouth was watering, but I held off tasting it until I gave Clare the news.

She took a big forkful of tart and I said, 'Your cake didn't have peanuts in it.'

'Really?' Her fork hovered in the air and she abandoned it on her plate.

'The Forest Bakery's Bavarian cream cake doesn't have peanuts,' I said, 'and Jemima made sure to tell them that you could not eat peanuts. In fact, it was underlined three times on the order. Look, see for yourself.' I presented her with the copy of the receipt.

Clare smiled as she read it. 'That sounds like my daughter. Jemima is thorough.'

'I also have the lab report right here.' I put a copy on the table, and told her what it said.

'There were trace amounts,' Clare said. 'That's enough to cause anaphylactic shock in someone like me.'

She looked confused. 'So how did traces of peanuts get into my cake?'

'I'm guessing this caused it,' I said, and gave her the bakery flyer promising the 'pea-nuttiest treats ever!'

'Those are all made at the shop,' I said. 'That's what Amy the salesclerk told me and it's also on the flyer.' I showed her the line at the bottom that said, 'Proudly baked in our shop for extra freshness!'

'Proudly baked!' Clare said. 'Stupidly baked, without a hint of warning. I almost died because of their carelessness. They have no idea the damage they did to my health and my family!'

Clare looked misty-eyed now. 'My children! I've been so angry at them I've been avoiding their calls.'

I remembered when she was going to declare Trey and Jemima guilty of attempted murder, without an investigation. A hardness lurked in the heart of the Forest. Clare's children would never know how close they came to being disinherited, and losing all that lovely money. Their mother wouldn't take their calls for three days.

Now she said, 'I'm going to call them right this instant.' Tears were running down her face.

'I'll go then, Clare.' I wanted to give her privacy, and I thought I might gag at this sudden show of maternal affection.

'Absolutely not. You finish your coffee and apple tart. I'll be back shortly.'

Clare left the room to make her calls, and I finished the coffee and the tart. The caramel-apple combination was luscious. I was wondering whether it would be polite to cut myself another piece when Clare returned, wearing a wide smile.

'Angela, dear, I'm so happy. You remember that I gave my children a test, telling them that I was having money problems? Well, when I talked with Jemima just now, she said I could move in with her and she'd give me the whole third floor of her home so I could have privacy. She even wants to install an elevator, so I won't have to deal with the stairs. She says my grandchildren would love having me live with them.'

Clare had somehow managed to polish off the whole slice of apple tart during that conversation, and she cut me another piece without my having to ask.

'And my son . . .' she was so overcome with emotion that she had to stop. 'My son said that the condo next to his was up for sale and he'd buy it for me.

'Both my children want me! I'm inviting them to dinner this weekend to celebrate and give them the good news.'

Charming. A real Hallmark moment. But what kind of mother 'tests' her children? I wondered. Had I idealized Clare because she'd been kind to my mother? Probably. Either way, my mission was nearly over. I would finish my apple tart and leave.

'Will you tell them what went wrong with their cream cake?' I asked.

'Yes,' she said. 'But only as a warning not to buy anything from the Chouteau Forest Bakery. And I'm also calling my attorney. The bakery should pay for my hospital bills, at the very least. There must be other people in the Forest with allergies. That place should learn. I could have died! That cake could have killed an innocent child with peanut allergics.'

Ah, now the weepy Clare had been replaced by a proper Forest reaction: Someone must pay – and she had a high-minded reason for her revenge. There would be money involved, of course. And it would go to her.

Clare and I finished our cake at a leisurely pace while she chatted about her grandchildren. She asked about my DI cases, but they were too grim to discuss over food. I did give her the inside gossip on Mario and Jessica Gray's murder. Now that he was free, I could talk about it.

'Blaming Mario for Miss Gray's death made no sense to me,' she said. 'He was so proud to be her hairstylist. I'm sure it was prejudice on the part of that police detective.'

I was, too. I thanked Clare for the apple tart and got ready to leave. Clare wrote me a check for the cost of the lab test and then tucked a check for five hundred dollars into my jacket pocket.

'Thank you, Clare, but I didn't do this for the money.'

'I know that,' she said. 'But everyone needs money. If you don't want it, give it to your favorite charity. I'll be insulted if you give it back.'

She sent me off with a hug and these words, 'Angela, your mother would be proud. You're just like her.'

I stepped out into the blustery day, warm and well-fed. Despite my feelings about Clare, those words meant more than the money.

THIRTY-THREE

Jessica Gray had arrived in the Forest with fanfare – luxury limos, splashy banners, police escorts, and hordes of reporters. She swanned around on-stage in sequins and glamorous gowns slit up to there. Everyone marveled at her timeless beauty.

No one noticed when Jessica left the Forest. Her ashes were sealed in a plain cardboard box. The Uber driver who picked up Stu and Tawnee for a trip to the airport had no idea the great Jessica Gray was in the footwell of his SUV.

Tawnee carried Jessica aboard the flight back to California, along with a turkey panini and her new purse. She deposited Jessica in the overhead bin, where the star spent the flight under a raincoat.

I wondered if Jessica had found peace in death. Was she once more young and beautiful, and spending eternity with her lover? Was she suffering the purifying fires of purgatory for all her petty acts, as the nuns had taught me? Or was she simply a pile of ashes and bone fragments in a cardboard box?

Whatever happened to her spirit, Jessica was finally free of the hated Forest, though their names would be linked in every article about her.

Monty returned Tawnee's locket to her. She said it was a gift from her mother and she must have dropped it when she was looking for Jessica's spray. I thought Stu palmed it as a petty punishment when she accused him of stealing the spray, but said nothing. Tawnee had agreed to be Stu's assistant while he settled Jessica's estate. The press had no interest in Jessica's widower, except for a brief mention that he was returning to California. Their stories implied there was something vaguely nasty in his relationship with Jessica.

The media was focused on Will, the make-up artist who had murdered Jessica, with stories like 'Oh, Artful Death.' Their interest was obsessive. Everyone wanted to know why he killed her. Missouri is a death penalty state, and uses lethal injections for its executions. Will was charged with murder one, and he'd heard the horror stories about botched executions. He knew about the Oklahoma inmate who took forty-three minutes to die, and it was a heart attack that finally killed him. And Ohio let an inmate gasp for death for an inhuman (and inhumane) twenty-six minutes.

Will was terrified of that gruesome ending – never mind that he'd condemned Jessica Gray to vomiting and spasming in the back of a black limousine. His delicate sensibilities couldn't bear the thought of his own death as an awful, long-drawn-out public spectacle.

So Ethan Heller, Will's LA lawyer, worked out a deal – life in prison without possibility of parole. Once the death penalty was out of the equation, Will talked. In fact he never shut up.

He said that Jessica Gray had promised to marry him and finance his line of cosmetics. When she was in the hospital, he accidentally found out that she had married Stu. Will confronted Jessica in her hospital bed, and she said, 'I saw you with that faggot hairstylist, and it wasn't the first time. Do you think I'd risk AIDS to marry you?'

'Then you won't finance my make-up line?' he'd asked her.

'Hell, no,' she said. 'Get one of your bum boys to fork over the cash for your schemes.'

She laughed at him. Will said it was a 'wicked, witchy laugh.'

Will brooded on her harsh words and broken promises until he decided to kill her. That night, when she was asleep, he stole both bottles of throat spray that Tawnee kept in her bag and poured vape juice into the blue one. Then he hid the fatal bottle and the harmless one in his make-up case. Will thought there was justice in that manner of death. After all, Jessica had decreed that her entourage give up cigarettes and vape.

Will said that Becky the homeless woman must have seen him make the switch. I knew she'd been lurking in the shadows at the hospital, waiting to steal from Jessica's sleeping staff. So did Will.

'Why didn't Becky say something?' people asked. 'She could have prevented Jessica's death. Maybe even gotten a reward.'

'Because she hated Jessica even more than I did,' Will said. 'She wanted her to die.'

Will hoped that Mario would be blamed for Jessica's death, but that didn't happen. He'd slipped the empty vape juice bottle into Mario's styling case at the hospital and was sure he'd get away with murder. But that didn't happen.

'Nothing worked out for me,' Will whined.

The Forest was relieved when Will's lawyer proposed that deal. (Between you and me, Will would have done better with a local attorney. Monty told me that the prosecuting attorney, Harper Jackson, was prepared to settle for a sentence of twenty years for Will.) A plea bargain meant there would be no publicity-packed trial. Will was quietly bundled off to prison, where he was quickly forgotten, except for an occasional 'What Ever Happened To?' feature.

There was also some interest in Becky's death, and much praise was given to the city police for 'solving a homeless person's murder.' Never mind that Becky was living in a hotel at the time of her death. She would forever be labeled 'homeless.'

In addition to dropping the charges for drug dealing, the Forest PD issued a formal apology to Mario. In return, Monty had agreed not to sue the PD for false arrest, and Mario vowed not to distribute drugs. I doubted he'd stop using, but I hoped he'd be more careful in the future.

After the national press departed and Forest life continued, Mario held a huge celebration at his shop – calling it his Grand Re-Opening – and invited all the Forest dwellers.

Monty and I were the guests of honor. Mario made sure I had the last appointment at his shop before it closed for the party – three o'clock. He did my hair and make-up 'as a gift to you, my friend.' He also presented me with a fabulous black Gucci pencil dress to 'make up for the one that was torn while you were fighting to save me.' And last – but certainly not least – he gave me new heels that could have been copies of the ones I'd lost running from Will's car.

'They're beautiful!' I said, and could think of no other words.

'Don't you dare cry,' Mario said, and smiled at me. 'You'll ruin your eye make-up.'

So I held off with the waterworks and thanked him. Mario said, 'You must honor me by wearing both my gifts tonight – the shoes and the dress.'

By that time, the florist had arrived, bringing in waterfalls of live orchid plants, and the caterer was starting to set up. I hurried home, and changed into my new cocktail dress. It fit like a glove, and the shoes worked, too. I knew they would.

Mario looked magnificent that night. His dark hair was long and lustrous, his body was lean in black with a Spanish silver belt and bracelet.

The catered food was probably the best ever served at a Forest party. There was something for every palate: mini filets mignon topped with blue cheese on crostini, chilled lobster rolls, and as a nod to his Cuban heritage, massive platters of arroz con pollo, ropa vieja (shredded beef in tomato sauce), and a giant avocado salad. Plus long loaves of warm Cuban bread, with lashings of salted butter. Desserts were cups of flan, cinnamon-and-sugar dusted crema frita (fried cream), apple pie, and chocolate cake.

And the wine! The servers poured wine and champagne as if they'd be fired for leaving a glass empty.

I saw almost all of the Forest regulars, except Detective Greiman, thank goodness. I met Monty and Katie at the party, and we sat together at a table near the DJ. Officer Christopher Ferretti was there, looking handsome in a dark blue suit.

He stopped by our table to say hello as the DJ played a Beatles' tune – 'Something.'

'Want to dance, Angela?' the officer asked, and blushed like a shy boy.

I hesitated for an instant and Katie hissed in my ear, 'It's a dance, not a date.'

She and Monty stood up to dance, and so I said, 'I'd be delighted, Officer Ferretti.'

'Chris,' he corrected me, and held out his hand. I went easily into his arms. As the Beatles serenaded us, he guided me around the salon, past the styling chairs, the tables piled with food, and the manicurists' stations. 'You look lovely,' he said.

'Thank you.'

'It's over,' he whispered in my ear. 'You've saved your friend and caught the killer of that poor homeless woman. You risked your life to do that. I'm so impressed. You're as smart as you are beautiful.'

His arms were strong and his chest was broad and it felt good when I put my head on his muscular shoulder. He smelled of Old Spice.

Soon we were in Mario's alcove, with Elvis crooning 'Can't Help Falling in Love' while we danced in clouds of orchids.

EPILOGUE

Jessica Gray's poison lingered in the Forest for a long time. The national press visited our enchanted area and slammed it brutally. A hip blog irreverently said Reggie's party 'featured a collection of local clench-butts,' but Reggie didn't deign to notice blogs. My favorite was this quote from the *New York Times*, which called the Forest an 'enclave of the one percent, the finest minds of the nineteenth century, barricaded in drafty mansions to avoid facing the problems of this new century.' The newspaper of record ruffled more than a few feathers, but no one canceled any subscriptions. The Forest preferred the *Wall Street Journal* and *Forbes* magazine, and neither had covered the event.

I agreed with the *Times*, but I had to keep my mouth shut, except around Katie, where we giggled like teenagers over the press slams.

After Jessica Gray's party, Reggie Du Pres was cool to his old friend, Clare Rappaport. She'd talked him into an expensive spread to honor the celebrity, and the only thing he got out of it was a few condescending mentions in the national press. 'The star collapsed during a party at the home of a local grandee and was rushed to the hospital,' was typical. One reporter sneered that the appetizers were 'the usual tired party fare – lamb lollipops and grilled octopus.'

The Forest was mightily impressed by the spread, but they were already impressed by Old Reggie. He was stuck with an impressive bill for more than twenty-five thousand dollars, including flowers, servers, and catering.

True to his word, Stu Milano had a huge memorial service for his wife, Jessica Gray, at the Beverly Hilton Hotel, with clips from her movies and photos of her timeless beauty. Guests ate and drank the food and wine, but didn't touch the samples of her Captivating line. 'I don't want to wind up like Jessica,' was a common quip. It was a ready-made excuse to avoid the ground kale and whatever else was in that junk.

Otherwise, Jessica would have loved her send-off. It was a weepy Hollywood spectacle, with dozens of Jessica's frenemies lying about what an enduring talent she was.

The memorial service was considered a success, except for the rejected Captivating samples and Stu's announcement that he'd be returning to Vegas with his own magic show in six months. He had flyers made up and gave them to all the mourners. That was considered 'tacky' and Stu was accused of 'trying to piggyback on Jessica's fame.' Many of Jessica's friends turned their backs on her climber of a husband, and refused to see or back his show.

Stu and Tawnee Simms flew to Maui to spread Jessica's ashes on the island where Stu and Jessica would have had their honeymoon. Tawnee was staying on as his assistant.

But the trouble started on their return to Los Angeles: Jessica's Captivate line crashed. Stu had inherited more than four million dollars from his wife, but her youth drink never survived the publicity after Jessica drank it on camera and then died in a spectacular fashion. Saks and Nordstrom dropped the line, and that was the end – nothing could persuade consumers that the green gunk was safe to drink. Besides, it was kale. Stu lost more than two million dollars on that debacle.

Stu used the rest of his fortune – two million dollars – to mount a show in Las Vegas called 'Milano's Marvels.' It failed miserably. The nicest thing any critic said was 'Stu Milano's show is where vaudeville came to die. Someone needs to put it out of its misery.'

Stu now manages Tawnee's career on the nostalgia circuit. He has the opening act in her show – fifteen minutes of 'Milano Magic,' which makes many eyes glaze over. The couple live together but so far they have not married. They are doomed to wander from one small town to another – Elk Horn, Iowa, and Hickman, Nebraska – in search of an audience.

Mario's comeback party was a success, and he was named Chouteau Forest Business Leader of the Year, the closest the Forest would come to an apology for his bad treatment during the Jessica affair. After all, the police had apologized. The title came with an award of one thousand dollars, which helped him cover the wages he paid his staff while he was in jail. Mario's business expanded rapidly in the next months. He had to hire three new stylists and two more manicurists. Even I had to wait a week for an appointment with him.

If he was hurt by Will London's betrayal, Mario never told me. 'Boys come and boys go,' he said. 'There will be others.' He's currently dating a handsome young man from Brazil. They make a stunning couple.

Will London was bitter about his plea deal for Jessica's murder. He felt he'd been badly treated by the star and the judge should have been more understanding. His only comfort was that he could smoke in prison. Will died of lung cancer twenty years into his sentence.

Tara Murphy, the woman who beat to death her construction worker husband Thomas Murphy, was charged with domestic assault in the first degree, a class A felony, and a host of other charges. Her father-in-law and her neighbors testified that she'd beaten and terrorized her long-suffering husband.

She was sentenced to sixty years. She is in the women's penitentiary, and has received several proposals of marriage. Two true crime writers tried to do books about the female spouse abuser, but neither project got anywhere. Her father-in-law campaigns to alert people to the signs of spouse abuse, especially in men.

Specialist 4th Class Harold Galloway, the homeless man who died in the lot on Shirley Circle, was given a military funeral by the Chouteau Forest VFW.

Lydia DePaul, the good daughter who spent her youth in the gloomy family mansion waiting on her dragon of a mother, the formidable Vera DePaul, inherited most of her mother's vast estate, and that was fine with her wealthy brothers and sisters. After all, Lydia earned that money the hard way, tending to their difficult mother. Lydia sold the old pile and tried to ease her grief by taking a world cruise. The ship's spa and the sea air did wonders for her. She eloped with a handsome Italian cabin steward who was twenty years younger than Lydia. The couple live in Tuscany, and he devotes his life to taking care of her.

Denise Sanders, the third homeless woman who was on stage for Jessica's show – the one with the shopping cart – was found dead in an alley the day after I saw her, the victim of a mugging. I hoped my twenty-dollar bill did not contribute to her death. Her shopping cart was missing and no one knew what was in those mysterious bags. Denise's body was never claimed and she was buried in the city's potter's field.

Suzanne Creighton – the legal name of Suzy the 'homeless woman' arrested for the murder of Becky (Rebecca) Barens – pleaded guilty to second-degree murder and was sentenced to ten years in prison. Suzy said prison was better than living on the streets – at least she got good meals. She is studying for her GED. Suzy mourns the loss of her suite in the Hofstedder Hotel, and with each description the rooms become more palatial. Losing that suite was the ultimate punishment for Suzy.

I donated the five hundred dollars that Clare gave me to a homeless shelter in St Louis, in Becky Barens' name. I donated another five hundred of my own money to Women's Work, to give the homeless hope.

Speaking of hope, Becky's ex-husband claimed her body. I met him at the small funeral service. He told me that he did his best to keep Becky off the streets, but I don't know if he was telling the truth. At the short service, the preacher read these comforting words from the Bible: 'In my Father's house are many rooms. If it were not so, would I have told you that I go to prepare a place for you? And if I go and prepare a place for you, I will come again and will take you to myself, that where I am you may be also. And you know the way to where I am going.'

I prayed that Becky was safely in a comfortable heavenly room, clad in white robes, and that she would never again know hunger or humiliation, and her earthly trials would be forgotten.

As I expected, after my dance with Officer Chris Ferretti at Mario's party, my friends practically had us married. Katie was the worst, insisting I should 'grab him while you can' – as if he was a Black Friday bargain. I admit I enjoyed dancing with him amid the orchids, and Chris felt good to hold – solid and strong. But I'd given my heart to Donegan, and my lost love still has it. I wish I could be with another man and not see Donegan. I consider myself lucky to have had one great love, and that should be enough. As for a new man, well, I'll keep on dancing around that subject.